SHADES OF HER

MONICA ARYA

*To **my husband, Sunny.** I love you more than words can say, and that alone should tell you so much since I've written a few books full of many words. Thank you for loving every shade of me, every version of myself, and growing up with me. My high school sweetheart, and my forever. I love you always.*

*My husband once said to me - **"You are insane. Literally. I love that about you."***

*To those who may not be proud of every shade of who they were, or who they are. May you chase the light even if the darkness finds you first because the sun will eventually rise again. More times than none when we feel lost, everything we may be searching for is right there inside of us. Including the light. **This is our now.***

CHAPTER ONE

*E*very so often, I feel this cold breath brushing against my neck and face. I feel someone's fingers trace my cheek, and when I open my eyes, I could have sworn someone was there. Someone wanting to wrap their hands around my neck or do something to me I can't figure out. I wake up confused, shaken, and covered in a cold sweat. Then I realize it's just a dream... or maybe a nightmare. Like the ones my children wake up from in the middle of the night and I reassure them it's simply a figment of our imagination coming to play when we are sleeping to torment us. I can feel eyes on me everywhere I go, but when I turn and look, there's nothing and no one. But what if it wasn't just a dream? What if someone is watching me? What if something is off, but life is just too damn busy for me to dig into it? After all, moms don't get a break and moms don't get to complain. We just keep pushing forward, even if... something truly and awfully wicked is happening.

We all know the type, the mom uniform—a shiny, pearl-white SUV, athleisure even though you haven't been to a gym since you had children. Oh right, children. At least two or three of those in the backseat, fighting over some toy they had forgotten about until that very moment. A husband who wears a dress shirt tucked into the khakis you got on sale, and a house that sits behind a white picket fence in the suburbs. Fall festivals, spring flings, and cookies with Santa replace the late-night partying, vacations, and fancy dinners. Friends with dreams and ambitions are replaced with realists who complain about how little sleep they got and how tired they are of their nine-to-five jobs they settled for. Mom friends who bitch about how their husbands don't help enough, how sleep training isn't working, and how all they do is cook, clean, and chauffeur their kids to school and activities. *Fuck, just saying all of that makes me realize how shitty it all sounds.*

But then again, it's just too bad, because it's my life. I'm that mom; the mom who swears under her breath, counts down to bedtime, when breakfast plates have barely been cleared and dreads when her husband's eyes trail from her face to her breasts, hoping to get laid in between the nightly news and the next episode of whatever Netflix show we are binging just to prevent conversations—which always, *always* turn into fights or some bickering. The tiara from my beauty pageant days that once sat on top of my head has now been replaced with a messy bun. Now, I'm just touched out and overstimulated—and not in the good way.

I wasn't always that woman. I was fun and lively, and even though my nights started at eleven p.m. for a different reason—and not because of a nursing or teething baby—I thought maybe, just maybe after getting married, having children, and moving to the damn suburbs I'd perhaps still manage to have a sliver of me. Well, that was the biggest joke ever. There is no "me;" it's just him and them. I can barely think straight most days, the television is booming with a catchy kid's song on loop, my phone is vibrating against the Carrera marble countertops we couldn't afford but replaced anyway—because everyone had them and we couldn't be less than everyone. The neighbor's dog is always barking at the delivery guy, the one who probably was bringing my two-day shipping packages that I one-clicked in the middle of the night, because why not buy another wine bottle opener or random sand kit that may gift myself three minutes of peace but thirty minutes of clean-up from my wild little ones. The kids are screaming in the background or whining about how bored they are. My husband is texting me about dinner and of course, he'll be home late... *again.*

Ah, the sweet life. The life you envisioned as a little girl lying in your pink, princess room, doodling in your journal. Sometimes I look around myself, in the midst of the chaos and commotion, and pause. *How in the actual fuck did I get here?*

"Sage?" My butt was pressed against the kitchen island and my coffee mug was warming my hands, just barely, since I've already had to put it down three times to break up the fights over who has more syrup on their pancakes.

"Sage, did you hear me? I need you to grab my dry cleaning on the way home from school drop off," my husband, Brody, said hurriedly while grabbing a muffin and shoving his thermos under our Keurig. I look over at him. His hair is still damp from his shower, he throws a suit jacket on over his dress shirt, and glances at his watch. He's a lawyer, but not those big fancy kinds. He could have been the big fancy kind, but he chose to settle for a more "upper-middle class" lifestyle and took on one too many pro-bono cases. He was a better man than I deserved. I guess really, I was the greatest pro-bono case he took on. Brody and I met at a bar while he was out with his law school friends. What he didn't know was that bartending was only a miniscule piece of my lifestyle. He thought that bartending was bad enough, and basically swooped in to save the sweet, blue-eyed bartender who had daddy issues and a drunk ass mother.

What Brody never knew, and could never know, was that bartending was saint's work compared to a shade of me he'd never see. My addiction—which I always lovingly referred to as a *hobby*—was one that would even make a sinner blush. Once I met Brody, I had to suppress those urges, secure my way out, and ensure he put a ring on it. That meant burying my darkest side and secrets as far as the earth would allow. *The problem with secrets is that they start as a small riptide in the ocean, but they eventually turn deadly, consuming you and anyone in its path.* My secrets were neatly tucked away inside of a dark coffin and placed under a mound of dirt, because luckily for me, the suburbs we'd moved to was not only states away, but it was one of those smaller islands off of Charleston where no one moved out of, so the people here had no way of knowing anything from the outside. Home sweet home. *The cleanest place for my dirtiest secrets.*

"Sage? Did you hear me? Dry cleaning, okay?"

"Sure babe..." I smiled at my husband.

"Bye, kids. Have a good day at school!" Brody called out to Andi and Tate. Andi was seven and Tate was six—though Tate was the result of "breastfeeding as birth control." I made Brody get snipped after Tate was born. Luckily for me, they were both in school now, and I was able to hit the gym—well, sauna—and actually take a shower without a child pounding on the door screaming. I also decided that maybe I could indulge in a new hobby, one that was a bit of a derivative of my original one. My hobby wasn't the usual mom hobby; hell, it wasn't the usual hobby for anyone. No, my hobby was all pleasure. It was as indulgent as the way it feels when you bite into a thick layer of chocolate covering a juicy, red strawberry. My hobby was delicious. The thing is, my hobby was once a hindering addiction—a lifetime ago, watered down to make it more morally acceptable. It was my brilliant way to indeed find that, no, keep that shade of me... *the old me.*

After putting Andi and Tate in their seats, I turned up some kids' edition of popular hip-hop songs that made my soul cringe, but they were bopping their heads to it in harmony, and as I drove, my fingers strummed against the steering wheel. This was my life. I pulled up into the infamous carpool line, the place I spent hours of my day in because idiots couldn't understand how to let their precious Susie's hop out, go into the school, and that she didn't need five hundred kisses and a whole damn cheer to go to kindergarten. Me…? I had places to be, and things to do… rather, people to see and oh, how I wish, people to do. Glancing into the rearview mirror, I smiled at my children, gently wiggling my fingers at them as they grabbed their bags, and the teacher opened their doors.

"Bye, guys, have a great day. Mommy loves you!" I sang out in a cheerily masked voice. Speeding off, my tires screeched shamelessly against the elementary school pavement and my music changed to 90s rap. I booty-bumped to even more shamelessly when no one was around. Eventually, I got back to our home. Kicking my shoes off, I ran up the stairs two at a time. The adrenaline rushed inside of me. I propped my leg on the rim of the bathtub after turning the water on. The pellets splashed near me as I generously lathered on shaving cream. Dipping my razor into the water, I kept my swift motions upward. "Ouch." My hand jerked to the cut that burned as blood trickled out. I froze for a minute before taking deep breaths in and out; I watched as my blood ran like a small stream down my leg and into the white tub. The sight of blood always triggered something inside of me.

Flashbacks to the past. Even the tanginess of the scent of blood alone permeated from my memories into the present. Shaking my head and repressing the thoughts, I sped to finish both legs. I rinsed them off, letting my hand stroke up and down the silky-smooth aftermath. Swiping on deodorant, I sat on the floor in front of the enormous mirror and unzipped my makeup bag. Carefully applying generous amounts of it, I made a blowfish face and contoured my cheekbones. Lining my lips in a bright pink, I filled them in, and applied a touch of lighter gloss to make them look fuller than they really were. Shimming into a tight, fitted black dress, I climbed into strappy, gold, sky-high heels. One quick spin in front of the mirror, I felt like a changed woman.

I was a changed woman.

CHAPTER TWO

"*H*ey neighbor! Wowza!" A whistling across the street ensued. The scent of spring grazed my nose, the leaves around were budding, and it was only a matter of time before a sheet of yellow from the endless pollen covered our cars.

With my keys clutched in my hand, I averted my eyes with a quick wave in the direction, but the footsteps grew closer. I tried to slide into my car, except I nervously double clicked the lock, and in return, looked like a moron pulling my door handle without it budging.

"Need a hand?" I glanced over, irritated. *Damn suburbs.*

"Hi, Harlow..." I cleared my throat and wished I

had grabbed a coat to conceal the fact that my boobs were spilling out of this dress. I wrapped my hands around my chest, which didn't do anything besides making me feel slightly better.

"Hey, sweets! How are you guys doing? We missed you both at brunch last weekend." *Harlow Davis.* She wasn't just our neighbor, she was also one-half of our closest friends in this suburban hell. She and her husband, Jake, owned Davis Reality, and pretty much had a monopoly of selling houses in the area because they were that beautiful couple with pearl-white smiles plastered across all the billboards and benches in a twenty-mile radius. They had three kids and were mostly tolerable and fun to be around. Okay, Harlow was my best friend and was probably the only friend who didn't talk shit about me behind my back. Her husband and Brody watched football together, while clinking their beers and yelling at the kids as they cut in front of the TV.

"Yeah, Tate had a cold, so we didn't want to leave him with a sitter. How are you guys?" I smiled through gritted teeth, tapping my heel aggressively against the driveway.

"We're doing good. Jake and I are heading to our anniversary dinner tonight. Ten years…" Harlow smiled at me, her eyes shifting up and down my attire, pausing on my face, clearly analyzing the excess amount of makeup slathered on. Her lips pursed.

"Well… I hope you guys have a blast tonight. We'd love to celebrate you both next weekend. How about dinner on Saturday?" I quickly turned and slid closer into my open car door, causing Harlow to step back.

"Really? Aww… Sage, you are the best friend ever! We'd love that." She threw her arms around my neck and pulled me in, the scent of her perfume overpowered my nostrils.

Patting her wrist, I forced a smile and nodded with my eyes bulging out of my head from her grasp. "It's a date!" I added chirpily just before letting my butt hit my seat and slamming the door behind me. The clicking of the gear stick sounded, and my heel slid against the rubber of the gas. Glancing into the rearview mirror, I saw Harlow walk back to her house.

Fifty-five minutes, six red lights, and four bridges later, I was parked in front of Hotel Besos. It was the fanciest hotel by the airport, which was a mile away. The greatest part about Hotel Besos was that it was home to no locals, no tourists, but usually one-night guests. *Passersby, which was exactly what I was.*

My phone buzzed inside my purse and I tugged it out, my long, painted nails clicking against the screen just before I triple-checked my location services and made sure it was off. Rookie mistake not to triple-check that, and I sure as hell was not a rookie at this game. No, this game... this game, I was its queen. You see, there is a secret piece of me no one really knows, not even my beloved husband. The husband I shared years of marriage and two children with. The husband I shared a mortgage that is too steep for us and bank accounts that could use a little bit of overtime. The husband I vowed for better or for worse...

Well, that husband of mine didn't know one teeny, tiny part of me. I'm a recovering sex addict. Ugh. Horrid, I know. I'm not one to falter at judgment. An athleisure wearing, messy bun donning, SUV driving soccer mom of two is what...? It's the truth. Judge away and click your tongue if you must.

Sage Miller... well, previously Sage Blake, is a recovering sex addict. I was insatiable before I met Brody. Call it deep-rooted daddy issues or attention-seeking behavior... I don't know. My many shrinks didn't seem to know either, but eventually, I ended up in a hotel room, drugged and tied up... and not in the way I liked. They say hitting rock bottom is a good thing because you only can go up from there, but I beg to differ. *You can always, always go lower, straight to the burning embers of hell that reside beneath rock bottom.* I just didn't want to be scorched by the flames quite yet, so I needed to find a better system. Maybe it's like those overly judgmental, so-called friends reassuring your worried parents when you're caught smoking weed, "Oh, she's not a drug-addict; she's just experimenting."

Maybe this was that concept for me. I just needed to purify my system, find a happy medium for who I was and who I needed to be. Except, then again, you can't truly change who you are. Besides, you shouldn't have to change who you are, even if judgement is showering over you. I'll never forget when Brody and I were newlyweds and I asked him to tie my hands to our bed post… you know, to spice things up. I wasn't asking him to gag or choke me, but still, his eyes grew wide and his jaw dropped. He told me I needed to remember there was a difference between the girl I was and the woman I needed to be. Let's just say I didn't try to add sprinkles to our very vanilla sex-life after that.

Opening my door, my heels clicked against the smooth cement underneath. The large weeping willow in the distance swayed with the cool breeze, which was rare but always welcome in the sticky spring heat. Usually, I could feel the humid, muggy air cling to my hairline and the ten pounds of hairspray I doused myself in because down in the south, "The higher the hair, the closer to God…." Except, I already had a first-class ticket straight to the blazing flames of hell, so I didn't know why I assumed hairspray may be my redemption. I walked toward the shiny gold doors and froze. My shoe stuck, I looked down and lifted my heel, finding a wad of clumpy pink gum stuck to my two-seasons' old Jimmy Choo's that I found at a thrift store. "Fucking hell…" I waddled to the patch of grass and violently brushed my heel against the grass. "Jimmy, you bastard…" I huffed under my breath as dirt clung to the gross glob.

"I'd hate to be Jimmy…" A voice behind me lifted. My eyes widened and I glanced over my shoulder. He was easily six-foot-four, light scruff lined his jawline and his brown eyes looked as cozy as a steaming cup of hot chocolate on a cold winter day.

"Yeah, Jimmy is a fucking prick…" I offered a small smile, planting my heel back down, while pulling the hem of my dress down.

"I believe you." He rubbed his thumb against his bottom lip and looked toward the hotel. "Are you a guest here, too?" His hands sunk into his perfectly pressed pants pocket.

"Um… no," I stammered.

"So, you just lurk around random hotels and curse out... Jimmy?"

"I mean, I'm not a guest here for the night, but if you must know, I was going to grab a drink." I clasped my hands together, knowing judgment would soon follow. What kind of woman, who has her life together, drank before noon? *Here it comes...*

"Well, how about I buy you that drink?" He shrugged, and I paused. This was a first. I mean, sure, the whole purpose of this stupid thing I did was to get male attention—to flirt, maybe a little thigh rub and an occasional ass grab, but I controlled the urge. I made sure to never, ever let it spiral. But this man... this man had *fuck me* flashing on his perfectly tanned face in bold red letters. *Turn around and go home, Sage. Look, but don't touch,* I repeated my mantra to no avail.

Clearing my throat, I straightened my shoulders. "Why would I agree to get a drink with a complete stranger?"

The mystery man studied me carefully. "Well, I suppose everyone you get a drink with at one point in time was a stranger, don't you agree?"

"Mm-hmm... how about that drink." I suppressed the smile that was creeping on my face. I liked his snark, his quickness. *This was going to be a disaster.*

"Vodka martini, two olives, and Suit over here is

buying, so definitely top-shelf." I slid into an empty bar stool and lifted two fingers up.

"I'll have what she's having." His eyebrows pinched together as he offered a curious smile. "Suit?"

"I don't know your name." I averted my eyes, knowing my cheeks were already warm, and they'd probably be as red as the maraschino cherries sitting by the bartender's quick-working hands.

"Archer Collins. Care to share yours before I nickname you Grey Goose or Jimmy?"

"Sage."

Archer leaned in and whispered, "Do you have a last name, Sage?"

My heartbeat quickened. "Nope. Just Sage."

"I like it… *just Sage*." The way his voice grew deeper, the way he clutched his glass, the way he leaned in and spoke with sheer confidence made me feel like I could wish away my real life and start over. *Young, wild, and free.*

"Can I ask you a question?" Archer took a sip of his drink.

I inhaled a deep breath and released it, straightening my back and turned toward him. Crossing my leg over the other I eyed him. "A question for a question," I replied, picking up the toothpick that stabbed through two shiny green olives.

"Deal." He smirked. "Business or pleasure?" He nodded in the direction of the main hotel lobby.

"Neither. I just come here to people watch." I paused, waiting for his expression to shift from intrigue to confusion, but it didn't. He still looked intrigued. *By me.*

"So, why do you people watch?" Archer rubbed his thumb against his bottom lip.

Taking a sip of my martini, I wiped the condensation from the cold glass and circled the rim, which emitted a soft, yet comforting sound. "Business or pleasure?" I looked up at him.

"Oh, I see… A question for a question." Archer laughed lightly. "I'd like to think both." His eyebrow lifted and he smiled in a way that made my stomach flutter.

I took a quick sip of the smooth alcohol, realizing water might have been a better option. Clearing my throat, I replied, "I people watch because it's fun to create stories about them and sometimes people watching turns into more…"

"More? Like what you and I are doing? Or more, *more?*" He crossed his leg over his knee and leaned into the bar, but his eyes were intently fixed on mine.

"No, not more, *more…*. Just forget it, this is stupid."

I grasped the cold glass in between my palms and tossed the rest of the cool liquid back.

"It's not stupid. Someone as stunning as you could never be stupid." Archer's jaw tightened, giving away little expression besides studying me like I was an animal at the zoo.

Crossing my arms over my chest, I lifted an eyebrow. "What does beauty have to do with brains?"

"The more beautiful you are, the more you can get away with, and you, Sage, know that all too well. You know that because you are so sexy, you can push the limits. You can push *my* limits." Archer grew closer to me, so close I could feel his cool breath laced with vodka on my face.

Flash. A bright light caught my eye.

"What the hell? Did you see that?" I leapt off my stool and sped toward the side door of Hotel Besos. Someone in a black hoodie and sunglasses took a picture of me. *Worse, took a picture of us.* Standing outside and catching my breath, I heard the screech of tires against the pavement before I saw a black car speed off. Fumbling in my purse, I tried digging for my phone. I squinted to see the license plate but whoever it was definitely didn't waste a minute before speeding off.

"What happened?" Archer came to a stop next to

me. I looked up at him; he was significantly taller than me, even wearing these heels, and I wasn't short by any means.

"Someone took a picture of us!" I yelled louder than I intended, pointing in the direction the car went.

"I didn't see anyone take a picture. Are you sure, Sage?" The way the words rolled off his tongue in a soothing way made me second-guess what I just saw.

Shaking my head, I rolled my shoulders back, hoping to compose myself. "I've got to go…" I looked up at Archer and swallowed the thick saliva that lingered in my mouth.

"Oh, okay. It was a great meeting you, Sage. I hope our paths cross again." Archer leaned in and let his hands drop to my waist, pulling me closer. "And when we do meet again, I hope it's nothing but pleasure…" he whispered against my ear, and I swore he could hear my heart pound against my chest.

Letting his hand drop to mine, he gripped it, and I felt something. Looking down, I saw his name and number on a business card nestled in my palm. "This is the vaguest card I've ever seen. Doesn't even say your profession… You don't even live here, so how would we ever meet again?"

Towering over me, he lowered his voice. "Sage, do you believe in fate?"

I swallowed and took a step back. "Yeah, I guess."

"Me too, and I know fate will definitely have us meet again." Archer winked and let his hand graze mine, which sent chills up my arm. Turning away, he walked back to the bar as I clutched my purse. Glancing over his shoulder, he called out, "Take care, *just Sage…*"

CHAPTER THREE

D *rip, drip, drip...*

My palms and clothes were covered in red. "Can you believe they make us do this shit? Like, get some damn volunteers..." Harlow rolled her eyes, groaning at the giant, freshly painted red wall inside our kids' elementary school.

"I mean, we *are* the volunteers. The best damn PTA moms in the state," I added with sarcasm in my voice. I was still shaken up by this morning's events between Archer and the potential psycho who snapped pictures of us. I barely made it back in time to wipe off my makeup and slide out of my skimpy dress into leggings with a fitted tank. I then stuffed my heels under the seat of my car and popped on my blush-pink Nikes.

"Look at Caroline over there acting like she is the damn cheer captain." Harlow elbowed me and nodded in the direction of the PTA president and doting mom of four.

"Shh...you're going to have us sent to the principal's office, Ms. Davis." I laughed as I bumped my shoulder against hers.

"Yes please, Principal George can punish me *anytime*." Harlow fanned herself. I quickly picked my paintbrush up and finished off the rest of the wall before Caroline stomped over to check out our work. "So, you going to tell me where you went bright and early dressed like Julia Roberts from Pretty Woman?" Harlow continued to paint beside me.

I froze and could feel the heat in my cheeks grow. "Well thanks, friend. I thought I looked elegant. But if my nosy neighbor must know, I met Brody at work... We've been trying to spice it up a bit. Please don't mention it to him though, you know he's so modest and all with his job." I licked my lips as if the deceit lined them and I needed to swipe it away.

"Oh, damn. That's hot," Harlow breathed, seeming impressed.

Hell, I'd be impressed too if a married couple with two young children could do something that fun for once.

It was far from the truth, of course. My hobby had

been one that I only had begun. A nice little warm-up jog for the true workout. I enjoyed dressing up, going to Hotel Besos, and simply flirting with random men. They'd give me attention and so far, I was two out of three on being invited up to their rooms. The third man being Archer, and I suppose if I hadn't run away, my score board would be a blazing three for three. I knew this was crazy, but I also knew I wanted more. It felt so damn nice to be wanted, to be desired and craved. Being a recovering sex addict didn't come easy. I tried; I really did. But now it was just like when you shake up a soda can… eventually you'll burst.

I needed more. I needed a release. I needed that high. Closing my eyes, I thought back to my teenage years and twenties before I met Brody. I was Miss USA, the most prestigious title you could get in the pageant world. I held state titles, every damn city and town title and more. Yes, my mom was a drunk and my father was emotionally abusive, but they knew how to put on a show and savor the nice checks I got from winning pageants. Well, they enjoyed those more than I ever did. Maybe that's why I am the way I am. Beauty pageants are a pit. You get extreme attention and praise because of how beautiful you are. I was praised for how good I looked in a teeny-tiny bikini and how so-called talented I was when I belted out

Amazing Grace. I hated pageantry and loved it. Truthfully, I never left it. After all, isn't that what life is? A giant show. We wake up every morning and choose a shade of ourselves—one to present to the world, one we know will be loved and adored. Is it really you, though? Hell no, and anyone who says it is, is a fucking liar.

"Sage?" Caroline Summers sang out my name. She was the mom all-star, but if I had secrets, I bet you a million dollars she did, too. Maybe not as trashy and dark as mine, but secrets all the same—you know the kind where she probably steals a pair of earrings at a boutique for a little rush.

"Sage? I said I need you to ask Brody if his law firm would be willing to sponsor the Spring Fling again this year?

"Oh, sure. I'll ask him, Caroline," I quickly replied.

She walked away with her sidekicks, and I heard them snicker. "She's always so dazed... probably on a bunch of anti-depressants or something."

Bitches.

Walking to the bathroom, I bent over to wash my hands in the super short kid-sized sink. The mirror was one of those distorted, plastic ones that wasn't even glass. The red paint drained slowly off my hands into the clean white sink as water pellets splattered around. A stall door creaked and my heart jumped. I looked up and over my shoulder. Grabbing a piece of brown, hard—and totally not absorbent—paper towel, I quickly wiped my hands. The stall closest to the door swung and creaked, and I slowly walked toward it. "Hello?" I called out, nerves rattling my voice. *One, two, three.* I counted slowly and gripped the bright blue door, pulling it open. Empty.

Releasing a hard breath of air, I chuckled. When the door swung shut, Harlow was there. My heart jumped and my hand flung to my chest. "Fuck!" I gasped.

"Shh, Sage. We're in an elementary school for Christs' sake. I've been looking everywhere for you. Your car… it's…" She looked at me with sympathy.

"My car, what?" I opened my hands, annoyed. I hated when people played dramatics. Just say it. If I needed the drama, I'd watch it on TV in my underwear with a glass of wine.

"It's… Well, you just have to go see it. Come on!" She laced her arm in mine and tugged me along.

And the Oscar goes to…

Moments later, the warm spring air and intense scent of pollen tickled my nose. The sun blazed into my eyes, making me squint. We walked up to my car, but my palms were already sweating because my shiny, beautiful, pearl-white SUV, now had red streaks all over the hood. My eyes widened and my heart raced as I took in the word *Whore* scrawled in red paint. I ran toward it and stared at the word and the streaky red paint. Tears pricked in my eyes, and I felt Harlow's arm around mine.

"Honey, are you okay?" She drew me in for a hug while I continued to look over her shoulder. "This has to be some stupid prank from one of those shit-head high schoolers from across the street," she added reassuringly.

"Yeah, probably," I squeaked. I unlocked my doors and quickly snatched a pack of baby wipes from the passenger seat. Pulling a handful out, I furiously scrubbed out the giant letters with all my might. Harlow quietly grabbed some to help. Meanwhile, without even turning, I heard a small crowd of moms behind me, gawking and whispering under hushed voices which only made my tears break free. Batting my eyelashes, I scrubbed harder.

"Ladies, get a life! Show's over," Harlow yelled behind us. "Oh honey, don't mind them. You know what PTA moms are like... vultures. They'll find a carcass and flock to it to rip it apart even more."

"Damn, Harlow, that's dark but so true..." I laughed between my tears.

Thirty minutes and one pack of baby wipes later, the visibility of the word was no longer there, but the white of my hood was now tinged pink. A car wash before heading home would probably fix that. It was almost time for the kids to get out of school, so Harlow and I hung out with my trunk popped open, splitting a bag of mini Oreos that Andi must have left from soccer practice.

"Do you ever miss it?" Harlow tossed back two cookies at once and looked over at me with her legs swinging.

"Miss what?" I wiped the corners of my mouth.

"Your beauty pageant days and life in the city?" She smiled at me, and I knew she was trying to lighten my mood.

"Oh, wow. I mean, no one knows besides you guys about all that, so it just feels like a totally different lifetime…" I opened my water bottle and took a swig. I could feel the Oreo cookie smashed between my teeth. Swiping my tongue against them, I tried to do a natural floss because I didn't want to be caught red-handed by my kids, who would definitely throw the world's most dramatic tantrum for more cookies.

"Yeah, but you have to miss it. I mean, you're not like the rest of us… Most of us were born and raised here and never left. We were basically made to do this, but you chose to do this."

"I mean, I guess when I met Brody in New York he made me think this could be my life, and I could be good at it. Turns out, I'm shit at it." I laughed and offered Harlow my water.

She shook her head and paused. "No, Sage, you're a great mom, wife, and friend... Hell, if I were you, I'd be a total bitch to everyone and wear my tiara in the car-rider line." She giggled and jumped from my open trunk. "You stay in your car; I'll send Andi and Tate to you, so you don't have to face the vultures," Harlow called out.

I couldn't have been more grateful. Springing out, I pressed my keys to shut the trunk and waited for my kids to come storming over.

Leaning against my door, I opened my purse to find some gum, because really, residual Oreos in my mouth felt gross. A small, ivory card fluttered and dropped to the ground below me. Bending over, I picked it up and traced over the numbers below his name. *Archer Collins.* The mere thought of him made me clench my thighs together.

"Mommy!" Andi and Tate screeched while plunging into my abdomen. My arms wrapped around them both, and I quickly shoved the card back into my purse. *Guilt.* The one word every single mother—no matter who you ask or where they are from—will say they feel. Working moms, guilt. Stay-at-home moms, guilt. Single moms, guilt. Married moms, guilt. And that was exactly what I felt. Instead of focusing on my healthy children and hardworking husband, I was sitting here dreaming about another man.

Once we were all locked and loaded into the car, which was my own version of an Olympic event between strapping them into their seats and being kicked in the ribs, I began driving. The chatter of my children radiated in the car, their favorite songs blasting and mixing in with all the noise. Smiling, I glanced in the rearview mirror as they sang along. Unfortunately, the bright faces of my children weren't what caught my eye... a black car did.

The black car.

No, now I was being paranoid. How could that same black car that sped away from Hotel Besos be here? How could the person who took photos of me find me almost an hour away? *How could they come to my children's school?* I shuddered at the mere thought of someone being after me, but my children...? I gripped the steering wheel tighter as lines formed between my brows.

Screech.

My heart jolted and honking blasted around me, mixing with screams from my children. I looked in front of me as my foot jerked to the brake. I ran a red light and was in the middle of a busy intersection, with horns blaring around me. "Mommy what are you doing?" Andi screamed while Tate cried for his dad.

Shaking my head, I slowly drove through and pulled over for a moment. I looked behind us and saw the black car, but it made a turn two streets back.

Sage, stop being paranoid.

CHAPTER FOUR

"Hey, babe, how was your day?" Brody gripped my waist from behind and planted a gentle kiss on my cheek.

I diced onions and watched the knife slide through. It was so satisfying and that either made me dysfunctional or a psychopath. The crackling of hot olive oil splattering against the pan and the scent of simmering garlic floated around us.

"It was… good." I smiled at him, pretending to busy myself with dinner prep.

"So, are you going to tell me why your brand-new car looks like cotton candy blew up on it?" He leaned against the sink and stared at me, his hands gripping the counter behind him.

"Oh… yeah, I was at the kids' school, and I think

some high schoolers from across the street did something." I wiped my eyes with my sleeve.

Damn you, onions.

"That's a weird prank... They just painted it pink?" Brody shook his head.

"Brody, can you please not put me on trial. I don't know. I'll get it washed after dinner. You know Tate is scared of the carwash place." I wiped my hands on the dish towel and dumped my diced veggies into the hot oil, causing it to splatter and hit my cheek. "Ow, shit!" I yelled out.

"Oh my god, Sage, are you okay?" Brody ran toward me. He looked worried as he rubbed my cheek. "We can't have this beautiful face getting damaged, now can we?" He kissed where the oil had grazed my skin.

"Why?" I pushed him away. "I won't be worth it if I'm ugly?"

"Oh, come on. You know I didn't mean it like that." He followed me.

"Well, it is why you married me, isn't it? A lowly ex-pageant queen who ended up bartending and never made it to college like you?"

"What are you even talking about, Sage?" Brody looked at me as if I had lost my mind. *Maybe, I had.*

"I'm tired of this shit. I'm tired of playing house.

Maybe… maybe you shouldn't have tried so hard to pull me into this hellhole. I'm suffocating!" I hissed at him, sounding possessed.

"Sage… what is happening here? I'm sorry… actually I'm confused. I'm sorry, I was not intending to upset you. Baby, you are beautiful, but you're also so smart and loving." He inched toward me and rambled off everything he could muster.

"Then why is it that you barely touch me or have a real conversation with me?"

"I… Look, Sage, that has nothing to do with you. You know the office is crazy-busy right now. We're getting a new boss soon, who has plans to change *everything*. Limiting pro-bono and increasing case revenue. I've just been stressed, and then you are always pissed off between the kids and house stuff."

"Well, maybe you should just talk to me and not treat me like some fragile doll who can't have a real and intelligent conversation."

Brody Miller was prince charming. *My husband.* He swooped in as my knight in shining armor and saved me, his damaged beautiful princess in a tower also known as a shitty bar while men gawked over me— the men who he perceived at as fire breathing dragons.

But what I didn't know and he sure as hell couldn't

know was, maybe, just maybe, I really liked those fire breathing dragons.

"Babe… look, I'll finish making dinner. You go sit down and relax with the kids," he offered.

"Relax?" I chuckled. "With the kids? You realize that's literally an oxymoron, right?" I paused. "You know what, I'm going to go to that car wash after all. Be sure to sign Andi's permission slip, too."

Grabbing my purse and keys and let the door slam behind me. I could hear my kids screaming behind the door—of course, their attention that was glued onto the TV shifted when mommy left prison. *I mean home, not prison… home.*

I drove and kept driving until I eventually landed in downtown Charleston. I glanced down at my outfit that consisted of leggings and a baggy T-shirt. Well, no classy bars for me.

I parallel parked and jumped out of the car. Tourists swarmed around me, their excitement surrounding them as they popped in and out of local boutiques and shops. The southern charm consuming them as they looked down at their phones, trying to decipher which restaurant had the highest rating on whatever app, while the scent of caramel popcorn intertwined with the aroma of fried chicken around us all. Whenever I came to downtown Charleston, I missed New York City a thousand times more—the stench of urine, sticky subway seats, and all. This was too Hallmark movie for a girl like me.

Except for my favorite part about downtown... turning my head, I observed a local woman weave beautiful baskets. Watching her dark fingers thread in and out of the sweetgrass, crafting a basket. Although it had imperfections and inconsistencies, it was absolutely breathtaking. After all, isn't that what life was? A beautifully woven creation that was crafted from all our imperfections, making us all that stronger?

Going into Bee's Bar, I slanted my body to make it through a crowd of friends, who eyed me, annoyed at my lack of manners. *Yeah, yeah, I'm not a Southern belle; I'm a mean-ass Yankee.*

"Look who the cat dragged in..." Mark, the bartender, wiped the off-white rag against the old, worn-down wood and nodded to an empty stool.

"Hey, Mark, it's been..."

"A year and two wheelbarrows full of dirt," he said in his thick southern drawl.

"That makes zero sense, and Brody thinks I'm the dumbest thing that hit Charleston." I laughed and gave him a fist bump.

"Oh, the husband called his beauty queen missus dumb, did he?"

"I hate when you call me beauty queen missus…" I rolled my eyes as Mark began making my go-to drink.

"One whiskey for the grumpy princess." Mark swung a towel over his shoulder and chuckled when I shot daggers from my eyes at him.

Pulling out the ivory card that had taunted me all day, I tugged out my cell phone. I tapped my finger against the smooth cardstock and dialed each number slowly, in hopes I'd reconsider. "Just Sage… it's nice to hear from you." His deep voice crawled through the phone as smooth as the whiskey in front of me.

"How the hell did you know it was me?"

"Because fate," he answered confidently.

"I don't know why I called you…" I whispered, cupping the speaker as Mark judged me. I rolled my eyes as I swatted at him before turning away.

"Well, how about I meet you and we can figure why out together?" His voice was deep and intense. I exhaled loudly. "I like the way you sound when you're breathing heavy," Archer said without a hitch in his voice.

I slid off the stool, flipping Mark off as he covered his mouth dramatically. Getting into the bathroom, I sat on the toilet. "That's inappropriate, Mr. Collins." I cleared my throat. "I'm a married woman." Instantly, I regretted saying those words.

"I don't really care about legal bonds in relationships… seems too patriarchal to me. I think you truly don't really care either, otherwise you wouldn't be calling me right now. Besides, I already knew."

Fuck.

I had hoped he'd hang up on me, tell me I was a skank and should go home to my husband and kids, but no. Archer Collins was tempting me, daring me to go back to the dark side—the side I missed, the side I craved.

"How did you know I was married?"

"Easy. Tan line on your ring finger."

I glanced down at my wedding rings. Balancing my phone between my chin and shoulder, I slid them off and immediately dropped my jaw. Damn, he was good. I mean, I knew that trick all too well, but I assumed the self-tanner I scrubbed on would have hidden it. The lightest line on my finger was definitely there, but how he noticed that in our very brief meeting was beyond me. But the fact that he noticed *me*… well, that made me feel amazing.

My phone beeped, and I checked the screen. ***Brody Miller*** flashed across my screen. "I've gotta go, Archer." I flipped over.

"Sage? What the hell is going on? The kids are going crazy, and you know Tate won't go to sleep without you." Crying in the background blurred with my husband's voice.

"I'm on my way." I picked up my pace. "Mark, put that on my tab!" I shouted as he opened his hands and parted his mouth, but before I could give him the chance to tell me that my tab is miles long, the jingling of the door slammed behind me.

Seeing my car, I stopped. "Shit." The pink glaze from the streaked red graffiti was still clearly embedded on my hood. No car wash was going to be open at this hour. Surely, Brody was going to lecture me about why we can't have nice things like I'm some silly toddler. *When it rains, it pours.*

Once home, I laid in bed with Tate. We were moving our fingers and hands into different shapes to make shadow animals on the wall. Tonight, he didn't fight sleep; he was just happy I was there beside him. Tiptoeing out, I immediately went to our bedroom. I could see the downstairs light reflecting into the stairwell and knew Brody would definitely ask me one too many questions if I went downstairs. Interrogation was his specialty, and I didn't want to be on the stand today, I just wanted to sleep. Climbing into bed, I peeled my socks off and once my head hit the pillow, I closed my eyes. Before I knew it, I was deep asleep.

"Mmm, not now, Brody…" I mumbled, wafting his

cold breath away from my face. My eyes were tightly glued together, and I was too cozy to move. His fingers grazed my face and rubbed my lips softly. "Brody... no." I swatted his hand away and turned into my pillow. His breathing grew louder, but more distant. Opening my eyes slowly, the room was pitch-black and a sticky warm breeze trickled in. I sat up and watched our curtains sway with the window wide-open. Chills shot up my spine.

"Brody?" I called out meekly. Glancing over to his side, I saw he wasn't there, the blanket still neatly tucked in. I checked the time, one a.m. My feet hit the cold hardwood and I slowly walked to the window. The stars were shining brightly, but the world was silent. Slamming the window shut and locking it, I walked downstairs, holding the banister as each step echoed in our quiet home.

"Brody?" I rubbed my eyes.

"Yeah, in the office, Sage," he called.

I walked toward his voice and saw him typing away with stacks of legal books next to him and a pen balancing in his mouth.

"Hey, were you upstairs?" I cleared my throat, my voice still scratchy from waking abruptly. "I felt someone touch me..."

"No... I've been working. Still have to get this

done." He glimpsed over at me, his eyes trailing up my face where I had just felt his cold breath.

"Did you open the window?" My voice shook as my body grew numb.

"Sage, is this important? I'm really busy. You were probably dreaming. Go back to bed; I'll be up soon." He shrugged as irritation grew in his tone.

I nodded and turned, shutting the door behind me. There was no doubt in my mind that someone was in my room. Someone was near me. But... maybe Brody was right? Maybe this was like when you have a dream where you are falling, and you swear you're about to fall over, but just like that, you wake up. The only issue was, there were still goosebumps across my skin where I had been touched. Grabbing a sleeping pill, I popped one into my mouth before getting back in bed.

I was losing my fucking mind.

CHAPTER FIVE

The weekdays blurred together; it was always the same thing over and over again. Morning madness, someone lost a shoe, someone was crying, someone was overwhelmed at work, and me... I'm just supposed to exist, supposed to be there for them all. Stretching myself thin like peanut butter over toast.

Finally Friday night rolled around, and Brody had the grill going and Jake and Harlow were over. Their kids were inside with ours watching a movie and eating pizza. The fire pit crackled near us as we sat around with some Trader Joe's wine. "Ah, this is nice. Thanks for inviting us over." Jake sipped his beer and leaned back into his chair.

"Of course. Congrats on ten years again," Brody

called out from the grill, lifting his beer toward them. The smoky air intertwined with the meat cooking.

"You guys are the best!" Harlow clinked her glass against mine.

"Definitely not the best, but I think we're decent-ish." I laughed.

These were the moments I thought—well, maybe this chapter; no, not chapter, this new book of life—was okay. *Okay-ish.*

"I'm going to go grab the salad from inside and make sure the kids haven't set the house on fire." I placed my wineglass on the table and tugged my off-the-shoulder sweater down more.

"Babe, will you run upstairs and get me my hood-ie?" Brody said over his shoulder as he flipped the sizzling burger on the grill. The spring air was cooler than usual tonight.

"Yeah." I gave him a swift kiss on his cheek and headed inside. The kids were building a fort and laughing, and they didn't even notice when I came in. Our living room looked like a tornado hit it, but this mess was worth my peace and some fun with friends. Harlow and Jake's kids were eight, five, and four, so it was a match made in heaven for our families. Gripping the banister, I ran upstairs and opened Brody's closet, pulling out his NYU Law hoodie before slowly shutting the door.

"Hey…" My heart jolted and I jumped.

"What the fuck, Jake? You scared the shit out of me." I planted my hand against the door as I took a deep breath.

"Sorry, I just wanted to see you… see how you were?" he whispered as he stepped closer. Jake Davis was a handsome man; he didn't have the dad-bod most men around here acquired at this stage of our lives. Nope, he had sandy blonde hair and tanned skin from his days surfing. He was basically the adult version of those Abercrombie and Fitch models you crushed on in high school.

"I'm doing good, Jake."

He put both hands on either side of me against the door, cornering me. His face grew closer to my neck, and he inhaled like I was a fragrance. Pulling his face away, he looked at me. Goosebumps streaked my arms, even though I had a sweater on. "God, I've missed you. I've missed *us*." He leaned in and brushed his lips against mine, opening slightly to kiss me.

I pushed him away. "Jake, our kids and spouses are literally downstairs. There is no *us*," I hissed. "Our affair was a huge mistake."

I ducked under his arm that wasn't budging, but he

gripped my arm and pushed me back against the door. "Sage… come on, beautiful. I know you need this just as bad as I do." His kissed me hard, spun me around, and pulled my arm to my back. Tugging my leggings down, I heard him unzip his pants behind me. My heart raced but I wasn't nervous and I wasn't scared. No, the thrill of this fucked-up moment excited me and that made me a monster.

Pushing inside me, he gripped my waist and pulled on my ponytail harder. A few moments later, he fell into me, exhaling just as heavy as his release. "Did you come, baby?"

I rolled my shoulders and tugged my leggings up. "No. And don't call me baby." I ran my hand through my hair and our shoulders bumped as I moved past Jake. *You're an idiot, Sage.*

"Well, that took long enough. Wasn't this just a bagged salad?" Brody looked at me as I gripped the salad bowl tightly.

"Oh, be nice, Brody. Bagged salad takes skill, too." Harlow giggled and grabbed the bowl from me.

"It really does." I smiled at her.

I was so messed up; I just fucked my best friend's husband against my closet while she was downstairs, and I didn't even feel remorse. I hated myself.

Jake Davis and I had a history. I suppose when we

moved here, we both found darkness inside one another. Jake and Harlow were high school sweethearts. Harlow had a miscarriage before they got married, and being the nice guy that he is, Jake married her very young. *He was trapped... just like me.*

So, we had sex a few times seven years ago. Eventually we stopped, but then we slipped up once last year and then again tonight. *Never again.* Honestly, it wasn't even good. I was a damn addict, and the drug was right across the street, wearing a sports coat and chinos. He was more like crack, though, not the cocaine temptation that Hotel Besos seemed to be serving.

Jake came out, donning a stupid grin on his face. "Hey, sweets, where did you go?" Harlow chirped.

"Oh, you know my stomach doesn't do well with cheese." He nodded in the direction of the charcuterie board we had set out.

"Aw, my baby. He's lactose intolerant and dairy shreds his poor tummy." Harlow got up and sat on Jake's lap, wrapping her arms around his neck. Jake looked at me and licked his lips with a wink.

Gross. Never. Again.

"So, you guys know Sage is writing a romance book, right?" Brody beamed proudly, setting plates in front of us.

Harlow dropped her jaw and shrieked, "What?"

"Wow, I didn't know that, Sage." Jake raised an eyebrow.

No two-pump, chump, it's not about you.

"Well, yeah… I'm writing. I didn't really plan on telling anyone yet." I shot an annoyed look at Brody.

"Oh, come on, baby… this is big. Y'all, my wife is not only gorgeous, but she's also so damn smart. I really hit the jackpot." Brody leaned in and kissed me.

"This is so exciting, Sage! How could you not tell your best friend?" Harlow shook her hands excitedly.

"It's not that big of a deal." I sipped my wine.

"You're writing a book. I'm pretty sure that's like, a huge deal. What's it about?" Harlow tossed back the rest of her wine and grabbed her burger, watching me like I was a celebrity.

"Um… it's a dark, mafia romance. I'm not really sure it'll be anyone's cup of tea in this town." Reaching for the wine bottle, I poured the last little bit into my glass, finishing it off.

"Oh, that's what you think, Miss New York. There are *plenty* of kinky couples behind closed doors. Isn't that right, Mr. Davis?" Harlow giggled as she nestled her head in the crook of Jake's neck, and his face turned red.

I cleared my throat, finished the last sip of wine,

and grabbed my empty glass. "I'm going to get more wine."

"Babe, eat something. My wife would survive off M&Ms and wine if it were up to her. I guess that's how she stays so skinny." Brody laughed behind me.

I got inside and found the kids were all asleep in their sleeping bags with the TV rolling credits. Clicking it off, I sighed. My phone buzzed and I flipped the screen over, finding a text from a private number.

Fucking your best friend's husband seems low even for you, doesn't it, Beauty Queen?

My eyes widened and I re-read the text. Looking around, my heart pounded harder. The glass in my hand slid and crashed onto the light hardwood floor. Spinning around, I could feel the hair on my neck stand.

Someone was watching me.

"Sage? What happened?" Brody ran inside and turned toward me. I quickly slid my phone into my pocket and looked at him. "Babe, you look like you've seen a ghost. Are you okay?" He immediately grabbed my hand and looked at me carefully.

Biting my bottom lip, I shuddered. "Um, yeah. I'm... I'm just tired."

"Shoot, girl, let me help you," Harlow whispered,

grabbing a broom and dustpan and immediately began cleaning up the mess. My mess. My best friend in this suburban hell was cleaning up my mess after I screwed her husband.

Remember when I said you can always go lower than rock bottom? Well, this... this is me grazing the blazing flames of hell.

CHAPTER SIX

*B*rody had to work over the weekend. He wanted to catch up on some cases before his new boss came into the office on Monday and shook things up. Apparently, he was from California and had invested a ton of money to transform the little firm into something bigger and better. I was excited because it meant limited pro-bono cases and more actual profit. *Hello, Dry Bar hair appointments and blow outs.*

My kids were with Brody's mom, who lived in Charleston and often took them once or twice a month on weekends so I could "write." I really needed to start getting words on paper instead of spending my free time at Hotel Besos—getting hit on and high off male attention, testing the limits of temptation. But then again, it was somewhat of a temporary band-aid to help my recovery, and I'd like to think a bit of research for my book.

Just Sage, I was wondering if you were free today? I'm back in town and would love to share another drink with you.

Part of me pushed Archer Collins far away from my mind because he was, after all, a passerby. I tapped my nail against the screen and slid my phone aside. I opened my laptop and began typing the next chapter in my romance novel. This was the only way I'd have steamy, hot sex—in my head and purely fictional. My phone buzzed again, and I hesitated for a moment. Eventually my curiosity overtook my willpower, and I read the next message.

I dare you.

My heart fluttered, and I, for one, am not known to shy away from a dare.

You're buying, Suit. Top shelf, Grey Goose martini. Two olives. This better be worth my time, I replied and slammed my laptop shut.

Business or pleasure? he replied.

I guess we will see... I confidently typed back to him —no trembling, no doubt. This was me. Just like a color wheel, we all have different shades that craft us into the human beings we are. The only problem is while some shades blend together and create something beautiful, others combine and the end result is nothing more than a hideous color. So, you must compartmentalize, separate the shades that cannot cross over together to ensure life is smooth and nothing gets messy.

I quickly run upstairs and looked at myself. I had been to Hotel Besos four times, each time I did my hair and makeup over the top and slid into a dress hidden in the tote box I had stowed away after having two kids. You know the box; we all have one... It's filled with the stuff you can't get rid of since it hurts too much because it either doesn't fit or it is closing a chapter of your life you so desperately want to grasp onto. Today was different. I already knew who I was meeting, so the element of surprise was gone. I vowed when I started this that I wouldn't be a repeat offender. No names, no sex, no numbers. Just flirting and some heavy petting. All those rules went out the window.

Archer Collins, he was different.

I kept my makeup natural and curled my hair. Sliding into a short dress, I tilted my head. It was true;

if God gave me one thing, it was beauty. *My strength and my weakness.* Maybe if I was unattractive, men wouldn't have flocked around me like seagulls on the beach; maybe I wouldn't crave their attention because you can't miss what you've never had.

My feet tapped down the stairs and I slid them into some wedges. I glanced over to the room on the side. Our peloton was sitting in it; I had done a pretty good job of keeping up with it and the reason being is this. My little hobby's only requirement was to *stay hot.* I opened the French doors and the opposing wall from my bike were shelves filled with rows and rows of my tiaras. Brody's law degree and college degrees hung neatly beside it. I supposed I hated feeling like I was some loser, so I displayed what was my identity for years. Letting my hand brush against them, I knew it was time to go—and not down memory lane.

Getting into my car, I started driving, turning up my favorite playlist that predominately consisted of Adam Levine. I took some deep breaths; I was actually nervous. My entire life, I was extremely confident—it came with the territory with beauty pageants and a dysfunctional family. I had to survive, so confidence was my armor.

Tapping my fingers to the beat of the song, I started to think about the text. The text where someone accused me of sleeping with Jake. *Accused?* Well, I guess it wasn't an accusation when it was the truth. Swallowing the lump in my throat, I could feel sweat beads budding at my hairline.

Who the hell could possibly know? Did Jake open his big mouth to a colleague or friend? No, he had just as much to lose as I did. That was partially why I thought it was a "smart affair." We were even on the playing field. *Damn, I'm fucked up.* This is the part when I should turn around and rethink my life choices, but instead, my strappy, wedged-heel foot hit the gas even harder.

Over an hour later, thanks to tourist traffic and crossing through bridges, I arrived in front of Hotel Besos. I chucked my keys at the valet, triple-checked that my location services were *off*, and walked in. Straightening my back, I glided against the cool marble floors and turned into the luxury bar area. It was decorated in emerald-green and gold, with velvet, smooth marble, and deep mahogany, which was far from the usually coastal décor that lined every other place in the area besides the historical attractions.

There he was. Archer Collins, the sexiest man I'd ever laid my eyes on and the sheer definition of trouble. Dressed in a sleek navy suit and cognac leather shoes, he was conversing with the bartender, and I couldn't help but smile. My Grey Goose martini was sitting there with two olives next to his own. Hearing my wedges against the floor, I instantly regretted not dressing up more.

"Sage…" His eyes started at my face and slowly dripped all the way down to my feet.

"Archer," I murmured, sliding onto the stool next to him. The bartender grinned while wiping a glass and turned away.

"You look…"

"I know, like a different person from the last time you saw me," I filled in, knowing I had significantly less makeup on.

"No, you look more beautiful than ever." His eyebrows creased together as his thumb swiped his lower lip.

My face felt warm, and I took a sip of my martini. "Mmm." I had forgotten what quality liquor tasted like. "Thank you for the drink, Suit." I turned back toward him, my legs spread apart.

His eyes glimpsed down and jerked back to my face as he tilted his head with a smirk. "The pleasure is all mine, Just Sage." He leaned into the bar, and I could tell he was thinking.

"So, this is pleasure, then?" I crossed my legs.

"Well, I don't see what business we have doing

anything else, do you, Sage?" The way my name rolled off his tongue, the way his hand gripped the bar, the way his eyes didn't falter from anywhere but mine... *I was a recovering addict, and he was my relapse.* All six-foot-four, hot chocolate brown eyes, shiny black hair, every inch of him was my damn relapse.

"What do you do for a living, Mr. Collins?" I lifted my drink to my lips and sipped.

"I observe people and judge them," he replied with ease.

"What?" My eyebrows pinched together as I paused before my next sip.

"A question for a question, Sage. Why did you come?"

I placed my glass on the dark mahogany bar and turned toward him, "But, Suit, I haven't come yet..." I let my breath brush against his face.

He turned, moving closer. His mouth was on mine, but we weren't kissing. "Let me..." he gripped my thigh and moved upward, "change that," he finished as his hand paused in between my legs.

For the first time, I saw Archer Collins shaken. I didn't have panties on, and he just discovered that.

Impulse. *Noun.* A sudden strong and unreflective urge or desire to act. Impulse is what makes or breaks human beings in any form of life. *Murder?* Impulse.

Sex? Impulse. *Marriage?* Impulse. *Having Children?* Impulse. *Affairs?* Impulse. See what I mean? It's imperative to human beings to be impulsive, because without impulse, we are irrelevant, boring. Impulsive behavior is what has me on top of Archer Collins, gripping his bare chest. His length hard inside me, my hips rocking in harmony to his deep groans, while he is repeating my name as if I were God. *Oh my, Sage...*

He flung me onto my back and gripped my ankles, perching them on his shoulders, teasing me with his fingers just before plunging back inside me, deeper than ever. Our sweat blurred together, our moans collided, and eventually, euphoria washed over both of us inside and out. My toes curled, my back arched, and I let myself go. For the first time in a long time, I truly let go. Archer crumbled next to me, and immediately turned his face to mine. Our noses touched and our heavy breathing mingled. "What are you, Sage, and where the hell have you been hiding?" He sighed with a laugh and ran his hand through his dark hair. Then, if this wasn't already enough of a high for me, he paused and tilted his chin upward, letting his lips miss my mouth and land on my forehead.

Chills raced up my arms. *I'm fucked.*

My phone shakes against the nightstand, but I don't want to move. I don't want to break out of this moment because I know all too well that this has to be the end. I prohibit myself from ever seeing Archer Collins again. That forehead kiss sealed the deal. The fact that I can't look him in the eye and even speak because my stomach is fluttering like a high school girl with a crush, hot glued the deal even more. Nope, this was it. I had my fix and now, this was it. I turned and looked at my phone.

Hey, sweetheart. I know we've both been in two different directions lately, but I want to take you out for dinner tonight. The new boss didn't show up today for the meeting so I'll be home soon. Hope you got a lot of writing done today. Love you. Brody texted me, and as if a sword tipped with guilt could do so, it sliced through my heart and soul. Tears taunted my waterline, and I turned away from Archer, tying the sheet around me.

"Hey, hey... Sage? You okay?" He body shifted toward mine to cradle me from behind, his strong hand rubbing up and down my arm.

Tears dripped down my cheeks. "My husband just texted me." I had cheated on Brody with Jake before. I had an affair, but I never even felt this way, this guilt. But that's because it was different with Archer. *I didn't want him to just fuck me, I wanted him to know me, and that made me the devil in wedges.* Emotional affairs are one hundred-fold worse than physical. Bodies connecting is just a temporary human need for fun, but letting someone have access to your heart and mind...? That's the most intimate piece of you that can be given.

"Oh, okay. Do you need to leave?" He pulled away, and I could hear him slide out of the bed and out of my dreams.

This was reality. I was a married woman and mother of two in my late twenties. I had a phone reminder to buy nut-free, dairy-free, gluten-free cookies for the annual Spring Fling at my kids' school for God's sake.

I looked over my shoulder and with words laced in anger, I spat, "Do you just enjoy screwing married women?".

Archer stopped, his briefs were already on. I hated that my eyes glued to how the black outlined his erection. *What was he, a sex Olympian?*

"Well, I've never done it before. However, I did enjoy..." he rubbed the light scruff against his jawline, "you." His words were as smooth as the buttery sheets under me.

"What are you doing back here? Are you stalking me?" I sat up and suddenly, fear pooled in my body, replacing the pleasure. The texts? The black car? How could I be so stupid as to climb into bed with a complete stranger when someone was stalking me, harassing me.

"Sage, may I remind you, that I don't even know your last name. I know nothing about you. Why would I stalk you? Is everything okay?" Archer pulled a white button-down on his tanned chest. His pecs were perfect and his fingers, the ones made of magic, began buttoning his shirt.

I quickly stood, holding the sheet around me, which I thought was always the dumbest thing people did. I mean, this man was literally inside of me and now I was a modest nun hiding behind a sheet? Archer turned away, giving me privacy to dress and probably to hide his expression, thinking he just slept with a psychopath.

"Everything's fine. I just need to go. I'm a mess..." Tugging my clothes and shoes on sloppily, I walked past Archer and paused. "It was really nice knowing you, Suit." I offered a half-smile and grabbed the cold door handle, but just as I turned it, I felt his hand on mine, warm and welcoming.

"I hope this isn't a goodbye, but rather a see you later, Just Sage..." He leaned down, kissing my lips.

My eyes closed, and I stood on my tiptoes, kissing him back. When you kiss back, you are officially equally responsible and have lost all impulse control. "You will want this to be a goodbye. I have more baggage than the airport you're heading back to." I turned away and left, closing the heavy door behind me, along with Archer Collins, for good.

CHAPTER SEVEN

*T*urning onto our street, I quickly moved my foot to the brake. Gripping the steering wheel tightly, I stopped. Our entire street was lined with police vehicles, fire trucks, and ambulances. My hands fumbled through my purse. I couldn't tell which house they were at. The kids had to be fine; they weren't even at home. *Brody?* Oh my god. Before I could even get to my favorites or recent call history, a text popped up on my screen.

I hope he was worth it. And then, as if the world couldn't have felt more suffocating, a picture tormented me. A picture of me, completely naked, on top of Archer. I could feel my pulse pounding and my palms sweating against the screen. Blinking as fast as I could, I counted my breaths in hopes this was all a nightmare, that this wasn't real.

My phone vibrated against my palms, reminding me this was all very, very real. "Brody?" My voice trembled against the speaker.

"Babe, I was checking on you. Our street is packed with cops. Mrs. Yang slipped and broke her hip or something. You might just want to park at the club-house and walk home."

I pressed my hand against my chest that was surely going to explode. I reversed my car, the tires screeching. Pulling over on the side of the main neighborhood entrance, I jumped out. My legs wavered like a baby doe while my head spun and my lungs felt starved for air. Glancing around, I felt eyes on me.

"You got caught, too?"

I jumped and turned. "Caught?" I hissed at Jake, who parked behind me.

"In the traffic on our street?" He squinted at me and pointed to the blocked road.

"What are you doing following me?" I stopped and stared at him. What if Jake Davis spray painted my car and sent me these texts?

"Sage, what are you talking about?"

I shook my head. No, there was no way... Why

would he when he was the other half of our affair? I started jogging away from him.

"Sage!" he called out from behind, forcing me to pick up my pace as I raced down the sidewalk to our home. Pushing open the door, I hunched over, catching my breath, but instead I choked on my sobs. My tears and snot intertwined and seeped into my mouth as I sunk to the ground.

"Sage? Babe, are you okay? Babe, talk to me…" Brody was wearing the silly grilling apron the kids had picked out for him last Christmas and had a spatula in his hand. He pulled me in between his legs, and I pressed my face to his chest, my nose clogged through my crying.

"Are you wearing cologne?" I looked up at him as he wiped my tears carefully.

"Well, it's date night…" He hugged me tighter with a smile. A smoky aroma wafted through the house from the back doors. "Oh shit!" Brody jumped up, leaving me on the floor, and raced to the back where I assumed he was burning some expensive steak.

I hated steak, I hated meat. I preferred veggie burgers, but Brody thought that was stupid. I was tired of him making me feel stupid compared to him, so I would eat it with a smile on my face while my stomach curled.

Peeling myself off the floor, I walked to the back-yard where Brody had two plates with, *ding, ding, ding* a medium-rare, charred steak on both plates. I sunk into the chair across from him as he opened a cheap bottle of Trader Joe's wine and poured it in the glass for me.

"Can you believe the new partner and boss at our firm didn't even show up?"

I looked down at my steak, cutting into the corner as small as I could. He didn't even care to ask why I was splayed out on the floor in hysterics. Stabbing my fork into a piece of asparagus, I took a sip of wine. "Maybe something came up?" I offered, my voice clearly hoarse from crying.

Brody's phone rang, and he tossed his napkin onto the table and grabbed it. "Brody Miller," he answered. "Hey. Yeah, of course... Mm-hmm... Perfect. Take care."

"Babe, I need to go and deal with a case issue." He quickly got up and left.

I looked down at my plate and pushed it aside as soon as he went inside. Leaning back in my chair, I looked out at our yard. We had a dense number of trees and a marsh-like area that ran behind. It was a huge reason I didn't want to buy this house with young kids, but Brody insisted the deal was too good to pass up. The sky was darkening, yet there weren't any stars. A starless night sky felt poetic, like it was just like me—dark and starless, with no glimmer of good.

Suddenly, a rustling penetrated my thoughts, causing me to jolt. I glanced behind me; our house lights were on, and Brody was probably tucked away in his office. Heavy footsteps cutting through water pattered again, and I turned back. My fingers trembled against my wineglass. What did that text mean, *I hope he was worth it?* Whoever was taunting me, whoever was trying to scare me was here, watching me. I looked into the dark shadows and stood. The light behind me probably crafted a halo around me, making it easy to see what I was doing, while I couldn't see what lurked right in front of me.

Taking a deep breath, I started to walk toward the woods. The sound of footsteps picked up, and I could hear them splash through the dark marsh water and mud. "Who the fuck is out there? I'm calling the cops," I hissed through my teeth, which were chattering with fear. The heavy steps grew silent and my rapid heartbeat started to settle.

Run, a low voice whispered, sending chills up my spine.

I slowly turned, but just before my feet could move

through the damp ground below me, my body was flung back. A ripping sound arose as pain radiated against my scalp. Someone grabbed my hair from behind, pulling me backward. Just before I fell, I looked up and saw a shine from the moon just before everything went black.

"Uh…" I groaned, closing my eyes tighter than they already were. My hand crept to my head. A light humming strummed next to me and I felt a wire taped against my skin. I let my tongue slide over my scaly, dry lips. Opening my eyes, my gaze darted back and forth. I wasn't home.

"Mrs. Miller?" My vision felt blurry. "Mrs. Miller?" the soft voice called out again. I looked over at the ridiculously handsome man wearing a white coat and stethoscope. His shiny black hair was brushed neatly, and his caramel-colored skin shimmered even in the low light of the stark room.

"What is going on…" My throat felt uncomfortably dry, causing my voice to crack between words.

"Mrs. Miller, I'm Dr. Shah. Your husband found you unconscious in the middle of the marsh located in your backyard." He paused, waiting for me to fill in the gaps.

"Sage Miler?" A police officer came inside the room and stood beside the doctor.

"Yes?" I replied meekly.

"Ma'am, we have to ask you some questions…"

I looked at Dr. Shah, who offered a small smile and nodded reassuringly like I was some kindergartner trying to go potty.

"Okay." I licked my lips again, and planting my palms next to my hips, I pushed upward. Dr. Shah moved quickly and handed me the hospital bed remote.

"Sage… You don't mind me calling you Sage, right?" the officer started, and I nodded in return. "Your husband, Brody Miller, brought you in last night, covered in mud and… blood." He paused with a smirk at his ability to rhyme.

Okay, Dr. Seuss, let's get to the point. What the fuck am I doing in a hospital bed and where is my husband?

"Do you remember anything from last night?" He tapped his pen against his lips and stared at me.

"No, I mean… all I know is that someone's been watching me and following me. Someone spray painted my car and—" I stopped as Dr. Shah and the officer looked at me like I was a complete idiot. I couldn't tell them about the texts, because then they'd know about my... *indiscretions.*

"So, someone is following you?" The officer scribbled something on the tiny notepad and looked back up at me with lifted eyebrows.

"Um... I think I remember someone had grabbed my hair, hit my head, and pulled me backward." Silence filled the room and I swallowed nervously. "Does... does anyone know where my husband is?"

"He's at work." The officer watched for my reaction.

Of course, Brody was at work. It was a Sunday, and he loved going in to have things prepped for the week ahead. And with the new partner coming in tomorrow, it meant he would want to make sure everything was perfect, all while I laid here, alone. "My kids?" I whispered, holding my tears of humiliation back.

"They are with their grandmother, and Brody was here earlier this morning..." Dr. Shah said kindly, unlike the prick cop.

"How much did you have to drink last night, Sage?" Officer Stick-Up-His-Ass asked me.

"I don't remember." I instantly regretted saying that because it made me sound like an alcoholic.

"Well, your blood alcohol level was very high, as in a full wine bottle and then some high."

Victim-shaming, nice.

"I was unaware that the legal drinking age had raised because the last time I checked, I'm over the age of twenty-one and wasn't driving," I fired at him.

The officer's face flushed, "Well, ma'am, it's taking police resources away when you're drunk and landing out in the marsh." My mouth parted, but I didn't have the strength to fight this misogynistic asshole.

"Okay... I think this is a good point to pause and let my patient rest." Dr. Shah began to wave the officer toward the door.

"Mrs. Miller... I'm going to go check on your blood work. I'll be back in a bit..." Dr. Shah said kindly.

"Oh my god! Sage!" Harlow charged through the door, pushing past the officer and doctor without a second glance, gliding with two cups of coffee and a giant monogrammed tote bag flung over her hand.

"Harlow..." I let my head crash into the pillow. I had never felt so alone in such a long time... until I woke up in a hospital room without anyone. I can't believe I was the world's shittiest friend, considering she was always the best. I was the black sheep of moms at the school, and she took me under her wing.

"Are you okay? What the hell happened to you? I told you to wait for me if you're going to be pounding alcohol." She offered a smile and handed me a warm cup.

"Harlow, I have no idea... I swear, someone grabbed me last night out back and they..." I nodded in the direction of where the cop and the doctor had gone through, "they think I'm some drunk stay-at-home mom..." I sighed.

"I mean, don't y'all have cameras out back?" Harlow sipped her coffee.

I shook my head and took a sip of mine, the warm liquid caressing my throat.

"Well, that's stupid, everyone has them now. I'll have Jake tell Brody which ones we have. It's going to be okay, honey. Maybe you just really had too much and went fishing..." Harlow giggled just before leaning in to kiss the top of my head. "Ooh, please, please wash your hair soon." She wafted her hand in front of her nose, making me laugh.

"You be sure to text me if you need anything at all. I'm heading back since the kids are with Jake, and he needs to go show a house soon."

I plastered a smile over my face but fear and anxiety laid underneath. *Jake.* He was the only one who knew about... knew about what? The fact that I stupidly had an affair with my best friend's husband or was even dumber for having one with a neighbor? You can't just throw a 'for sale' sign in your yard and run away. I was trapped, and what in the hell was I supposed to do? But then again, Brody wasn't here. Brody left me outside and magically moments later, I was attacked. Did he lace my wine with something? Did he find out about everything? My head was spinning with assumptions.

Nice job, Sage. You wanted more of a ride in your life and now you've got yourself a whole damn theme park.

I spent the next two days in the hospital, eating bland food and flipping through random shows on the tiny TV hung on the stark wall. It was sad because this was the closest thing to a weekend getaway I had since having children. Nurses caring for me, doctors checking in on how I was doing. Brody came by twice and even brought flowers, which only made me think he was overcompensating for trying to attack his wife and the mother of his children.

The gash in my head made me pause playing detective and just rest. I also kept checking my phone obsessively to see if Archer had texted, but I suppose he was long gone to where he was headed or wherever he was supposed to be.

Eventually, the getaway ended, and I was back home. Andi and Tate had decorated the living room with colorful banners and balloons, and the three of them greeted me so excitedly that I felt guilty for enjoying my stay in the hospital. Besides the fact that I couldn't sleep well, considering every time I closed my eyes, I heard that callous voice taunting me to *"run."*

The next two days flew by between packing lunches, loads of laundry, peloton rides, and carpool. I behaved myself because I realized that maybe boring was good. *Boring was safe.*

"You look so much better, Sage." Harlow pushed her shopping cart next to mine. We did our bi-monthly Costco trips together because we shared a membership card.

I know, I know, gag me.

I glanced at her. Harlow was wearing a fitted black workout tank and bright pink fitted leggings, finished off with a perfected messy bun and some crisp new Nikes. "I guess when you wash blood, sweat, and mud out of your hair, you look like a brand-new person." I paused. "So, how's Jake been? I haven't seen him since the dinner and he's usually out doing yardwork or something…" I reached for an oversized box of gummies, also known as bribery for my children, and put it in my cart.

"He's been out of town, I thought I told you…he's

looking into getting his North Carolina real estate license, too. You know, since I've cut back so much to be with the kids more... well, we need to expand, expand, expand." Harlow placed a massive box of cashews in her cart.

"Oh... okay." That was fucking sketchy as shit. Before I could push and pry further, my phone rang. Probably a telemarketer, because honestly, who called anyone these days? If you didn't text me, you wouldn't hear from me. Glancing at it, I froze. I recognized the area code from our texts, though I didn't save his number because I figured I'd be better off if I just forgot it completely. *Resist the temptation...*

"Answer your damn phone, Sage!" Harlow cinched her brows and looked at me.

"Watch my cart," I mouthed and walked away.

CHAPTER EIGHT

"*H*ello?" I mumbled under a hushed tone, making my way outside the massive box store.

"Sage, how are you?" Archer's deep voice cut through the phone. "I've been meaning to call... I'm so sorry for the way things were left." He sounded... different.

"Archer, please don't call me again. I am married, I have kids... I can't... I can't do this," I pleaded, hoping he'd end the call and never want to talk to me again.

"Because you have more baggage than the airport?" he asked, and I could envision the sexy smirk on his face.

"Yes." I chewed my bottom lip nervously.

He paused, then said, "Turns out, I'm pretty strong and can carry a lot of additional baggage." He rolled each word without any doubt in his voice.

I swallowed. "Archer."

"Sage—"

"Sage Miller!" A sharp voice pierced through this moment, a moment I wanted to bottle up because of the exhilaration coursing through me was incredible.

Quickly ending my call, I paused between syllables. "Car-ro-line."

"Did you ask Brody about the Spring Fling? I never heard back from you, which is very irresponsible I may add." She pursed her lips obnoxiously and stared at me.

"He… he said his law firm would love to." I hated the way my voice shook in front of her. I stood in front of thousands of people, wearing a tiny bikini and strutting my ass over runaways, wearing a thin sash and balancing a crown on my head and now, I was stammering in front of the damn PTA president from our school.

Her thin lips smacked together. "Sage, I mean this in the nicest way possible… but you really are lucky to be so…" she poked my shoulder, "pretty." She clenched her eyes together and shot them open.

"Girl, I just paid for your stuff…" Harlow was behind me, our groceries combined into one cart.

"Oh my gosh I'm so sorry." I quickly moved to help her push it.

"Caroline, I see your still bullying Sage. Get a life," Harlow shot at Caroline.

I moved past them both and heard Harlow follow me to the car. "You need to stop letting her put you down…"

"But it's true, I don't fit in…" I pointed in front of me. "Brody married me because he wanted a pretty little wife with no brain and just…" I sighed, popping my trunk open and flinging the giant value boxes inside. The parking lot was jam-packed, and I was hungry. All I wanted to do was go home and relax because I had to go to a work dinner with Brody to meet his new boss tonight.

"That's not true, honey… He loves you; I love you." Harlow finished helping me pile our stuff into my trunk just before we jumped inside.

I began driving, turning up the music in hopes this discussion could just be ignored. My signal light clicked as I made a right turn, and glancing into my rearview mirror, I saw a black car. *The black car.*

I sped up and turned again. The car continued to

follow me, and I gripped the wheel tightly as I let my foot slide over to the brake. Slowing, I watched the car grow closer. "Harlow, I think this car has been following us." I didn't take my eyes off the mirror, until suddenly, the car turned just as she glanced over her shoulder.

"Which car?" She looked back at me.

Shaking my head, I sped up and pulled up to Harlow's house. I offered to unload her groceries but she insisted she'd be fine. I waited as she unloaded and stared at the house in front of me. The Davis house was a little smaller than ours, but stunning. My eyes moved up toward a shifting curtain upstairs. Squinting and leaning in closer to my steering wheel, I looked up. It was a man. Jake? He was home? Why would Harlow lie?

"Thanks, hon, for the ride. Hope y'all have fun tonight." I glanced at Harlow through my open window.

"Sure will..." I smiled and reversed my car, looking back up at the window—there was no doubt Jake was home. The curtain quickly pressed together tightly as my tires hit the bump at the end of their driveway. Anxious, I twiddled my thumbs against the leather of the steering wheel. I needed to go home; Brody's work dinner was in two hours and by the looks of how I rolled into Costco, I'd need that time to get ready and set the kids up with the sitter.

"Mommy!" Andi's sweet voice shrieked when I came through the door. The way she and Tate gripped my legs and hugged me always made me feel emotional. I had always felt like the only reason I kept up this role was because I had to. I had two kids who depended on me. My mother was either drunk or pushing me to "maximize my beauty" to help with the bills. I had to grow up so quickly.

I squeezed their cheeks together in between my index finger and thumb, leaning down to kiss them both. As much as I thought of this as a prison sentence —you know, an eighteen-year term—looking at this life, I realized I didn't need to fit with them, I wanted to.

But I also wanted something of mine, too.

Humming upstairs, I let the steaming hot water wash away the impending neck pain I felt. I couldn't believe the police didn't care to further investigate into how I landed in the hospital. They just assumed I was a stay-at-home mom who had one too many. Someone once told me that I was so lucky to be beautiful and that it was a weapon; I agreed but not in that sense. No, beauty was a weapon that shot me first. No one ever took nor takes me seriously because I'm just a pretty face, and now even worse, I'm just a pretty face with a pretty little life.

Using the tips of my fingers, I scrubbed my scalp. Lining up hair wash days with plans was my go-to. Tilting my head back, I sang softly as I washed the soapy suds off. As my eyes slowly parted, I saw something. Panic washed over me faster than the water from the showerhead as I took in a shadow outside of the shower curtain.

"Brody?" I called out. Frozen in fear, I took a deep breath and jerked the curtain open and just as I did, the lights went out. My heart knocked against my chest cavity as fear sent chills inside me. "Brody..."

My feet tapped against the cold floor as droplets flaked off my body, puddling where my feet trailed. Reaching for my towel, I wrapped it around. I could hear light echoes from my kids downstairs and... *Brody.*

If they were all there, then who was here? Finally reaching the light switch, I clenched my eyes shut, the ticking of the switch taunting me. A noise closer to our bedroom erupted, and I spun, gripping the wooden frame of the bathroom door and peered out.

No one. Nothing's there.

Sweat beads collided with the water droplets that covered my body, and sinking onto our bed, a long breath escaped my mouth. Shaking my head, I got up and knew Brody would freak out if he saw me like this when we had to leave soon. Maybe it was Andi or Tate just playing silly games with me.

I'm okay. Everything is okay.

I painted my face with makeup—fake lashes, contour, highlighter, the works. If there was anything I knew how to do, it was makeup, hair, and fashion.

"Wow, you look beautiful, babe." Brody's reflection rose in the mirror in front of me.

I smiled while lining my parted lips. The silk robe covering me was partly open, revealing the curves of my breasts. Turning toward him, I looked at him. "You don't look so bad yourself, handsome." I fixed his tie and tugged his jacket in. Reaching up, I kissed his lips and then the side of his neck.

"Oh, babe, we've got to go soon." He turned away. "Please get dressed. I don't want to be late."

Heat rushed to my face as embarrassment pounded my body. I craved being touched and wanted. Sex was what relieved the tension and anxiety that suffocated me. This wasn't a part of my addiction, this was me—a fucking human with basic fucking needs. Annoyed, I aggressively grabbed my black dress from the back of the door. Sliding into it, the slit ran up my thigh just enough to be sexy yet classy. The fit hugged my curves but showed off my flat abdomen. Tilting my head to the side, I shrugged with a sigh and walked downstairs.

"Mommy, you look like a princess." Tate grinned at me with pizza hanging out of his mouth.

"Thank you, my sweetheart." I kissed the top of his sandy blonde hair, fluffing it with my fingertips.

Brody grabbed his keys and hugged the kids while I reached for my clutch and phone, which instantly vibrated against my palm. Looking down, my heart stopped. A picture of me, with my eyes closed in the shower... *The shower I just took.* The shower that a shadow was outside of.

I looked up at Brody, who was strapping on his watch, his phone sitting on the kitchen island next to me. "Brody..." I started. What was I supposed to say? I was digging my own grave. This person knew I had too much to lose, and they were enjoying this sick game. Anger replaced my fear. *I'm calling the cops.* What if they were still in my house? My kids were going to be here.

Spinning, I raced in all directions, opening closet doors and squatting under beds upstairs. My phone buzzed again with another picture as my foot hit the top stair. This time it was an old photo of me asleep in a hotel—the same hotel I was in with Jake Davis.

"Sage? What the hell?" Brody appeared in the door. I probably looked like a deer in headlights.

"I was... looking for my earring." I stammered, gripping my earlobe. "Oh, look, found it." I smiled, showing him the gold hoop.

"We're going to be late, let's go." He rolled his eyes with disappointment and left the room.

"Just give me a minute. I'll meet you in the driveway," I huffed. Just as I turned out of our room, the curtain fluttered. I walked toward it and tugged the curtain away, finding the window was wide open. I pressed my hands against the window and looked down. A ladder. *A fucking ladder.* I had to tell Brody, but how? These texts would ruin me, especially since Brody wasn't a man of forgiveness. I couldn't let my kids grow up with *his house, her house, their kids, my kids'* kind of life.

"Andi, Tate! Leah?" I called out and ran back downstairs. "Leah, I want you to take the kids to Harlow's. You know Mrs. Davis, right?" I looked at the high school babysitter who mumbled while busying herself with some social media app. "Leah!"

"Sorry, Mrs. Miller." She stood quickly. "I'll take them over. Are we supposed to stay there until y'all get back?"

"Yes, I'll pick them up from there and pay you then,

too." I ushered them all out of the house in front of me. Just before shutting the door behind me, I glanced over my shoulder and a shudder racing up my spine.

Brody was in the car, and I tapped his window. "I'm just going to run the kids over to Harlow's. Don't ask." He rolled his eyes as I sprinted them over to her house, my heels skidding across the driveway covered in chalk masterpieces and hopscotch outlines.

I repeatedly pounded my clenched fist against the pale blue door with a giant "D" hung from it. Harlow opened it with a giant smile. "Hey girl… Damn, you look smokin'."

I laughed but glanced over my shoulder and to both sides like a paranoid psycho. "Thanks, Harlow. I know this is so last-minute, but our air conditioning isn't working and we don't have time to mess with it. Can the kids stay with you? Leah will help." I nodded in her direction. "I'll pick them up as soon as we get done with dinner." I clasped my hands together, begging.

"Sage Miller, stop that mess. You know I love these kids. Come on in, babies." I pulled Harlow in and gave her a swift hug before tugging the hem of my dress down to jog in my five-inch heels back to the car.

I slid into the passenger seat and looked over at Brody. "Do I even want to know what that was about?"

He turned the key and swiftly reversed out of the driveway.

"The kids just wanted to play over there, and besides, Leah's so careless. Her eyes are never on the kids and always on her phone. I need to find someone older to babysit," I rambled, spinning my wedding ring around my finger.

There was silence between us, though it wasn't unusual. Brody and I never really had much to talk about. He was a man who loved tennis, studying legal jargon, and talking about politics. Meanwhile, I could tell you how to layer Vaseline on your teeth to make sure your lipstick doesn't streak onto them, and how double-sided tape will hold your bikini in place or give your pants a quick hem in a pinch.

"So, how is your book coming?" Brody stared straight ahead.

"Um, well… I've been busy with the kids, so it just got you know, pushed on the back-burner." I anxiously tugged the hem of my dress.

"Well, haven't you been going to some hotel or bar to work a few times a week?" He glanced over at me.

I was completely caught off-guard; I had never told Brody where I went and he never asked. "Oh, how did you…" I started but regretted my interrogation, which made me sound guilty.

"Sage… you know I'm a lawyer, right?" The way his eyes latched to mine made me suddenly realize maybe Brody Miller wasn't just the nice guy… maybe he also had pieces of himself that I didn't know.

Pulling up to The Shell—Charleston's nicest restaurant—I waited because Brody insisted on opening my door for me. I knew deep down it was in case anyone from work saw us out here.

I couldn't make eye contact with him as I murmured, "Thank you…"

The doors were held open for us, and we strode inside. We were directed to a private room in the back. "Sage, make sure not to say, 'um and like' so much," Brody hissed into my ear.

My back instantly straightened and my lips parted, but words didn't come out. This was what Brody did. He was that sweet guy you wanted to be with, but then he would crush your soul and make you feel inept in two seconds flat.

Walking into the crowded room, I shook hands and shared hugs with people Brody had worked with over the years. I knew the entire firm was trying to do a complete revamp to make more money.

"Sage!" A friendly voice called out. Brody's secretary Callie turned toward me. Callie was so much like me when I first moved here—young and out of place—which was a huge reason we connected.

"Callie, it's so wonderful to see you, girl!" I chirped, but instantly caught Brody's side-eye. He hated when I got too close to his co-workers, and he especially hated when I said "girl."

"Have you seen the new partner... well, boss? So confusing, like he's a partner but the boss, too. Anyways, oh-mah-god... drool worthy." Callie turned my body and pointed toward the back of a tall man who had a glass of whiskey in his hand. "Did you?" Callie leaned into me.

"Did I what?" I stuttered, my eyes fixed on the back of the silhouette of Brody's new boss. My hands trembled and I laced them together.

"Callie, may I borrow my wife?" Brody intertwined his hand in mine and led me away.

My feet dragging behind, but I kept moving forward. *Please don't be him. Please, please, please...* My mind spun with a million ways to run or how to just feign an illness. But just before I could piece my scattered thoughts together, he turned... and so did my stomach.

His creamy, chocolate brown eyes widened slightly as he locked onto mine and his brow slightly arched. My chest clearly heaved faster than it did after a marathon. I slid my hand from Brody's because it was slathered in sweat, while my legs trembled in the heels I could usually walk miles in.

"Sage, this is our new partner and owner of our firm..."

And just before Brody could finish his introduction, the voice in front of me cleared. "Archer. Archer Collins." His hand—the one that had traced every inch of my naked body—reached out to mine.

I looked down at it and looked back at him. He wasn't supposed to be here, he was supposed to be a passerby. Suddenly, I felt confused and lost. Everything started spiraling out of control ever since *him*. Secrets I had expertly buried were being unearthed. My smooth sailing life was now trekking on unkind, crashing waves. Archer Collins was my demise, and now he was here, as my husband's new boss.

"Sage?" Brody spoke through his teeth and nudged my hand. I looked at him and back at Archer's lingering hand.

"Sage." I shook his hand, his fingers gently grazing the inside of my palm as his eyes stayed on mine. Heat grew between my legs as his fingers circled my palm, reminding me how they felt inside me.

"Just Sage, huh?" He smirked, tilting his head to the side and letting his eyes fall all the way down. "So, what do you do, Sage?" He knew he had me in a vulnerable spot. This wasn't question for a question. My husband was standing right here, making sure I was polite to the person who was about to sign his paychecks.

"I am a…" *What was I? A whore you slept with? A sad, lonely suburban mom and wife who was a recovering, no wait… relapsed sex addict?*

"Sage was Miss USA and is writing a book," Brody spat out. "She even had a modeling contract with a huge makeup company, but I swooped in and charmed her into coming down here and being my wife." He chuckled at his own charm.

"Wow, a beauty queen and a novelist? You're a woman of many wonders, Sage Miller." Archer lifted an eyebrow and took a sip of his whiskey—the drink I always preferred when I was alone.

"Oh, I'm so sorry, Mr. Collins. I'm going to have to go and say hello to Martin Jones over there; he's a huge supporter of the firm. I'll be back soon. Sage." He nodded at me, eyes wide adding a non-verbal warning to make sure to not embarrass him. I smiled at him with my lips folded.

"You take your time, Brody. I'll go get your beautiful wife a drink." Archer creased his elbow up, signaling me to take it.

Licking my bottom lip, I let my arm sew through his. His touch sent a current through my body. "I thought you were a passerby?" I hissed through my teeth.

"I never said I was." He grinned at me. "Two Grey Goose martinis, with two olives in each." He tapped his finger against the bar in the corner of the private dining room. The bartender nodded and quickly busied himself crafting our drinks. Sliding onto a stool, he did the same, but never took his eyes off mine. "So, how are you, Mrs. Miller?" Archer smiled and let his thumb rub the scruff of his jawline—the jawline my lips had grazed, the thumb that circled me and made me scream his name.

I lifted my drink and took a sip, hoping it would coat the excessive dryness that coated my throat. "I'm good. How are you?" I said mid-sip.

"Well, I'll be honest, I was dreading this dinner party—they always bore me. But now… business has become pleasure."

His hand rubbed against mine, and I quickly pulled it away, glancing around the bustling room. "Archer…" I hissed.

He smiled confidently. "Sage."

"What happened between us can never ever happen again, and no one can ever find out." I straightened myself up and took another sip.

"So, our little secret. I like sharing things with you, Sage," he whispered, leaning in towards me enough for his cool breath to brush against my face.

I pulled back, balancing my ass on the stool, hoping I wouldn't fall backward but definitely testing the limit. Something I seemed to have a knack for.

"Hi, babe…" Brody approached and smiled proudly. Of course, he wouldn't be jealous. He was thrilled I had impressed his new boss and wasn't embarrassing him. But then again, why would any husband be jealous? He wouldn't naturally assume his wife had already screwed his new boss before the first day working with him.

CHAPTER NINE

I was sitting next to Archer and across from Brody. The three of us made a right angle that couldn't be more wrong. The clamor of legal verbiage, mergers, and cases all blurred together. Everyone was intrigued by Archer, and why wouldn't they be? Archer Collins was from California, he was a top, cut-throat attorney, and had owned his own firm in Calabasas. The rich and famous adored him—all their petty crimes, major mishaps, and image issues *poof* went away because of Archer's talent. After spending so much time with the vein of society that stuffed his accounts with millions, he decided he wanted a change. A change of pace, here in Charleston, South Carolina. At freshly forty, he was too young to retire, so why not buy out a small law firm and be the boss—because clearly, that was what normal people did to downgrade their stress.

I stabbed my fork through the crispy kale in front of me and took a bite. Brody was immersed in conversations between his lawyer friends and paralegals after devouring Archer's story of success. You could basically see the drool trickling from everyone's mouth as Archer described high-profile cases with ease.

Archer leaned toward me and whispered, "You don't seem impressed."

I looked up at him, pausing my fork at my lips. "I'm more impressed by how the chef managed to keep the kale this crisp." I grinned and let my lips part, and Archer's eyes fixed on my lips.

Suddenly, a cool hand and fingers ran up my thigh through the slit of my dress. My heart quickened and I looked over at him, warning him with my eyes and a light shake of my head. Clearing my throat, I threw my napkin over my lap and pulled myself in closer to the table.

His eyes lit up, just as his fingers reached higher. "I'd love to learn what would impress you, Mrs. Miller," he said smoothly.

I looked around us; everyone was enjoying their meals and conversations, but this... This was risky, this was bad. *So, very bad.*

His fingers pushed inside of me, my mouth dropping as he added a second. "Mmm…" I let out a soft moan, immediately grabbing another napkin to cover my mouth.

He knew exactly what to do. My thighs clenched together as sweat beads built against my hairline. I looked into his eyes; he had never shifted his gaze off of me. *Was he not worried or nervous?* Pushing inside of me harder and faster, my breathing great heavy and I stuffed my mouth closer to the napkin. I shuddered as warmth washed over me completely. Letting out a mix between a moan and cough, I swore the room grew in on me.

Grabbing the wine in front of me, I took the longest sip ever. Brody looked at me and smiled just before going back to his conversation. I smiled back with both rows of my teeth showing, like some competition poodle at a dog show.

"Mmm… delicious." I turned and looked up at him. He had placed his fingers in his mouth and winked at me.

"You like the food, boss?" Brody laughed, and I basically could have died.

"I've never had something more delicious. Charleston definitely has hidden gems that I'm so thrilled to have found," Archer replied, taking a sip of his wine.

My face felt like an oven burning, and I quickly excused myself to go in the bathroom and slap myself back into reality. Standing in front of the mirror and sink, I grabbed a paper towel and wet it, wiping behind my neck. I planted my hands on the granite vanity in front of me. Inhaling and exhaling the fragrant aroma around me, I paused. Even the damn bathroom smelled like roses in this upscale restaurant. A woman wearing a cream-colored fur coat came inside and moved into a stall. The coat on her was stunning, it emitted wealth.

I closed my eyes thinking back to winning Miss USA. One of the luxury items I won was an incredible, soft, silky mink fur coat. Look, I love animals and think it's so screwed up, but something about that coat meant so much to me. I was the kid who stood shivering at the bus stop since mommy dearest was too hungover and my dad was too busy screaming at us while working double shifts. That fur coat showed me I could take care of myself, and maybe my beauty wasn't a weapon aimed toward me, it could be aimed to protect me.

One cold, New York morning, I went to my mom's house since I hadn't still moved all of my things out. I went to my old closet to pull it out, but it was gone. Storming to my mom, who reeked of shitty four-dollar Burnett's vodka, I shouted at her. She smiled in a way that made me clench my fist. She had sold it for money... money she was pouring down her damn throat.

They say everything has a silver lining, and that is true. That was the morning which turned into the night I was working at the bar when I met Brody.

My ticket out of my personal hell—into a new hell, one with a white-picket fence. I thought maybe he'd be the cure to my addiction to sex—my repulsive need to have male attention, even if it was negative.

But if there's one thing I had truly learned was that there's no antidote to a problem embedded in your soul. It's just who you are, and you can't change that. No one can.

What happened with my mom in the morning just hours before my shift at the sticky-floor bar was something that would haunt me for the rest of my days. It was the reason I went from messed up to an absolute shit-storm. It was also the reason I lived every day in fear. *Fear that if anyone ever knew, a flip of the switch could turn on my life and I would sit behind a new prison... a real prison.*

Breaking out of my thoughts, I focused back to dinner, I realized many people were done and flocking to the bar. Brody was still talking his head off with someone from work, and Archer was nowhere to be found. I passed a young waitress and grabbed a champagne glass off the silver platter she held.

"I thought you ran away…"

I turned around, almost spilling my champagne. Looking up at him, I couldn't help but roll my lips to suppress my smile. "You can't run if you have nowhere to hide…" I offered back to Archer.

"Well, I think you always have a place to hide." He brushed his finger against my cheek just before another law firm employee came over to kiss his ass.

"Hey, babe, you ready to go?" my doting husband asked. "Harlow called and said she's bringing the kids back to our house because Tate went ballistic for his room." Brody wrapped his hand around the small of my waist.

I looked up at him. "Yeah, I'm tired…" I glanced over my shoulder and met Archer's curious eyes, he followed Brody's hand that was resting on my waist and I could have sworn his fist clenched. Getting to the car, I tightened my seatbelt over me, and sunk back.

"You did amazing, sweetie. Archer thinks so highly of you. It'll really help me at the firm." Brody had pride glowing from his face as he maneuvered the car out of the lot.

Yes, honey, I'm wife of the damn year. Your boss just fingered me at dinner and you're thanking me.

The car ride was spent with Brody rehashing and relishing every single detail and conversation he had. His voice lined with excitement because apparently, Archer had big plans for the firm. I guess Brody had tapped-out from all the pro-bono cases and realized the life we lived came with a hefty price tag. He was rambling about the kids' college funds and retirement, but I didn't hear much. I watched the bridges connect, the water passing by, and the dark sky hover over us. I also couldn't hear much besides recollecting the moans I had to suppress in my napkin at dinner when Archer Collins had his hand up my dress.

When we got home, Harlow was finishing up some dishes I had left in our sink. She smiled at me but put her index finger against her lips, pointing the other hand up. "They are finally asleep..." she whispered.

"Harlow, thank you so much for watching them." I came to the island, letting my fingers trace the slivers of gold embedded in the countertops. "Hey, is Jake home?" I looked over to double-check, but I knew Brody had already gone upstairs to change and get ready for bed.

"No, he's still in North Carolina, remember? He'll be back tomorrow. Everything okay?" Harlow paused with the drying towel in one hand and the shiny plate in the other.

Maybe I didn't see anyone...? Harlow wouldn't lie to me. "Yeah, yeah…" I hesitated. "Where are your kids tonight? I feel terrible that you had to come over here when Jake's not home to help with yours." I looked at her.

"Oh… my dad is over. He always comes and stays with us when Jake's gone. I'm too scared to stay home alone." She laughed and came around, pulling out an island chair and sliding into it.

I let out an over-the-top sigh and smacked my hand against my head. "Oh shit, that explains it." I laughed and got into the chair next to her.

"Explains what?" Harlow opened a bottle of water and looked at me curiously.

"I… I saw a man in your upstairs window after our Costco trip, and I don't know… I wondered if I should have mentioned it before sending you in to possibly find a serial killer or something." I rubbed my lips together feeling embarrassed.

"Well, yeah… I'd appreciate you telling me that next time, Sage." She lightly punched my shoulder and we both laughed. "Anyway, how was tonight? How was Brody's new boss?"

"Um, it was good. The food was great, and his new boss seems... *nice*. I didn't really get to talk to him." I spun my wedding ring around on my finger. "There was this lady wearing a fur coat...you remember my weird love for fur coats, don't you?" I smiled at Harlow.

"Oh honey, of course I do. The story about your mom selling the one you won from your big pageant win?" Harlow's hand flung to her heart as if it were breaking for me.

"Mm-hmm..." I sipped some water.

"Why don't you just buy one for yourself?" She shrugged.

I thought about it so many times. "They are so expensive, and where on earth would I wear a fur coat in Charleston? Besides, I think it's also unethical..." I shrugged. "Honestly, it's almost like a young Sage repression thing. I just want it because it was taken from me and God, they are beautiful." I hugged myself.

"What is your favorite animal?" Harlow asked.

Without thinking twice, I replied, "*Men*."

She laughed so hard, some of the water she was drinking went up her nose. "You are a naughty little housewife, Sage Miller." She snorted between laughs.

I covered my face and laughed into my hands. "Ugh…I'm just tired and need to go to bed. Thanks so much for watching the kids, I owe you."

I stood and walked her to the front door, letting her out. After shutting the door, I leaned against it. I felt happy, a stupid grin was plastered on my face, but fell soon after. I was happy because I got off tonight by my husband's boss' hands. I was happy because, as an addict, I had found a new high.

My new drug of choice? *Archer Collins.*

"Andi, Tate! Move it!" I yelled as I scrambled to pack lunches and grab my keys. Speeding through our neighborhood, we were late, which was a good thing because the car line had cleared and dropping my kids off was drama-free. I quickly turned out of the school and headed toward downtown Charleston. I had to meet with someone, someone who might be able to help me with whoever the hell was trying to scare me. Well, trying was a soft word considering I was fucking terrified. I tossed and turned in bed all night, once the excitement of Archer wore off and I flipped through my phone. Seeing the images sent to me just hours before. The picture of me in the shower? Pictures of me with both Jake and Archer. These were things I couldn't make up. The worst part was, this person knew I couldn't afford to tell my husband or anyone. They had something on me that connected me to everyone and everything—enough to destroy every relationship I had. *What if they knew more?*

"Hey, beauty queen. Ain't it early for a drink?" Mark's Southern drawl instantly took the edge off, more than the drinks he served.

"Mark... I told you not to call me that." I took a seat on the smooth, stool in front of his worn-down bar and tugged out my yellow Chapstick tube before gliding it over my lips just to buy myself time before telling him what was going on.

It was too early for tourists to flock in to get a taste of his Southern charm and fried chicken served with the popular IPA's. Mark was wiping some shot glasses clean. "Lady, if I won Miss USA, I'd have my fuckin' tiara and sash on every damn day. For the record, you told me not to call you 'beauty queen missus' no more." He put his hands on his hips and stood tall before lifting one cupped hand, waving like a pageant girl.

I shook my head with a laugh. "Mark, listen, I have to be quick. I have to start writing more of my book before Brody wonders what I've been doing all day."

"Well, what *have* you been doing?" Mark lifted his dark brows that were streaked with gray.

"None of your business, nosy old man." I shook my finger at him. What was I supposed to say? I spent my days scoping out men to potentially sleep with or flirt with at a hotel, then eventually fucked my husband's new boss at said hotel before I found out he was his boss. My stomach curled at what my life had become. *'Be careful what you wish for' cut deep right now.*

"Okay, baby doll, whatchya need?" Mark planted both elbows on the bar and leaned in. His wrinkles were deep around his reddened face from years of spending time in the ocean without sunscreen.

"Someone is following me, stalking me, taking pictures of me..." I showed him my phone. He squinted as he swiped through the messages. "It's gotta be personal. I just don't know what to do." My voice trembled. Mark was the only person I knew who wouldn't judge me, and the only person I knew who could potentially help me.

"You don't want to involve the cops?" His voice grew serious, yet hushed while his eyes darted side to side, making sure no one was listening,

"No..." I shook my head.

"Okay, come on with me." I slid under the loosened bar counter and followed him to the back. "If it gets worse, or you think this man is gonna hurt you, don't you dare think twice. You hear me?" He closed the door to his small office and punched in a code on the large metal safe.

I sunk into the wobbly chair across from Mark's desk and he slowly turned towards me. A heavy sound clanked against the table, and my eyes snapped onto a small, shiny black gun. My heart quickened. "Mark—"

"Look, beauty queen, I know you're lil' Miss Liberal but this... this is your life. If you ain't going to tell the cops, and I don't wanna know why... then you better be prepared. People like that..." he tapped my phone, "don't give up. At least not 'til they get what they want... *blood.*"

My body shook at his words. I had thought this was some idiot trying to scare me, taunt me... but now I was realizing the magnitude of this. Without any further words, I slid the gun into my purse. "Do ya know how to use it?" Mark rubbed his chin.

Shaking my head, I felt like a small child. "I might just watch a YouTube video or something," I replied, swallowing the thick saliva in my mouth.

Mark let out a loud laugh, "C'mon, sweet thang, we're gonna have a little old-school lesson."

I pulled into the kids' school after dropping off my new accessory Mark had kindly gifted me after shooting lines of soda cans. Today was PTA volunteering for the upcoming Spring Fling, which was partially sponsored by Brody's firm. I got out of the car and headed toward the doors. The main lobby was bubbling with excited moms, a few dads, and some grandparents. The Spring Fling was on a Saturday, and I couldn't think of a worse way to spend my weekend.

"Sage! Sage!"

Oh, great. "Hi… Caroline." I spoke through the fakest smile I could plaster.

Her blonde ponytail swung behind her as she scanned me. "Oh, look how cute you are. Love those shoes!"

I glanced down at my pink Nike Air Jordan's, which topped off the all black athleisure I had on. "Thank you." I paused.

"So, you didn't tell me he was sponsoring the entire Spring Fling and donating a hefty check to the PTA! Oh, Sage, you are magic!"

I blinked hard, making sure I wasn't hallucinating, and it really was just bitchy, Caroline Summers in front of me, not some alien in Lululemon. "He?" I questioned.

"Sage, that handsome piece of man-meat over there, Brody's new boss." Caroline tilted her head and my eyes lifted, scanning through the crowds.

Fuck my life.

Archer Collins was standing there, wearing fitted jeans and a white V-neck with a brown leather jacket, helping some little old lady hang a banner. "Yeah, it was no big deal," I replied to Caroline.

"I mean, it is... You never really contribute to the success of the PTA," she said in the most condescending tone.

I pushed past her, picked up my pace, and ran over to him. "What the hell are you doing, Archer?" I hissed through my teeth. The little grandma next to me looked appalled at how I was speaking to Mr. Handsome Handy Helper.

"Why hello, Mrs. Miller. It's a delight to see you here... such a wonderful surprise." He smiled at me, growing closer.

"Oh, okay..." I cornered him against the wall. "You mean you're surprised to see me at my *kids' school*? This is crossing the line."

"You look beautiful..." His eyes trailed me, sending chills along my arms.

"Archer, this is not okay."

I heard a voice clear behind me. "Hey, bestie..."

Spinning around, I saw Harlow holding a giant box of bubbles. "Harlow, hey..." I stepped away from Archer, not realizing how close our bodies were. She glanced between the both of us and widened her eyes at me. "Oh, Harlow, this is Brody's new boss at the firm. Archer Collins, this is Harlow Davis, my best friend and neighbor." I spoke like I was at some work meeting, hoping the robotic tone would help the fact that I was hovering over Archer just moments ago.

"Oh wow, nice to meet you." Harlow smiled huge and looked at me, mouthing, *he's hot.*

"It's a pleasure meeting you, Mrs. Davis." Archer shook Harlow's hand.

"What grade is your kid in?" Harlow asked Archer.

"I don't have children, actually. I always saw myself in more of step-dad role. I'm just here volunteering."

My jaw dropped slightly. *What. The. Hell.*

Harlow let out a loud laugh. "Oh, you're funny! I'd have preferred the step-mom role myself. Let the real parents do all the dirty work, am I right?" She lightly slapped Archer's arm, giggling like a schoolgirl.

"Oh-kay then. It was nice to see you, Mr. Collins, but Harlow and I need to go and help over at another table." I grabbed Harlow's arm and pulled her away. This was stalker status. I glanced over my shoulder, finding Archer's eyes firmly on mine.

"Um… earth to Sage. How could you not tell me that Brody's boss was a GQ male model? I'd play dirty secretary for him anytime." Harlow tossed her head back, laughing at her own joke.

I released the grip I had around her arm. "Harlow, I think he's stalking me…" I'd never felt so scared in my life until I realized my lack of impulse control and addiction was going to potentially affect my children and their lives.

Harlow looked over at me like I was insane. "What?" She grabbed my arm and pulled me to a corner, placing the box of bubbles down.

I wrapped my arms around my abdomen, feeling sick. "Harlow, I… I slept with him." I choked on my words, feeling mortified. "Someone's been sending me texts and pictures… Pictures of me in the shower, and I'm…" I breathed heavily, sweat pooling against my face, yet my body felt cold. Just when I thought I couldn't sink any lower, I was about to have a panic attack in the middle of my kids' elementary school. Harlow's eyes were stuck on me, her lips parted, but she was processing the massive bomb I just dropped. Harlow was the woman who would take an item back to the store if the cashier forgot to ring it up, she was the person who entered Facebook giveaways and participated in book clubs. She was the mom with kids that had names that all started with the same letter. She had morals, unlike me.

"Sage, why didn't you tell me?" She wrapped her arms around me, pulling me closer.

Tears stung my eyes. "I'm so ashamed, and I don't know what to do. Brody can't find out. He'll leave me, and he's..." I cried lightly against her shoulder. "He's a lawyer, Harlow. He'll get full custody because he'll learn about my past and how I am an addict and..." I was stammering.

"An addict?" Harlow rubbed my back, holding me closer.

"I'm a recovering, well... not recovering, but a relapsed sex addict."

She pulled away and stared at me. "What? Sage...?" She tilted her head, and I knew that look—it was the look someone gave you when they realize they don't know you at all. It's the look of betrayal.

"It's not at all better than drugs or drinking, it's the same... it's hindering." I wiped my tears away.

"Honey, you need to tell the police about the texts." Concern was painted across her face. "I mean, how could you not tell Brody about someone breaking in?"

"Because this is personal. And now, I know it's Archer." I glanced over my shoulder and realized I'd have to handle this myself. I couldn't afford to break my family apart. As much as running from this suburb hell sounded fun, I truly had nowhere to go. I couldn't do that to my kids, I couldn't be my mother.

I just had to hope and pray I could figure out what to do before he figured out what he wanted to do to me.

CHAPTER TEN

*T*elling Harlow felt like a small weight was lifted off my shoulders, and just knowing someone knew the truth in case something happened to me was also a sick form of reassurance. Sitting at the dinner table, Andi and Tate were whining about the broccoli and grilled chicken in front of them, while Brody scanned his phone and ate. I took a bite of my salad in front of me and took a deep breath.

Brody looked up at me mid-bite. "Did you see Archer today?"

My fingers trembled against the grip of my fork. "Why would I have seen Archer?" I spat out defensively.

"Because he said he saw you at their school." His forehead creased as he glanced over at our kids.

I leaned back into my chair. "Oh, yeah... sorry, I thought you meant..." I placed my fork down, the clink against the plate mimicked the pulse in the side of my forehead.

Brody looked at me carefully. "Meant what?"

"I don't know. I just... it's been a long day. I did see Mr. Collins at their school briefly. That was nice of him to volunteer." I smiled.

"I mean, I think it's strange out of all the schools he chose to drive out from downtown Charleston where he lives, to volunteer here. Don't you, Sage?" Brody clasped his hands together and studied me, the way you watch a fish in the tank at a Chinese restaurant.

Tears stung my eyes, but I blinked them away quickly. "Maybe he knew our kids go there and he wanted to... help because he respects you?" I wiped my mouth with my napkin and looked down at my plate.

"No, no... I think he likes you..." Brody didn't take his eyes off me, nodding at his declaration.

I choked on my own spit, and I coughed to clear my throat. "What?" I croaked and took a long sip of water.

"I mean, seriously, I'm not an idiot... The way he was engaging with you at the dinner party. I definitely think he has a crush on you." Suddenly the seriousness that lined his face melted in a smile. "Which is great for me, because he just gave me the case I wanted that I was certain would go to Linda."

My heart slowed. *A crush.* A harmless crush. That's what my husband picked up from one interaction between Archer and me. *It would only be a matter of time before he knew it wasn't just a crush, and if he did, he'd use everything in his power to crush me.*

"Andi, please eat one more bite, and then we will go do baths." I looked over at Andi, who was moving her food around her plate in circles.

"Tater-Tot, let's go head up." Brody stood with his arm around Tate.

I smiled at him and rubbed his soft blonde hair. "How is this kid so blonde?" Brody laughed and I looked back at him. "My mom had blonde hair, so maybe it's that skip a generation thing," I replied.

He looked between both of us and nodded. Brody and Andi both had dark brown hair, but Tate had sandy-blonde hair with bright blue eyes. His eyes matched mine while Andi had her father's hazel eyes. I normally had my hair dyed blonde, but I was a natural brunette.

"Let's go, kiddo. Andi, you meet us up there. I'll help you out tonight and do bath so you can clean up the dishes, Sage."

Oh, wow... thank you for the honor, sweetheart.

"Sounds good." I stood and grabbed the plates off the table as the kids giggled and followed their dad. Clearing the plates into the trash, I brought them to the sink and turned the water on, scrubbing the dishes while I hummed along to the song that radiated into the kitchen. The window in front of me was dark, but the stars were twinkling in the night sky. I leaned down to load the plates into the dishwasher.

When I stood back up, my eyes shot open, my hands flung to my mouth as I shrieked. A dark, hooded figure stood at the window watching me. Lifting his hand up, he waved. He was standing far enough to not be made out, but close enough to know he was clearly watching me. Chills skyrocketed through me and the plate in my hand shattered against the floor beneath my trembling feet. I ran as fast as I could to the front room and lifted the top box from the closet that held stacks of my pageant sashes, grabbing the cold, hard gun out. My fingers fumbled but I held it firmly.

Opening the front door, I raced outside and to the side, aiming the gun in front of me as my heart pounded. My finger trembled against the trigger, and I used my opposing hand to hold it steady. It was too dark. I couldn't see anything...or anyone.

Run, a voice whispered, making me fling around with both hands fastened against the gun I couldn't remember how to even properly use.

I screamed so loud it cut through the evening air. My eyes clenched together, but my finger remained frozen on the trigger.

"Sage!" His voice made my eyes dart open, finding the gun pressed against his chest.

I stared at my husband, his face was pale, his shirt damp from bath water. "Sage, what the fuck?" he screeched, pushing the gun downward.

"Oh my god, Brody..." Each word came out heavier than the next.

"Sage, why the fuck are you outside with a gun?" He flailed his arms around. "Where did you get the gun?"

"I was... I was doing the dishes, and there was a man outside... Brody, someone was outside watching me," I fumbled my words and dropped the gun into the grass, falling into the moist ground before bursting into tears. My hands pressed against my face as I sobbed.

"Sage, get up. The kids are inside, probably freaking out. I heard a scream and a dish shatter, so I had to drain the tub and run out here, only to find my wife waving a gun around like a fucking lunatic. Get.

Inside. *Now,*" he seethed at me through clenched teeth, his eyes open like an animal eyeing its prey. "A gun? Are you crazy?"

Through my sobs, I pulled myself off the ground and Brody swooped the gun up and tucked it into his pants. "I cannot believe you… I have a career and an image to maintain as an attorney, Sage. What the hell is going on with you? You need some fucking help." His words dug into me as we walked into our house to two crying kids wrapped in towels with dripping hair.

"Mommy! Daddy!" they screamed through their tears. I wiped my nose and eyes against my jacket sleeve, feeling like the biggest fucking failure in the world. Catching a glimpse of Brody's eyes before he lifted Andi into his arms, I knew he wondered who he married. More so, *what* he married.

I was the devil driving an SUV and playing mommy to his kids.

The thing that gets me the most about parenthood is that no matter what the hell is happening in your life, or in the world, if your kids are young and oblivious, then that means you have to always keep your shit together. A bloody meteor could come coursing through the night sky about to blow the town to smithereens, but you better believe if those kids want fifteen bedtime stories, a song, and a third snack, then you're going to fucking do it. So, after a psychopath was lurking outside my home and my husband found me with a gun outside, what did we do? We divided and conquered the bedtime routine for our kids.

I sighed, carefully closing the door behind me—the creaking always made me slightly anxious in fear Tate would wake up and I'd have to restart the whole ordeal to get him to bed. Andi preferred Brody put her to sleep, and Tate always favored me. Heading down the stairs, I gripped the banister as I heard clicking. Peering behind the wall that connected to our stairwell, I saw Brody wearing his glasses that he rarely wore, rapidly typing on his laptop at the dinner table.

His eyes met mine as soon as my feet hit the cold hardwood, and he pulled his glasses off, setting them on the table, "Sage, we need to talk."

Nodding, I looked down at the floor and trekked toward the table, the way a child would getting called to the principal's office. Pulling the chair out, I sat down and stared at my fingers.

"Sage." His voice rose with frustration.

"Look, Brody… I can explain." I laid my palms out in front of me and closed my eyes, unable to make eye contact with him. I felt like I was on trial, which would happen to you when you married a lawyer.

"Sage. Look, you're the mother of my children…"

The pause in his voice made me all that more nervous. "I have an image to sustain here more than ever, especially now since Collins is changing and making our firm essentially blow up. When I married you, I figured you'd change from your old ways—a bartender in booty shorts and a bra, basically begging to be—"

"Be what?" My body ignited. "Oh, fuck off, Brody. Be *saved*? I'm not your goddamn charity case. I was outside with a gun because if you cared enough, you'd know I'm being stalked." Hot tears stung my eyes as I slid my phone over to him. I had deleted Archer's texts already, but the anonymous ones were still in my phone.

Brody looked emotionless as he picked my phone up and scrolled through. His eyes met mine. "Sage, what am I even looking at here?" He passed my phone back toward me.

"Did you not see the picture of me in the shower? The threats?" I parted my lips and hurriedly checked my phone and my jaw dropped even more. "What...?" I whispered almost inaudibly. It was all gone—all of my messages were just gone. "I just saw them... just moments ago. Don't these go to some cloud thing? Brody, I swear I think someone's out to get me, wants to hurt me..."

Brody planted his hands on the table and pushed

himself up. "You know what I think? I think I married a girl from the wrong side of the tracks who never realized she should just shut her damn mouth and be thankful she didn't have to parade her tits and ass down a stage to make a buck and get some fucking attention."

I'd never seen this side of him, and I stared in disbelief as tears streamed down my face. "I was in pageants... it's not like I was a fucking stripper."

"Oh right... Beauty pageant queen who worked nights at the sleaziest bar in New York City and dropped to her knees the first night I met you... So respectable, sweetheart," he scoffed at me and turned away. The way he looked at me made me feel like I was putty, being smashed and molded into his palms, and then slammed under his shoe.

"Brody..." I cried, salty tears dripping down my cheeks into my mouth. Shaking his head, he left to go upstairs. What was I supposed to do? What was I supposed to say? The man I married, the man I had a family with, thought I was nothing more than disposable trash. No one believed me, and that was the most terrifying thing I'd ever felt. *I was the girl who cried wolf.*

He halted mid-way up the stairs. "And Sage... I don't want to know where the hell you got a gun, but as usual, I have to clean up your mess and get rid of it tomorrow." He sighed. "Foolish woman." The stairs crafted an echo around his feet as he went to our room.

I felt defeated, I felt weak. No, I was weak, and the only thing that made me feel strong was a high. *Even if getting that high was by playing with fire, I'd risk being burned. I was already in a furnace, blistering each and every day.* I lifted my phone and did exactly what I shouldn't have done… I lit that match.

"Mrs. Miller…" His voice was low and deep. I didn't say anything as my breath picked up. "Meet me at 602 Stoney Avenue. I'll send a car for you…" He clicked his phone off and I planted my face against the smooth wood of our table. I absentmindedly traced the sticky patches that remained from dinner with the kids. I closed my eyes as tears continued to seep through my lids. Yet, all of this wasn't enough for me to rethink my decisions.

Less than fifteen minutes later, bright lights flashed through the front window. I swiped my fingers under my eyes—which were guaranteed red and swollen—then grabbed my purse and phone. I didn't care to change my clothes or fix my hair; I didn't care to cake on makeup. My lips were dry and chapped, my eyes burned, and my face was clear of nothing but streaks of tears. This was me. I didn't need to be in a fancy dress or tiny bikini for a man to want me. Brody had no idea what he was saying. I wasn't desperate. I was wanted and craved and needed just as badly as I needed those things, too.

The driver offered a small nod as I got into the car. I pressed my head against the cool glass window and watched as houses passed by. Another car turned in, coming back into the neighborhood. A black car, identical to the one I saw at the school. I squinted as hard as I could. It was definitely a man. I tugged my seatbelt off and turned to see where the car was going. The car pulled into a driveway.

My driveway. No, maybe the house over?

Before I could even think twice, we'd already gotten onto a bridge over the water. Shit. Why didn't I tell the driver to stop? I pulled my phone out and opened our Ring doorbell camera. Nothing showed in the driveway.

Was Brody, right? Did I need help?

Black cars weren't a crime, and I didn't even know the make or model. Shaking my head, I buckled myself back in and leaned against the soft leather. I let myself focus on my breathing until my body relaxed. Unfortunately, I wasn't like a normal human where mindful-

ness and meditation helped calm nerves and anxiety…
but I knew what would.

The car came to a stop in front of an enormous
house, an oceanfront property. I thought Archer lived
downtown? Where was I? Suddenly uneasiness took
over me.

*The problem with addiction is that you'll pursue it, even
if your life is on the line, because either way, the withdrawal
will kill you, so you might as well enjoy the chase.*

CHAPTER ELEVEN

*S*tepping outside the car, I swallowed the lump in my throat as I looked at the driver. What if this was the last person I'd see? What if Archer Collins was a psychotic murderer and brought me to his oceanfront mansion to drown me in the ocean? Before I could even think of an alternative plan, the driver sped away, leaving me behind.

I turned toward the house. Pristine white with coastal-blue shutters. Palm trees lined the driveway with lights brightening the dark pathway, leading to the house sitting high up on the tall stilts. It was so silent I could hear the heavy ocean waves crashing against the moonlit shores and almost taste the saltiness from the sea.

"Just Sage..." His voice cut through the silence. I

looked up at his porch, finding him wearing gray joggers and a fitted black V-neck, barefoot. He looked… so normal.

"I guess it'd be stupid to call you Suit… and, Jogger, well, that just doesn't seem right." I offered a crooked but forced smile.

He let out a light laugh and nodded toward the house. "Please, come in."

If he was the last face I'd see before dying, then death may not be so bad.

Walking inside, my jaw dropped. This wasn't a cozy house on the coast; this was a massive, modern mansion. The inside was bright yet masculine, the hardwood was light and immaculate, and as I followed ahead, I saw sleek furniture and pops of sea-green and blue. The middle of the living room had a massive chandelier that looked like coral reef, but a million-dollar coral reef.

"Like what you see?" The husky voice in front of me called out.

I took my eyes off the ceiling and looked back at Archer. "No, no… it's all hideous," I said sarcastically, covering my eyes.

A smirk lined his perfect pink mouth, and he rubbed his bottom lip carefully while watching me. "How old are you, Sage?"

I tilted my head, the question throwing me off-guard. "Twenty-eight." He looked stunned and I clarified, "I met Brody at a bar when I was twenty-one. I got pregnant with Andi shortly after, and we had a shotgun wedding. I guess he thought the slutty bartender had trapped him. But I won Miss USA before I met him. I had so many contracts lined up and was supposed to move into this awesome apartment. The night I had met him was supposed to be one of my last shifts. You just can't do much modeling or be Miss USA when you're knocked up." I shrugged.

Archer sunk into the couch and rubbed the spot next to him, listening as I spoke. *Okay, there was no way this man was my stalker or trying to kill me.* Who would be dumb enough to give all this up for the life of crime? I sat next to him, sliding my sandals off and pulling my feet up on the couch, tugging my knees to my chest. I already looked like shit, might as well act like my normal self.

I turned my head slightly. "How old are you?"

He shifted his body toward me. "Forty." I nodded carefully. Brody was thirty-one and I thought that was an age-gap. "And for the record, no man could ever be trapped with you, Sage. Being with you is... *holy.*" He leaned in closer, cupping my jaw in his hand, rubbing it slightly with his thumb.

My eyes dropped to his lips. "You're crazy. I don't get why you're even interested in me... You could probably have every woman in the state..."

Scooting closer to me, there was an inch between our faces, and my heart was pounding as his deep brown eyes bounced between my lips and eyes. "I don't give a fuck about any other woman, except for the one in front of me." His mouth pressed against mine, but he didn't kiss me. "You're broken like me, Sage, and so damn perfect," he whispered against my lips, pushing his tongue through them and kissing me hungrily.

I let my hands palm his cheeks, his scruff grazing my hands. I moaned out with my head tossed back as his lips traced my neck.

He pulled me onto his lap so I could straddle him. I rubbed back and forth against him, feeling how badly he wanted me. He sighed as he guided my hips over his pants. "Sage..." The way my name rolled off his lips, the way he looked at me...

Archer Collins was the kind of man you sold your soul to the devil for.

Lifting me, he carried me down a long hallway before we entered a massive bedroom. His bedroom. He tossed me onto the end of the neatly made bed, and without words, we both began stripping without taking our eyes off one another. I leaned back and let my legs fall apart. "Fuck…" Archer's voice was loud and desperate. "Sage…"

I titled my head slightly and watched him stroke himself just before plunging inside me. My voice cracked as I let out a muffled scream into the crevice of my elbow. Lifting my legs up to my shoulders, he went deeper and kept his pace steady. Within moments, I clenched my eyes shut as warmth washed over my entire body. I had never felt so alive.

"Sage, fuck. Sage…" he chanted my name just before he let himself go completely. Seeing him so out of control was invigorating because I did that to him. I was in control of his body and his pleasure. I was more powerful than Brody even knew.

I woke up to my phone vibrating somewhere between the sheets. Wiping my eyes, I looked over. Dim light was seeping in through the floor-to-ceiling glass wall in Archer's room. I hadn't noticed before when it was so dark, but the ocean was literally his backyard.

Turning my head, I bit my bottom lip to suppress a smile. Archer was deep asleep next to me, breathing slowly and his thick black eyelashes slightly fluttered as he slept. My phone continued to vibrate, so I pushed the sheets off me and looked through my pile of clothes on the floor before finally finding it. It wasn't a call, it was a string of text messages. My heart crashed onto the floor underneath my shaking feet. I flung around, looking in every direction, clutching my phone against my bare chest.

"Sage?" Archer lifted onto his elbows as his eyes filled with sleepiness. My body shook as I walked to the bed. Handing him my phone, I crawled back into the bed, pulling the blanket over my body, feeling more exposed and vulnerable than ever.

"Who… who sent you these?" Archer's forehead creased and his eyes darted between my phone and my face.

"I-I don't know. Someone's been harassing me…" Tears trickled out.

"Sage, why didn't you tell me? We have to call the police." Archer got up and grabbed his pants, pulling them on before grabbing his tablet off the nightstand.

"No. I can't." I cried softly. "If Brody finds out… he'll take my kids," I stammered.

"That's not how it works, Sage." Archer rapidly scrolled on his tablet.

"It is when you sign a contract binding you to that. I guess my husband knew his wife couldn't be trusted." I closed my eyes.

Archer's finger paused on the screen and he looked at me. "What? What did you sign?"

"If I'm ever unfaithful, Brody gets full custody." I began crying.

"Sage, I can get you out of anything." Archer paused.

"No, it's not just that." I sniffed. "Brody... he'll expose me, he'll find out about my past and... he'll make sure I pay."

"Your past?"

"Archer, my mother... She was a really bad woman. She used me to... I just, I don't even know where to begin." I hated this conversation; I hated talking about her.

"Sage..."

"I'm not looking for your pity. I'm just telling you I cannot involve the police, and you have to promise me to stay out of it, Archer. Promise me!" I was nervous, knowing the last thing I needed was any law enforcement looking into me. Hiding away in the suburbs was the best gift this place gave me. The police briefly investigated before assuming my mom was murdered by some junkie boyfriend. When they interviewed me, I was the doe-eyed beauty queen in distress, and no one thought twice. Beauty is the ultimate weapon for a woman, and I knew how to arm and discharge it. "I'm just fucked up, okay? You have no idea. I lean on men because I'm too weak to stand on my own." I averted my eyes.

"Sage, have you... been with anyone since me?"

I looked at Archer, who sat on the bed close to me. I shook my head. I wasn't going to tell him about Jake, besides that was before we had slept together. "Brody hasn't touched me in weeks," I mumbled.

"Sage, listen to me... You have to let me tell the police. I just scanned through my security cameras and there was no one here. I have no idea how these pictures were taken." Archer rubbed his face.

I picked my phone up, images of me hours ago straddling Archer on his couch, images of me standing outside his house. I shuddered and reached for my shirt, pulling it over my head.

"Please don't get the police involved. I'll handle it. Please." I tugged my pants on quickly and looked at my phone. "I have to get home. My kids are going to be up soon and school..." I rambled. "I told you I have more baggage than the damn airport. You need to stay away from me, Archer." I looked in my phone to order a ride, but I felt a warm hand grip the exposed skin between where my leggings and my shirt didn't meet.

He turned me toward him. "I'm not staying away."

He tilted my chin up and brushed his lips against mine, sending chills throughout my entire being.

"You have to…" I whispered against his lips.

"I won't."

I made it home just before anyone was awake, exhaustion pooling inside me. Scanning through the photos on my phone, I thought of everyone I knew. I wasn't really well-loved or well-liked here. Caroline thought I was an abomination to mothers, Jake thought I was the neighborhood slut, Brody thought I was an embarrassment, and even Harlow looked at me like I was a total mess that she was always helping to clean up. But I didn't think I had an enemy so great that they'd want to hurt me or destroy my life.

I had exactly thirty minutes before tiny feet pattered and small voices screamed my name. Grabbing a coffee pod, I opened a cabinet to get a mug and closed it carefully.

"Sage." My heart jolted. His eyes were dark and fixated on me, his undereye bags deepened. "Where the fuck did you go?" He paused, his voice heavy and tired.

"Brody," my hand clasped my chest, "you scared me." I exhaled with a small smile.

His squinted as his gaze went down to my smile, and something like a switch flipped inside him. You could see it clear as day.

I screamed as he gripped my throat and pushed me into the counter, my head slamming against the cabinet. "I asked where the hell where you last night?"

I dug my nails into the skin of his hands and my eyes darted down as I watched his knuckles turn white from the tight hold around my neck. "Bro...dy," I choked, gasping for air and pleading with my eyes, which felt like they were going pop out of my face.

"You fucking whore," he spat through gritted teeth. His spit splattering against my face as he shook my neck hard before releasing his hold.

Tumbling over, I coughed, gasping for air as he walked away. "And Sage... before you think of doing anything stupid, remember I know all about how your drunk ass mom really died." I collapsed onto the ground, letting my tears drown me.

The problems with any secret is that the person who knows them will do one of two things... They'll either protect you fiercely or fiercely destroy you. And then, that person will forever know they have control over you, over your life, and that will haunt you until they choose what to do with your secrets. The holder of your secret can choose to keep a firm hold around your freedom, and there is nothing more frightening than that.

The door slammed shut and I peeled myself off the ground because I heard the echo of little feet upstairs. Grabbing the hand towel, I wiped my face and caught a glimpse of myself in the window reflection. The whites of my eyes were red, my face was streaked with residual mascara, and my face visibly puffy. I let my hand trace where Brody had choked me, and I couldn't help but laugh at myself. I used to sleep with complete strangers, letting them pin me to walls, choke me, and slap me to feel sufficient and now… I was being choked by a man, my husband, who hadn't touched me in weeks. Brody Miller was a man I didn't really even know, and that man was my husband. He knew everything about me… *He knew too much.*

I raced upstairs to wash my face and swipe on deodorant before chasing Andi and Tate down to brush teeth and get dressed. No amount of makeup would be able to help with my disaster look today, and after being physically assaulted by my husband, I didn't think I cared enough to impress some damn moms at the school drop-off line. "Come on, guys, we are running late!" I covered my eyes in oversized sunglasses and threw on a fitted tank and fresh leggings.

"Mommy, why does Tate have yellow hair and my hair is brown?" Andi's sweet voice penetrated my buzzing, racing thoughts.

I glanced up at them in the rearview mirror. "Um, my mom had blonde hair… yellow hair." I fixed my eyes back on the street.

"Where is your mommy?" Tate questioned, sticking an old lollipop from his seat into his mouth, which made me cringe, but I didn't have the fight in me.

"She…" I cleared my throat, "she's not here anymore." I skipped coffee this morning—well, unintentionally—and this conversation should have been happening after a strong, hot cup of coffee or not at all.

"She's in heaven, Tater-Tot," Andi added reassuringly.

"Mm-hmm." I didn't want to lie to my children. Their so-called grandma wasn't in heaven, she was definitely in the blazing flames of hell… and I helped her get there.

A car honked loudly at me, and I realized I was sitting at a green light. *Shit.* I waved and turned into the school. We were late again, meaning I'd have to go inside the school, which was possibly the worst timing ever. Getting the kids out and throwing their backpacks over each of my shoulders, we walked inside.

"Long time no see, beautiful…"

I gripped Andi and Tate's hands, swiftly turning to the voice behind me. My face fell. "Jake…" I squinted at him in shock. Andi would for sure repeat his words to her father.

He grinned and came closer to us. "Hey Andi-girl and Tater-Tot." He rubbed Tate's golden blonde hair, making my pulse race.

"We're running late, Jake. Good to see you." I ushered my kids through the front office but heard his footsteps behind me. *Not today.* "Bye, kids!" I kissed their cheeks and quickly turned toward the door, pushing past Jake.

"Sage, Sage…" he called after me, but I picked up my pace and cut through the front doors.

"Jake, this is far from appropriate." I halted in my spot, pointing at him.

"Sage, how are you. God, you look so… good." He touched my shoulders as his eyes trailed and landed on my chest.

"I haven't showered in two days, and I slept three hours last night, so I'm assuming you're talking about my tits... I don't have time for this shit." I spun around, but his hands fell to my waist.

"Oh, come on baby, let's go to my car."

"Have you been texting me? Taking pictures of me?" I moved closer and pushed my sunglasses onto my head.

His face dropped and flushed, "Sage... I've been meaning to talk to you—"

"Oh my god, it's you..." I gasped. "You're sick, Jake. Leave me alone, you motherfucker or I'll call the cops." I shoved him and ran to my car.

Sinking inside, I felt an emotion I couldn't believe. *Relief.*

I was relieved that it had to be Jake Davis—the suburban dad across the street with a crush that had turned slightly obsessive—and not some maniac from my past or worse, Brody. It was over; I wasn't some mouse in a game with a big, bad cat chasing me. The only thing that still bothered me is the way Jake looked at Tate, as if he saw something in him I prayed he never would.

I hope no one would ever see it.

Pulling into our driveway, my eyes caught a glimpse of a large bouquet sitting on our doormat. I quickly jumped out and walked toward it, gripping my keys hard, the metal cutting into my palm. The small white card attached shook in between my fingers.

Roses are red...

I lifted the bright red bouquet into my hands and looked around. "Damn you, Jake Davis." I walked to the trash can and threw it inside before the lid slammed shut behind it. I'd have to make it clear to him that I wasn't some little bitch he was going to torment into fucking him.

"Hey girl, hey!" I turned and saw Harlow checking her mail, giving me a big wave. I wiggled my fingers at her and quickly went inside. Holding the doorknob, I waited at the door for a moment.

Knock, knock, knock.

I needed to move to some large, secluded land with no neighbors to sleep with and no friends to make.

"Hi..." Harlow shook her head, her eyes widening. "You gonna let me in or just ignore me?" She pushed past me.

"Sorry, it was a shit-show morning, and I haven't even had coffee yet."

She walked to the kitchen, immediately grabbed coffee pods, and started the machine up. "Honey, that's what friends are for. You know you can vent to me anytime." She smiled and opened the fridge, pulling out eggs.

"You hungry?" I asked as I sunk onto the island stool.

"No, but you probably are, skinny mini. I never see you eat, so let me fix you something while you tell me what the hell has your panties in such a wad." She laughed and started busying herself in the kitchen.

"Brody and I got into it this morning. I don't even know… Anyway, I saw Jake at the school."

"Yeah, he was there dropping off the donation check we raised at the office." She glanced over her shoulder and smiled.

"Are you guys doing good?" I asked as she slid my coffee over to me.

"Yeah, really good, actually. We started marriage counseling, like couples' therapy or whatever, and it's really helped us just… conversate better. If you and Brody need the number… lemme know."

"I think Brody and I are way, way past therapy." I watched the steam rise from my coffee and let the warmth heat my ice-cold hands.

"Like, divorce?" Harlow dropped her jaw and placed her hands on her hips as the eggs cooked in front of her.

"No… Brody would never let me divorce him, and I think he likes having me around for an image. You know he eventually wants to run for something political or whatever. A divorced dad of two isn't really appealing." I sighed, feeling more trapped than I ever felt, even during my ruthless days in New York.

"I think you guys are in a rough patch and will be just fine by the summer. I mean, look... kids, bills, keeping up with the Davises, it's all tough shit." She smiled and made me laugh.

"I hope so..." I sipped my coffee as Harlow slid over a plate of fluffy eggs and toast. "Wow, this is great. Thanks, Harlow." I smiled at her.

"Honey, you had babies so young. I'm thirty-three and I still feel like I have no idea what I'm doing. You just need to give yourself a break, and if Brody needs a come-to-Jesus-moment, you know I'm your girl." She leaned in on her elbows and grabbed my hand.

Maybe she was right. Brody and I had kids young, then I was plucked from my bustling city life and thrown into a small suburb of Charleston, South Carolina. I never had a chance to process how much my life had changed all at once.

I could fix this. I could fix us.

More than anything, I had to fix us... Brody Miller knew one of my two secrets. He could ruin me in the snap of a finger.

CHAPTER TWELVE

"Mrs. Miller, it's been so long. How are you? You look stunning as always." Jessie, the receptionist, smiled at me. I had showered, applied a generous amount of makeup, and slid into a cream-colored fitted dress with my hair in giant loose curls. It was slightly pathetic, but isn't this what a good wife did? Dress up and bring her husband lunch to his office.

"Hey, Jess. Yeah, the kids and the PTA life has kept me busy." I clutched the take-out bag in my hands.

"Oh, I bet. When my kids were that age, I felt like I was constantly running." She pushed her glasses up the bridge of her nose.

"Brody said you're writing a book?" she sang out in her Southern drawl.

"Mm-hmm… I am. It's a slow process but it's been fun." I glanced at Brody's office door down the hall.

"Well, you know I'm going to buy a copy. I love a good romance…" she leaned in and whispered through her fingers, "especially the steamy kind."

"Thanks, Jessie." The bag crinkled in my hands.

"Mr. Miller is in his office, just head on in. Nice seeing you."

"You too, Jess." I walked down the hall and took a deep breath before releasing it. *Should I knock? God, I sucked at this whole doting wife role.* But then again, he wasn't winning any awards for husband of the year, either. I subconsciously rubbed my neck. Instead of a hickey, my husband left a light red mark around my neck from his morning suffocation attempt.

Opening the door slowly, I plastered on my best smile. "Hi babe…." My words fell out just as fast as my jaw dropped.

Brody looked up at me, confused. "Sage?"

"I brought you, er… us lunch." My fingers shook against the brown bag as I lifted it up like some damn gameshow host showing off the ultimate prize. My eyes darted between Brody and Archer Collins, who was sitting across from Brody, sifting over stacks of paper.

"Sage, you remember Mr. Collins, don't you?"

Archer stood and buttoned his suit jacket, reaching his hand out. "Mrs. Miller, it's so nice to see you again. What's it been? Since the dinner party, right?" He smirked.

"It's good to see you, too, Mr. Collins." I shook his hand with my head hung low, not daring to look into his eyes. Brody cleared his throat, and I immediately pulled my hand back, brushing my hair with it.

"How are you doing, Mrs. Miller?" Archer stood firm. Clearly, he was a dominating force in any room... not just the bedroom.

"Just Sage is fine..." I shifted my eyes to his face for a moment, feeling my cheeks heat. "And I'm doing well, how are you?" I replied as emotionless as possible.

"Well, Sage, I had the most enchanting date last night. She was... absolutely mesmerizing. I'll have to have you both meet her." His eyes glimmered with excitement; meanwhile, I thought I would unquestionably have a heart attack.

"That would be great, Mr. Collins. We will have to get a double date in the books." Brody had kiss-ass written all over his face.

"Absolutely. My girl is usually busy, but when she's with me it's as if no time has passed. Anyway, I won't keep you both. Enjoy your lunch." Archer's jaw ticked, and I felt my palms moisten at the words, *my girl.*

Suddenly, I felt like I was cheating on Archer with Brody, and not the other way around.

"Sage, what are you doing?" Brody spoke under a hushed but agitated tone as soon as Archer closed the door.

"Look, Brody. Please, I want to make this work… make *us* work. We have children together."

"Child," he mumbled under his breath.

"What did you say…?"

"Never mind. Look, I'm sorry. I shouldn't have…" His eyes dropped to my neck, and I closed my eyes, hoping the tears wouldn't stream out.

"I brought your favorite from Indigo's Café on Sullivan's Island… I even got a slice of their famous blueberry pie." I smiled and lifted the bag.

His eyes softened and he nodded towards the seat Archer just left.

Sliding it over, we sat and talked minimally, but it was something. A start. *Ultimately, a start was better than the end.*

After leaving Brody's office, I caught a glimpse of Archer at another part of the office. I tried to walk past him, but he spotted me. "Sage…" he called and scanned from my face down. I knew he was undressing me with those dark, delicious brown eyes.

I shook my head, knowing I needed to just go home. He nodded and smirked at me, looking at a door. *His office.*

The rules of recovery for an addict are pretty much the same across the board. An addiction is an addiction, no matter what your choice of drug is. For someone who is addicted to sex, professionals advise not to necessarily refrain from sex completely, but rather, refrain from compulsive and destructive sexual behavior. Was sleeping with my husband's boss considered destructive and compulsive? I guess I'd have to compile more evidence to find out…

"Archer, what if someone sees us?" I whispered against his face as he backed me into his office. His mouth was already on my neck, his dark brown scruff pricking my skin, igniting a slight amount of pain that was all the more pleasurable.

"I don't give a fuck…" he hissed into my ear before biting my lobe. "God, you're so sexy…"

Lifting me into his arms, he slammed my back against the wall, which caused his fancy rows of diplomas in fancy frames to shake. I ran my fingers through his thick, dark hair, his eyes not moving from mine. Pushing my dress up with his hands—the same ones that felt so good on my bare skin only hours ago —he licked his bottom lip.

"Do you ever wear panties?" he whispered into my ear, every word slower than the next through his heavy breathing.

"I swear, it's the darnedest thing... They simply melt off when you're around." I smiled at him, keeping my voice low.

Letting one hand fall, he caressed me slowly. I turned my body, letting my palms plant against the wall as he lifted my hips up higher and pushed inside of me.

He picked up his pace, causing my head to hit the wall harder. I moaned so loud, I instantly slapped a hand over my mouth to cover it.

"You're so tight, baby..." he panted.

"Archer, please..." He pushed harder, slamming inside and pulling out before repeating every push and pull, teasing me.

Something ran through me when he was inside me. *Completion.* Why did he do that to me? Sex was never emotional for me, ever. I never got attached. It was an obsession, an impulse. But with him... it felt more. That scared me because as much as Brody controlled me through my secrets, Archer controlled me emotionally, and I didn't think there was deadlier weapon than that.

Holding me up while still inside me, he turned and with one swift motion, swiped his desk clean of papers. Lying me down on the sleek wooden desk, he lifted my ankles and placed them on top of his shoulders, smiling down on me. I closed my eyes. "Sage, look at me." His deep voice rattled me. "Sage…"

I kept my eyes closed and shook my head. He laughed and pressed back inside me. The way he moaned, the way I felt his pulsing… it shook me, overtook me. When I finally gained enough courage to open my eyes, a ripple ran through me and I got my rush. My high, my fix. I covered my mouth and screamed into my arms. The sensation was too much; he was too good. Collapsing next to me, he let out a light laugh.

"Fuck…" He sighed, running his hands through his hair. Sweat glistened against his perfect, broad shoulders. "I think I'm falling in—"

Taking my index finger, I put it over his lips. "Don't you dare." I frowned at him. Sliding off his desk, I pulled my dress down and looked over my shoulder. "Thanks, Suit." I winked at him.

He looked at me curiously and began to laugh before lying back on his desk, shaking his head. I shut the door behind me, and knew, this time, I wasn't going to lie. I had knowingly opened the flood gates, and Archer Collins came crashing into me, washing over me, embedding into my dark, dirty soul.

Walking out of Archer's office, I looked around carefully, running out the back door before speeding off. Maybe the thrill of it all made me all that more satisfied. The idea of being caught...? I didn't know for sure, but it was something different here.

Once I got to our neighborhood, I noticed Jake's car wasn't at their house, so I decided to surprise Harlow. Ringing their doorbell, I waited patiently, smoothing my dress out but stupidly smiling, thinking of Archer.

"Sage!" Harlow opened the door and her face lit up. "Um, okay... I didn't get the dress-code memo." She wrapped me in a hug and led me inside.

"I went to surprise Brody at work with lunch, hoping to..." I started but sighed.

"That's so sweet." She smiled at me.

"What have you been up to?" I looked around their spotless house. A giant family portrait hung over their fireplace—one that could have passed for an ad for a dental commercial.

"I was upstairs in my craft room, just working on

some of the kids baby books and what not... I really should be looking at some listings to help Jake. Poor guy has been swamped, and I'm just enjoying not rushing from house to house for marketing." She brought over a sparkling water for me, and we both sunk into the couch.

"I didn't mean to take away from your quiet, crafting time."

"Girl, please. I love seeing you. You're my best friend." I smiled and leaned back into the soft couch. "So, did you see Archer? I mean, you literally left me hanging with all of that..." She waved her hand in the air. "You went from telling me you slept with him and he's stalking you to... nothing?"

"No, I think I was just PMS-ing when I said all that. I... Yes, I fucked up and slept with him once, but it's not anything more, and he's definitely not the one stalking me." I sighed, looking at the family photo again.

"Then who is?"

"Maybe no one?" I looked over at Harlow. "Do you ever feel like you're so far in your own head that things that shouldn't be anything turn into this mountain of madness?"

"Uh, no... that's called psychosis." She leaned into her arm and laughed.

"Maybe that's just me...psychotic." I shrugged and sipped my sparkling water.

"No, you're just in the trenches of life. I'm glad no one is really stalking you, because I'm not trying to be interviewed for a segment of a crime episode."

I laughed and threw my head back, sinking lower into the couch. Jake wasn't a killer stalker; he was a bored man with a crush on his wife's best friend. I was definitely not worried. The texts, the pictures, the flowers... disturbing, sure, but I knew I could handle this if it was Jake Davis.

Harlow flipped the TV on and put her feet up on the coffee table. The local news flashed in front of us with a bright red strip. "Breaking news just in, a man found murdered at the Besos Hotel. Police are asking anyone who knows Payton Smith to immediately come forward for questioning. Mr. Smith is a frequent guest of Besos Hotel and was here on business." A picture appeared on the screen and my blood froze.

"Oh my gosh, how terrible..." Harlow's hands covered her mouth.

I closed my eyes as memories washed through. Payton Smith was the first man I'd ever been with after Jake. When I started going to the Besos Hotel, I swore it was just to flirt, to satisfy this void that my addiction had left. But Payton was interesting and sexier than most. So, when he led me to his room and fucked me in the shower—and again on the hotel bed —I didn't bat an eye. I never heard or saw him after. He told me he never came into Charleston. It was the perfect scenario to never have to run into him again. Now, he was dead? At the Besos Hotel? I blinked rapidly, re-reading the headline.

"Sage?" Harlow's voice broke through my thoughts. "Honey, you've gone pale." Harlow rubbed my arm.

"I… That's terrifying. I'm going to head home. I have to… start some laundry before getting the kids." I swallowed and immediately stood. "I'll call you later," I said robotically before running into my car and racing home. Would they check security footage? Would they post that on the news that they were looking for me? My heart thumped against my chest and my hands grew slick against the steering wheel. What if I got arrested? My kids. I hit my head against the steering wheel as tears strummed down my face. Brody was right… I was nothing more than a stupid, foolish woman. Selfish, just like my mother.

"I mean, Collins wants the case. He said it'll be excellent publicity for our firm. I agree, yeah… mm-hmm. Apparently, they said the murder weapon was a knife, and then get this... some kind of metal piece was jammed into his chest. Mm-hmm, knife is missing. Yup... and the murderer is definitely some psychopath because they shaved the guy's head completely and took the hair with them. Can you believe that sick fuck? Yeah, I know..." Brody was on the phone in our office, and I had my ear planted against the doors as my body convulsed in terror. My kids were playing with magnetic tiles and eating the pizza I had ordered because there was no way in hell I could cook something considering my life was exploding right in front of my face.

The door flung open and I fell over. "Sage, what the hell are you doing?" Brody helped me stand up straight.

"Oh, I... Brody, I saw what happened on the news. I didn't know you were going to take on the case," I stammered nervously.

"Well, Archer is going to be the lead prosecutor, but yeah... we're taking it. Why?" His eyebrows lifted and suddenly, a glimmer from behind him caught my eye.

"Um... oh, you know, just excitement with it being on the news." I clasped my hands together to help stop fidgeting.

"You're excited that someone got brutally murdered?" Brody asked flatly.

I let out a small laugh and slapped his shoulder. "You're silly."

He looked at me like I was crazy and stepped around me. "Right... I'm gonna go eat with the kids now," he said slowly and left. I glanced over my shoulder and heard the kids giggling with their dad, buying me what I needed the most. *Time.*

I chewed my fingernail and said a quick prayer under my breath, not really sure to whom but I need every supernatural being on my side. Walking to the shelves that displayed my tiaras, I froze in front of the one from Miss USA. The only problem was... it wasn't there. My greatest win and a title that was supposed to change my life but ultimately didn't because instead, I chose to be involved in the gruesome death of my mother, meet Brody, and get pregnant. Life in the spotlight wasn't something I could ever have again. I had to stay away in the shadows.

My breath grew heavier as I ran my fingers over the other tiaras. My eyes darted all around the shelves. Did Andi take it? I looked at the top shelf; there was no way she could have been in here and reached it. I ran over to Brody's desk and opened my laptop—the one a book should be written on, not searching for, *Payton Smith, murder.*

I waited for it to load but nothing came up. Brody knew things early because they were working the case. Shit. Did he say something shiny was found in the body? Now I'd truly lost my mind. A tiara at a murder scene? No. This was crazy. I shut my laptop and heard light movement, and when I glanced up, my eyes met Brody's.

"Sage?" Brody looked at me carefully and walked to the shelves that housed my pageant tiaras, and his hand immediately went to the empty spot at the top. His fingers glided against the vacant place as his eyes stayed on mine, causing my breath to halt and my pulse to race.

"Brody..." I whispered, my forehead creasing. *What was happening?*

"Mommy! Tate took my doll!" Andi screeched. I was frozen in the chair and Brody laughed lightly before he smirked at me and turned away. "Mommy?"

All the noise around me blurred as I faintly heard Tate crying in the background. *Was my husband setting me up for murder? Did he know about everything?* I glanced all around the room. *Was he the one watching me?* My chest felt tight and stomach acid rose, teasing my throat.

"Sage! The kids want you," Brody yelled shaking me from my panic attack. Jumping up, I raced out.

Brody Miller was hiding more than I knew. He had something so sinister planned, and if I didn't follow his rules, he'd destroy me.

CHAPTER THIRTEEN

*T*he next morning after dropping the kids off at school, I came home and opened the trashcan outside. I pulled out a bag and underneath were the bright red roses. Tugging them out, I reached for the card.

Roses are red.

Flipping it over, I saw the name of the florist, and a quick Google search later, I was on the phone with them. "Ma'am, it seems that a Mr. Jake Davis had the roses sent to you." I was right. Jake was obsessed with me, but then why was Brody acting suspicious?

I didn't know what to think anymore, but maybe Brody was just testing me? Maybe he'd hidden my tiara. What was the metal shrapnel lodged inside of Payton's chest? I had officially lost my mind, and there was one person who may be able to help me. But before that, I had to press pause and pick up dairy-free, nut-free, gluten-free cookies for the annual Spring Fling today.

"Can you believe this shit? It's like eating air." Harlow took a bite of a cupcake she had picked up from a local bakery. "I mean, it's free of everything good. We might as well eat dirt." She stuck her tongue out in disgust.

I laughed. "Well, Caroline insists that every item be vegan and nut-free, so you know, I just dropped fifty dollars on a dozen cookies." I rolled my eyes and carefully moved the boxes to the bake sale table. Kids were running around everywhere; bounce houses took over the soccer field and bubbles floated carelessly in the air. "I would have loved this as a kid." I closed my eyes and smiled, taking in the smell of popcorn and the sounds of innocent laughter.

"Y'all didn't have Spring Flings in New York?" Harlow looked at me.

"Well, I started pageants and modeling at a young age, so I missed a lot of this kind of thing. My mom was so set on having me be her golden ticket away from my dad, but she'd spend every dollar I won on booze. I guess I had to grow up a lot faster than these kids." I nodded in the direction of the laughing children in front of us.

"Damn, I didn't know it was that bad, Sage." Harlow looked at me with sympathy.

I hated that look; I wasn't some sad little girl who needed pity. "What doesn't kill you makes you stronger... or impulsive and fucked-up," I added, pursing my lips.

"Hey, look there's Jake and Brody!" Harlow excitedly waved at them.

I quickly busied myself stacking cookies on plates, and for the first time, I was thrilled that Caroline was storming our way. "Ladies..." Her shrill voice was almost comforting.

"Caroline, hi." I smiled with both rows of teeth.

"So, you brought in the most money for us and the Spring Fling, thanks to your hottie, Mr. Collins... who spoke so highly of you that I've decided you should be my VP." She reached for a cookie off the tray.

"Oh, wow... Well, he's not my... Mr. Collins. He's just Brody's...." I started.

"Who? Hi, Caroline." Brody leaned in and gave her a swift hug, which lit her overly Botox-ed face up.

At least someone is getting affection from my husband.

"I was just telling your wife—"

"Caroline asked me to be the PTA vice president,

and I'm honored to do so," I cut in, reaching my arm around Caroline's shoulder and tugged her closer to me.

Harlow choked on her water and began coughing hard. "Are you okay, honey?" Jake rubbed her back.

"Yeah...yeah..." Harlow shrugged him off her. "Just in awe of the PTA king and queen over here..." she added sarcastically.

"Oh-kay then, I'm leaving. Rule number one, don't touch me with your cookie-crumb hands, Sage. See you at the meeting tomorrow night." Caroline quickly walked away and had already found her next victim by the face painting table.

"We haven't gotten together in forever. You guys want to come over for dinner?" Jake said to Brody.

Say no, say no, say no.

"Absolutely. How about Friday? And, Jake, you better be making your chicken parmigiana." He waved his pointer finger at him.

"For my best friends, of course. You like my meat, right, Sage?" Jake sneered and stared at me.

My lips parted, and my eyes darted between Harlow and Brody, who busted into laughter. "You're a pig, Jake Miller. I'm sorry, Sage, please excuse my husband's perverted sense of humor." Harlow leaned in and kissed his face.

"Okay, you boys need to go to the kids, Sage and I have to watch the baked goods table or Caroline will definitely stab us." Harlow moved to me and gripped my arm.

"You sure Caroline will stab you? I think my wife would be the expert at that." Brody snickered and turned away.

Harlow looked at me confused and I shrugged. "He's joking… Let's go sell some air cookies." I glanced over and saw Brody walking with Jake toward the kids.

What the hell was his deal?

We sold off brownies, cupcakes, and cookies galore. I watched as Brody chased our kids, throwing them into the air as their faces lit up. Would life always be like this for them? When we started dating, Brody told me that divorce was never an option with him. It meant losing, and he certainly wasn't a loser. He made me sign an iron-clad prenuptial and custody agreement. I was young and in a vulnerable place when I signed it, so I didn't think twice.

I would have signed my soul over to him if he would have asked me to, knowing he'd get me out of New York.

My parents had divorced and then my mom died, so I basically never talked to my father. He was an emotionally abusive man and in return, my mom emotionally abused me. I was her scapegoat, and she was his.

A toxic family. All I thought I wanted for my children was to not have a toxic family, but the truth was neither of my children were planned. I didn't even think I wanted to be a mother until I had no other choice but to be one. The first thought that ran through my mind when I found out I was pregnant with Andi was that no man would want me again. *That's the drawback with compulsions... it becomes the light to your darkness, and you don't even see that it's just darkness shadowing any chance of light.*

"Oh, hello..." Harlow paused in between counting the stack of cash in her hands. Her eyes were glued in front of us, and I followed them. Archer was standing out in the field with Brody, shaking hands with Jake. I tilted my head and realized I had slept with all three of those men. What kind of person could say that on their kids' elementary school field? I rubbed my hands against my face, hoping they wouldn't come over here.

Wishful thinking.

Archer Collins strutted his sexy ass down the elementary school field, looking like he was on the New York runway. His hands were tucked into his suit pockets, his jacket was open, showing his crisp white button-down. "I'm not saying I'd ever be unfaithful, but if that man wanted a night with me, I might forget all about my kids and husband... Jesus, I don't blame you, Sage." Harlow moved her fingers across her face and chest in a cross.

I forced a light laugh as my heart turned with each footstep he took. I grabbed the cash from Harlow and busied myself with counting each bill slowly, hoping it'd prevent me from drooling over the baked goods.

"Hello, Mr. Collins, how are you today?" Harlow sang out with her Southern accent intensified.

"I'm doing well, how about you, Mrs. Davis?" His deep voice shook me to my core, but I didn't dare look up. Instead, I licked my finger and counted each bill again.

Oh, well, you know... Just busy with the bake sale portion of this amazing Spring Fling you so-kindly sponsored." Harlow giggled. "For a man with no children, you sure do show a lot of interest in our school..." She nudged my shoulder.

I glanced up and found Archer's eyes were fastened onto mine. "Hi, Sage." A sexy smirk slowly grew on his face.

"Hi." I swallowed, my word coming out cracked and hushed. Licking my finger again, I started counting a new stack of bills.

"Sage, we can do that in a second. Don't you think

you should offer Mr. Collins some complementary goods?" Harlow's eyes widened and she mouthed, "You're being rude."

"Mr. Collins, what would you like?" I stood and shift my eyes from his heavy gaze.

"I don't see my favorite dessert on the table…" He smiled again, heat rushing to my face which I was sure was red.

"How about you just take one of each, sweetness?" Harlow began packing the baked goods into a bag and handed it to him.

"Thank you, Harlow." He leaned in and hugged her, giving her an extra pat on the back. She gripped him tightly and giggled so hard. Letting go of her, he had to use extra force to pull away. "Sage, always a pleasure." He walked toward me, and I realized he had only hugged Harlow so he could hug me without a second thought. I licked my finger again anxiously, trying to count the next stack of bills, but Archer leaned in closely. "I wish it was my dick instead of your finger against your tongue…" he whispered against my face. My eyes widened, my lips parted in shock.

My entire body shuddered and I looked at his face and then back to the table. The heat between my legs competed with that on my face. I swallowed again and pulled back, rolling my lips together. I watched as

Harlow busied herself serving another parent before I cleared my throat and mumbled, "I heard you guys took on the Payton Smith case."

"Yeah, it's been a shit-show." He nodded.

"Archer, can I… Can we talk later in private?" I whispered.

"I don't know about talking, Sage…" his eyes dropped from my face and slowly traveled down before flicking back up to my lips, "but I'll do anything with you in private."

"Archer." I paused, anxiety racing through my veins faster than the kids around the field.

His face grew serious, and he realized I wasn't messing around. "Of course. Name a time and place. I'm there." He rubbed my arm, and turned away, glancing over his shoulder once again. I wiggled my fingers at him.

"So, how is he in bed? I know it was more than once."

"What?" I dropped my jaw.

"Oh, get real, Sage. You both have sex buddies written across your foreheads when you're in one another's presence. I have to know." Harlow threw her arm over the chair and leaned back, watching me.

"That's a very disrespectful accusation, Harlow. One I'd never expect from my best friend. I told you because guilt is wreaking havoc inside me. It was one time, and a huge mistake. I don't need you rubbing salt in my damn wound." I threw a bag of cookies down and stormed off.

*I wasn't mad because she accused me of something I wasn't doing. I was mad because she accused me of something I **was** doing.*

I walked up to Brody and Jake which was probably worse than Harlow outing me and Archer. Was it that obvious? Is that what Brody was so mad about? Did he know? No, he wouldn't kiss Archer's ass if he knew. Brody was a man with an ego greater than God, and he'd be fuming. He'd be working on ripping me to shreds.

"Mommy!" Tate screamed and jumped up. I caught him in my arms and held him tightly.

He was getting so big, I nestled my face in the side of his thick blonde hair and smiled at him. I saw Brody watch us carefully. Jake stood beside me, and I saw Brody's eyes flick between the three of us, which plagued me with anxiety.

He tilted his head and looked at me in a way that made my stomach curl. "Can we please leave now? I'm over this whole field-day fun-day." Jake threw his head back, and I so badly wanted to slap the lovestruck stalker out of him.

"I agree, we should go." Brody called out for Andi, and she came running. Lifting her in his arms, I followed in his shadows with Tate.

Once in the car, the kids were dozing off from spending the day running around in the heat and having overstuffed themselves on every kind of carnival-style food possible.

"So, any recent developments on your case, B?" I whispered but kept my eyes straight ahead.

"Since when do you care about my work?" he scoffed.

"Brody, please. We have children and a life together. I'm sorry if I hurt you in any way, but I want this. I want us to work… please." I looked over at him, and when his eyes met mine at a stop sign, he let out a defeated sigh and nodded.

Offering a small smile, I rubbed the back of his hand. This is what I had to do. I couldn't afford to have Brody plotting against me when someone, most likely Jake, was already harassing me. Not to mention that I could potentially be a murder suspect.

"Payton Smith was stabbed at Hotel Besos. We have no clue where the weapon is, but a metal item was found in the deceased's body. Beyond that, we have no motive and no leads." His voice lowered as he glanced at the kids in the rearview. "The creepiest part is that his head was perfectly shaved… yet the hair was gone. We're thinking the killer is trying to craft a trademark for future…" he paused.

"I shouldn't be telling you any of this, but this case has me fucked up. I swear to God, Sage, you better keep your mouth shut. This is a breech in confidentiality, and I could lose my job." His eyes widened with warning.

"I wouldn't tell anyone… Craft a trademark for future, what exactly?" I asked.

"Murders. This has serial-killer written all over it."

My pulse raced. *This had nothing to do with me,* I reminded myself. "What is the metal thing they found in the body?" My voice cracked between words as my mind flashed back to my missing tiara.

"No idea…" Brody sighed again. "It's definitely broken off of something, but it's with the police." I swallowed the lump in my throat, nodding slowly.

Pulling into our driveway, I stared at our house. When I was younger, I would have never believed I'd get to live in a house like this. When I won Miss USA, my world altered, but then just as it changed for the better, it flipped for the worse between my destructive behavior with men and my mother's sudden death. I had to pull out of the light and hide away in the darkness. The darkness was safe, the darkness would allow me more hope than any light could ever give. The darkness brought me here.

After dinner, I got the kids to bed, which was surprisingly smooth and quick since Brody didn't look at me like he was going to choke me to my death. I took a long hot shower, and the water felt amazing over my body from where the stress and anxiety had pooled inside. My facewash stung my eyes because I refused to close them while showering—after all, someone had been in here once before. When I mentioned the ladder by our window, Brody swore he had put it there when cleaning our gutters out. Easy access.

"Hey…" I felt hands grip my hips from behind, and I turned as my fingers were laced through my soapy hair.

Brody was naked and smiling at me. I couldn't remember the last time we had sex. Maybe that's why I had relapsed? Would my addiction be rampant if my husband actually slept with me? Then again, my affair with Jake, and Payton were both when Brody and I were at our happiest.

"You're so hot…" Brody's voice was filled with

desperation as he pushed me against the shower wall.

My eyes lifted to his. "Brody…" I didn't want to have sex with my husband, because suddenly, I felt like I was cheating on Archer. "I'm tired…" I whispered as soap bubbles pooled by our feet.

He pulled my face to his and kissed me, and I could taste the bitter alcohol on his breath.

"Brody, you're drunk."

He was wobbling and laughing with the white of his eyes slightly red. *He had to get wasted to be intimate with me.* "Sage, you're my wife." His erection pushed against me.

I closed my eyes. I wanted this, but not him. I wanted the sensation, the high. I was sick in the head. I turned and planted my palms against the shower wall. Closing my eyes, I pictured Archer. If this was me getting high, I'd at least control what my drug of choice was.

Feeling him push inside me, he jerked my hips over him, moaning so loud I clenched my eyes shut. "Sage, yes…" he panted against me, letting his hands shift upward to my breasts as he pounded me from behind.

"Harder," I demanded. He picked up his pace to what I so badly wanted. I so badly needed a release, but it didn't happen because Brody let out a long, satisfied sigh before pulling out of me.

"Fuck, that was amazing." He chuckled before leaving the shower, and shortly after, I heard the bathroom door shut.

"So amazing," I muttered under my breath, rolling my eyes. Getting out of the shower, I dried myself slowly, hoping that by the time I did my entire skincare routine, Brody would be snoring. Facing men after sex was my least favorite part. I didn't want to be their cheerleader and caress their precious male ego.

Opening my palm, I dripped my face serum into my palm, watching the deep golden liquid melt into my skin before I rubbed it all over my face. Finishing up, I slowly opened the door and peeked out. A light snore echoed through the dark room. Sneaking out of our room, I went downstairs. The house was silent and dark; I usually enjoyed the silence but today it made me feel nervous.

My phone buzzed in my hands and I looked down. Opening the text, my heart stopped.

Boo.

Something crashed behind me. I flung around, clutching my phone tightly. Racing to the light switch, I turned it on and dashed to the butcher's block. Plucking out the biggest, sharpest knife and clutching the handle tightly, I tried to ease the tremble in my hands. I saw a picture frame shattered from our living room console. Walking to it, I flipped it over. It was a picture of me—my bridal portrait. The glass shards scattered all over.

"Ouch." I dropped the frame and lifted my index finger. Blood was pooling at the tip and a gust of cooler than usual air dusted across my neck. Fear drained from every limb and I felt like my breathing was booming amongst the silence. Frozen in my spot on my knees, with my bleeding finger in my mouth, I was terrified because…

Because I knew, in this very moment, *I was being watched*.

Taking a deep breath in, I slowly turned my head with my body trembling. I collapsed, letting my legs fall over to the side. Tears trickled down my cheeks from the exhaustion of this torment. The back door was wide-open. My teeth dug into my lower lip anxiously.

This wasn't a break-in, this was someone trying to break me. And it was working. I was tethering on a very thin thread. My eyes caught a glimpse of something on the countertop. I walked toward it, my chest heaving.

Sage. A bundle of sage, neatly tied with red string, and a small note attached.

You're going to need to start burning this, baby. XO.

CHAPTER FOURTEEN

Stop fucking texting me, you sicko. My fingers hammered away at the screen. I had spent twenty minutes cleaning every tiny piece of glass from the frame, double-locking every door, and finally sliding into bed next to my oblivious husband.

What are you talking about? Jake's text came through immediately.

Tormenting me, breaking into house, the tiara... I know you're a desperate, blue-balled jackass who thinks I'll be at your sexual beck and call, but I'm not kidding. Enough is enough. We were a stupid mistake, and it was because I was too weak to realize what a big, fucking mistake you'd be. Fury blurred my eyes.

Sage, I seriously have no clue what drug you're

on. **Maybe you're not just a sex addict, but also a drug addict who is on some serious shit right now. Do I need to be worried? I'm not trying to wreck my life with Harlow and the kids. You better delete these messages.**

Before I rushed to reply with another hate-filled text, I paused. He had a point. I mean, why would anyone, especially a suburban, doting father and husband want to throw himself under the bus? Why would he torment me when he knew Brody was an attorney, who was not only a good friend but also provided his real estate business with tons of free legal help.

While he wasn't off the hook, I did think maybe I needed to loosen my grip and think twice before pointing a sharp finger at Jake Davis. Maybe it was someone closer to me… I turned my head and looked at my husband. His breathing was slow and shallow. He seemed so full of spite toward me, but could the man I married and the father of my children hate me enough to want me to spiral out of control? Could he be trying to uncover my worst-kept secrets to unravel me? My head spun, and before I knew it, sleep took over and for a few hours, I was able to drift away into oblivion where no one could hurt me, not even me.

Brody took the kids to school in the morning,

which was the greatest gift of all time. I woke up, brushed my teeth, washed my face, and changed my clothes without sweating from racing between the kids to make it on time. The doorbell rang, breaking me from my steaming hot coffee that instantly warmed my soul as soon as it touched my lips. Was it not sad what luxury had become after becoming a mother and wife? Drinking my coffee while it was still hot and showering without screaming children was a gift. Basic human necessities were my silver lining.

The doorbell sounded again, and I quickly got up. I usually ignored it because solicitors were always trying to sell pest control services or religious patrons were always telling me how I needed Jesus. These visits were more common than actual friends visiting, and Harlow was definitely at carpool.

Placing my coffee down on the table in front of me, I trekked over to the door, standing on my tiptoes to peer through the small half-moon window at the top. My eyes instantly widened at my visitor. Shit.

Definitely not pest control and definitely not a church-goer. I quickly smoothed out the oversized T-shirt I was lounging in, cursing myself for not putting on pants. With a quick fluff to my hair and a deep breath, I opened the door.

His dark eyes scanned my entire body, and I could

have sworn they were like lasers leaving goosebumps wherever they landed. "Hi…" He brought his sexy gaze back to mine.

"Hey…" I tugged my faded T-shirt down and tilted my knees inward. A car passed by, and I realized this wasn't me at my New York city apartment; I was married with kids, living in a neighborhood with HOA dues and a yard of the month competition. I grabbed his arm and tugged him inside, then checked left and right before slamming the door shut behind him.

"Archer, what if someone sees your car?" I shook my head, realizing just how stupid it was that I even let him in my house.

"I parked at the clubhouse and strolled over." He smirked at me.

"Strolled over… looking like that." I titled my head and took him in. A fitted, gray-pinstriped suit, crisp light blue button-down, and shiny cufflinks on the end of his sleeves.

"You are… breathtaking." Archer gripped my elbows as he stared at me with intensity. The thing that shook me to my core with Archer, was that unlike other men I'd slept with or dated, I actually believed him.

"You shouldn't be here," I whispered.

Moving closer to my face, his eyes stayed fixed on my lips. "Then tell me to leave, Sage."

My eyes dropped to his lips and darted back up, then he tilted me into his arms and kissed me. Moaning into his mouth, he picked me up with urgency, his hands resting on my ass. This time I was at least wearing panties. I could see mischief dance in his eyes as he climbed the stairs two at a time. Pausing in the hallway that connected all the bedrooms, he looked at me. "Where am I supposed to go?"

I laughed and pointed to my bedroom. *Our bedroom.* My heart sunk at the thought of what I was willing to do—sleep with Brody's boss, in the bed we shared as husband and wife. This is the part where women with morals put their feet on the floor, cry, and say no. This is the part where women with morals realize they need to be happy and grateful with what they have. This is the part where women with morals *think twice.* But the thing is, I'm not a woman with morals, I don't think about what I need... it's more so what I want.

And right now, I want Archer Collins in between my legs.

Flinging me onto the bed, he doesn't even think twice as he rips the condom between his teeth and then he's inside me. The moans coming from me sound primal. I grip the sheets as I watch him lose himself in this moment. The way he looks at me, the way he craves my body makes me feel alive. I can't tell if that's me going back to my old ways or if this is me just knowing what I really want. Lost in a haze, moments pass in a blur, and when he collapses and says my name while breathing heavily, I think to myself that this is what life should be like.

Addiction: *noun*—the fact or condition of being addicted to a particular substance, thing, or activity. I never thought sex could be the rival of a drug or drink. I watched my mother drink her entire life away to the point she'd fall unconscious after my dad screamed hideous names at her, demoralizing her minute by minute. She'd waddle into my bedroom, my heart would stop, and my chest would constrict as I'd hear her hand against my doorknob. The turn and click would make me wish for death. She'd come in holding a giant bottle of shitty alcohol, and she'd look at me, laughing hysterically and call me a dumb bitch, or basically tell me I'd be dead in a ditch if it weren't for my pretty little face.

The day I came to look for my fur coat and noticed

it was missing, I stormed out into the living room. My dad was long gone by then—we never heard from him. Fast food wrappers were strung along the floor, bottles of liquor emptied in her stomach, lining the table like souvenirs as she laid on the couch, one arm grazing the stained carpet below. Soap operas and dated game shows blared as she snored. I was paying her bills through modeling gigs, pageant wins, and bartending. I'd throw myself at every man to get a bigger tip, just so I could pay for my place and hers. Why? I don't fucking know. That's the sad thing about family. You give the shittiest people second—and third... and twentieth—chances, just because they share the same blood as you. Even if they'd never do the same if the tables were turned.

"Mom, where is my fur coat? The fur coat I won from Miss USA," I shouted at her, tears already brimming my eyes. It was the one thing I didn't want to give up, just one. Maybe those repressed feelings and memories of my skinny legs trembling at the bus stop before school haunted me, because she'd forget to put me in a jacket, and eventually, she would forget to buy me one... or maybe it was something inside of me waiting to be unleashed.

She finally woke up and tilted her head. "Oh, did the beauty queen get her wittle heart bwoken?" she said with a nasty smile on her face in the dumbest baby voice possible.

"Mom, please. I'm going out tonight, and I must have left it in the closet here... Please." I hated that I was begging, pleading for something I had won. Not just won, I fucking busted my ass for it. You didn't just win a pageant; you had to own it. Every step you took, every piece of your flesh on display, being judged.

"Ugh, stop pouting. I sold that ugly junk." She lit a cigarette and pressed it against her dry, chapped lips.

"You are spiteful. I'm done paying your rent." Burning tears poured from my eyes as anger raced through every vein in my body. I turned, grabbed my purse, and promised I'd never come back here. Just as I was leaving, a strong hold tugged my ponytail. My hands instantly shot up to my scalp. "Ah!" I screeched.

"You little, ungrateful bitch." I landed on the floor, my mother standing over me with a sharp, shiny knife. My eyes grew wide, my mouth parted, but the words were stuck in my throat. I pushed against my heels and elbows, scurrying backward as she wildly waved and stabbed into the slots of my body. This was the woman who was supposed to love and protect me, but the same woman showed no remorse in attempting to take the very life she had given me.

"Mom! Please, no! Please! I'm so sorry. Please, don't...." I pleaded through hysterical sobs.

Her laughter was wicked, crackling through the smoky air around us. Just as I was beginning to stand, the blade almost pierced through me. I pushed her back with all my might, while the screams of my dwindling strength towered around us. This wasn't me; this was me as a child shaking in bed, fearful of the yelling. This was me as a teenager, scouring through racks of thrift stores for a dress to parade myself in for a pageant. Trying to please her, trying to get her to love me.

I shoved her back and everything blurred in front of me. My hands flailed and blended with hers. Screams I didn't recognize were strumming from my own body while the air left my lungs. I stood over her body, my feet firmly planted on each side of her. The knife gripped in my hands—they weren't shaking, they weren't trembling. I was strong. I was lucid. With one swift movement, I slammed the blade into the center of her body—the same body that gave me life but also ruined mine. Her eyes widened, her mouth dropped. I flung it out and in once again. Over and over, while blood painted my hands and my bare legs. I couldn't stop. A sheet of madness covered my entire being.

Blinking my eyes violently, I waited. I waited for

tears, but they didn't come. I looked around and realized the woman in front of me had wrecked my life enough, and I wouldn't let her be the reason I spent the rest of my days behind bars. My fingers ran across her pulse, but nothing was there.

I quickly grabbed the knife from her body and wrapped it in my scarf, sprinting out into the cold, unforgiving New York winter. Clutching my thin coat tightly with one hand, I ran as fast as I could, my feet sliding against the black ice.

Less than thirty minutes later, I ended up at Wildberry Park. I used to come here and hide when my parents would fight. Glancing side to side, I was thankful it was an otherwise abandoned park, home to the homeless and perfect drug dealing spot. Once my feet crunched down against the frozen leaves in the middle of the woods, I viciously dug into the cold dirt. My nails ached as they acted as a shovel. Once the dirt broke and a hole was made, I laid the knife in the ground, then refilled the hole, packing down the icy leaves. The winter would bury it further, and honestly, no one would give a shit to dig that deep into my mom's death. She was an abusive junkie who had no friends, besides bottles of alcohol. New York City had bigger problems and crimes to manage. Many people came to New York to disappear, ironically, and I'd need to leave to be hidden. Her face would probably be plastered on a local station's bulletin board with a shitty reward for any information. I was finally free.

Maybe fifty shades of fucked-up, but free.

"So, want to get some lunch?" Archer's voice broke me out of my trance as he stood next to my bed, carefully buttoning his shirt over his impeccable body. I leaned up against my elbow and watched him.

Looking over his shoulder, a smirk grew on his face. "Enjoying the show?"

With a laugh, I rolled over and out of the bed. Slowly walking over to him completely naked, I lifted onto my toes and began to knot his tie with my eyes fixed on his. His thumb rubbed against his bottom lip, but he didn't dare break his gaze from me. This moment was even more intimate than the sex we just had.

"Let's get lunch," I whispered against his lips before letting mine brush against his. A smile grew under our kiss on both of our faces.

"Sage, I think I'm in lo—"

I put my index finger against his lips quickly. "Don't you even think about finishing that sentence,

Suit." He let out a small laugh and shook his head, watching me in awe.

One hour later, we pulled up to a restaurant near Hotel Besos. There was no way in hell I'd be going back there, but the area around it was the perfect place to not be seen. It was predominately tourists and easy to blend in. Brody was going to pick the kids up and take them to his mom's house for a quick visit after school since he thought I was spending my day writing my romance novel.

Glancing up at Archer over the menu, he caught my stare. "So, what is that you wanted to talk about?" Archer unbuttoned his jacket with one flick of his fingers.

Placing my menu down, I parted my lips, but the waitress came up to take our orders.

After she turned and left, I looked up at him. "The case you and Brody are working on… Payton Smith?" I don't know why it came out more like a question than a statement.

Archer clasped his hands in front of me and squinted. "Sage, I can't discuss an ongoing investigation or any case for that matter."

"Archer… why did the murderer shave his head? What's the metal souvenir they leave behind?" My heart pounded against my chest.

Tilting his head, lines grew between his brows. "Why are you so interested?"

"I spent a lot of time over at Hotel Besos, and it's… just creepy." I tucked hair behind my ear and looked away.

Archer leaned in closer, his voice dropped as realization grew over his face. "Sage… did you know Payton Smith?" His hand reached for mine. "Sage?" Looking into his dark brown eyes, I could hear my pulse in my ears. Slowly, I nodded. Archer's mouth dropped. "Sage… were you there when he was killed?" His grasp around my hand grew tighter, and I could have sworn if he was a cop, he'd have slapped on a cuff around my wrist in an instant.

"No," I whispered, staring at my shaking hand in his.

"Did you sleep with him?" His voice cracked between words.

Letting out a long sigh, I whispered, "Yes."

"While you and I have been together?" He pulled away as if he wanted to put a bigger distance between us than the small table for two could give.

"No," I answered again, shaking my head quickly.

"Sage, what the hell is going on?" Archer stared at me like he was looking at a complete stranger, which wasn't a far-fetched sentiment.

"Archer, please. Just tell me what you know…" Hot tears brewed in my eyes.

Archer glanced side to side before leaning in again, letting out an exhale. "The victim's head was perfectly shaved, and the hair was nowhere to be found. Additionally, a shiny, metal object was found in his body. He was pretty mutilated. We have detectives working on finding the source of the metal and matching up the shaving of the victim's head with a potential trademark of a serial killer. It's all confusing and a fucking mess. Now, tell me the damn truth."

"I slept with him when I first started going to Hotel Besos just to…"

"Just to what, Sage? Why did you go there, dressed up every week?" He poured his question out rapidly as if he knew he had me in a vulnerable spot.

"A question for a question, huh, Suit?" I offered a sad smile.

"Sage… baby…" He caressed my hands carefully.

"I'm an addict." I shuddered at the stupid label that made no sense.

"An addict? To drugs?" He cinched his brows together, trying to conceal his nerves.

"No…" I looked up at him, "sex."

A small grin let out on his face. "I'm sorry, what?"

He chuckled lightly and took a sip of his drink before swishing the liquid around in the glass.

"It's not funny. It's gotten me almost killed before. I have a compulsive need for sex because it's the only way I feel... alive. I don't find it to be an intimate connection; I find it to be a way that validates that I'm wanted." I let my face fall into my open palms. I had never told anyone that before.

"Damn, Sage... I didn't know... I would have never..."

"Never slept with me?" I peeked out from the cracks of my fingers. "Never talked to me?"

"No... I would have never slept with you if I knew it'd hurt you. But talking to you... that's been even better than the sex."

I frowned. "Well, then I must be terrible at sex."

"No, definitely not." He grinned.

I cleared my throat and eyed him carefully. "Archer, you need to stay away from me."

He stood and slid his chair closer to me, leaning in and tilting my chin up with his index finger. "The problem is, you're not the only one with an addiction, Sage." His lips ran across mine, and in that moment, I didn't feel alone. "I'm addicted to you, baby."

Maybe I could trust him...because I knew he had

feelings for me, deep ones. The kind that makes you stupid shit, and act even more recklessly.

"Now, why do you want to know about the Smith case?"

"Someone's still sending me photos and messages... I don't know, I'm just worried and hoping there's no connection between the Smith case and whoever is messing with me." I dug my fork into the leafy salad in front of me.

"What? Why didn't you tell me? I assumed you had handled it?" Archer's voice was laced with anger.

"Because you don't need to be involved in this mess... my mess."

"Like I told you at the beginning, you need to get the police involved, Sage. If someone's harassing you... I mean, do you have any idea who it could be?"

Shaking my head, I chewed slowly so I didn't have to pour out all my insane assumptions between my husband and my best friend's husband. Archer would definitely lose all respect for me if he knew about Jake. Hell, I had lost respect for myself. "No police. I can't, and please don't ask why." Deep down, I knew bringing the attention of the police on me was asking to incriminate me.

The problem with your past is that no matter how hard you try to leave it there, it won't stay where it should. The past is embedded in who we are and is a piece to your own puzzle. Without it, you'll be incomplete.

"Fuck, Sage…" Archer ran his hands through his dark hair. His meal sat completely untouched. "Look, we have some leads for Smith's murder, and your name hasn't come up. If you…"

"I didn't kill him, Archer. I'm an ex-beauty pageant queen and now a stay-at-home-mom of two, driving an SUV and hosting bake sales… I'm not a murderer. Am I a fuck up? *Yes.* Murderer? *No.*" To that, he took a bite of the burger in front of him, and I knew he believed my life.

Did I kill Payton? *No.*

Had I killed someone before? *Yes.*

CHAPTER FIFTEEN

"*A*ndi, Tate! Dinner!" I called out. I could hear their little feet racing from upstairs. This was the first year they both had been able to somewhat play together without me constantly breaking up fights. It was a new sense of sanity and freedom, cooking dinner or doing the dishes without two crying children on you. Brody was typing on his laptop at the table, his keys clicking quickly against his fingers. "Wow, you're swamped tonight." I stirred the steaming spaghetti noodles with the thick red sauce.

"Yeah, it's that damn Smith case," Brody replied flatly without moving his eyes off his screen.

"Any new leads?" I asked in the sweetest voice I could muster.

"Mmm..."

"Kids! Dinner!" I yelled again. Their pitter-patter came echoing down the stairs. My phone buzzed against the counter. Quickly wiping my hands against the hand towel that was flung over my shoulder, I licked the sauce off one finger. *Perfect.*

Wow, you look beautiful. I re-read the text once again. My chest tightened as I looked over my shoulder.

Brody was still typing on his laptop.

The spaghetti looks just as delicious as I imagine you'd taste. I did a full spin, clutching the phone tightly.

"I'm hungry, Mommy!" Andi called out as Tate took his fork and began pounding it into the table, chanting with her.

Looking for me?

I turned again so quickly, and the whining of my children collided with the fear coursing through my mind. With my elbow, I knocked the giant, glass jar of spaghetti sauce onto the ground. The crashing competed with the sound of my heartbeat.

"Sage! What the hell?" Brody jumped up and raced over. I tucked my phone into my pocket and quickly bent down. Without thinking, I began to scoop the sauce into my palms, a shard of glass slicing into my flesh.

"Ow!" Blood mixed with the red sauce, and suddenly the screams from my past haunted my present. Flashes of my mother's dead body and the blood that stained my hands as I plunged the knife in and out of her body. Chills shot through me, yet sweat was beading on my forehead.

"Sage? Move, I'll clean it." I looked up at Brody, who was watching me intently. "Sage... go wash up." His eyes darted to Andi and Tate, who were both watching over the backs of their chairs like I was some sort of wild animal lurking in their home.

Nodding, I walked down the hall and washed my hands, specks of the diluted sauce and my blood swirling around the pristine, white sink.

Looking up at my reflection in the mirror, I could see a surge of anger flooding through my eyes. I peeked out toward the kitchen and could hear the kids cheering for their spaghetti as Brody served them. I needed to handle this shit once and for all.

Tip-toeing toward the front door, I placed my palm on the back of the door, twisting the cold knob with the other, hoping to stifle the sound. Standing outside, I looked and saw Harlow's car wasn't in her driveway. She had women's bible study once a week, and I knew she'd be there. Her kids always went with her and hung out with the other children, meaning that would leave Jake, the goddamn terrorist, home alone, fully able to harass me as his new hobby. Storming over there, I banged my bloody, clutched fist against his door.

Within a minute, he opened the door and looked at me in shock. "Sage? Hey, everything okay?"

I shoved his chest, almost knocking him off his feet. His hands flung up protectively. "Whoa! Sage, what the fuck?"

I kicked the door shut behind me as hot tears streamed out my eyes. "You are a sick bastard!" I screamed, letting my fist hit his chest.

"Sage, stop!" He grabbed my flailing fists, which landed aimlessly on his body. He held my clutched hand and looked at the blood. Leading me to their kitchen, he grabbed some paper towel and wrapped it. "Sage, care to explain why you just barged into my house like a Category 5 hurricane?" He nodded to the island and pulled a stool out for me.

Sliding my phone over to him, his eyes widened as he read the messages. "If you sent these to me, I swear to God, Jake, I'll kill you."

"Sage… this is crazy. Who sent you these? Did you tell Brody?" The blood from his face drained as he read through the messages again. Seeing Jake's reaction was a telltale sign he didn't send them to me, and he wasn't my stalker.

But if Jake Davis wasn't stalking me and watching me... then who the hell was?

Chills shot up across my entire body. "No, I didn't tell Brody, and I can't. He'll dig, and he'll definitely find out about us, so don't you fucking even think about it, Davis." I jammed my pointer finger into the center of his chest.

"Shit… yeah. Got it." He rubbed his hands against his face. Silence fell between the both of us because what was there to say?

Whoever was doing this to me knew I was the perfect person for their sick, fucked-up game. I couldn't ask for help because help would mean my life being exposed, and that was something I couldn't risk. Death would be better than putting my children through the wrath of my ugliest, darkest secrets.

I put my elbows on their kitchen island and ran my fingers through to my scalp. "I'm scared, Jake…" My voice shook with each word.

No matter how secure you are in your life, it's nice to know you can run... The problem arises when you have nowhere to hide.

Charleston was where I ran to; Charleston was

where I thought I could hide, but just like a game of hide-and-seek, someone had found me. Someone knew my past and present, and someone was doing everything they wanted to do shred any chance at a future I had.

The ring of my phone cut through the doom that clouded around us. "Hello?"

"Sage? Where did you go?" Brody hissed through the phone.

"Oh, sorry, I'm at Harlow's. They needed me to help for a minute. I'm coming home." I quickly ended the call before he could pry further.

"I'm hoping the rage and fear you may feel can turn into... some, I dunno... revenge sex?" Jake's finger traced down my arm.

No, Sage. Just say no.

Anyone who says sex isn't an addiction doesn't know the concept of addiction. It's an overpowering compulsion. When your drug is right in front of you, even if it's the cheaper version of what you prefer, it's impossible to reject it. I didn't have a heart, yet inside some small portion of the good in me screamed for me to say no. But my actions would always speak louder than my words.

I stood up off of the stool and tugged my leggings off. Leaning his back against the kitchen island, his gaze remained on my naked lower half before he tore his pants and briefs off. "Come here you, dirty little whore... I've missed you."

This is the part where any normal woman with a shade of shame would slap the grin off of his face and run home—to her husband and children. To her home nestled behind the white picket fence.

But I wasn't normal. I was the chipped China teacup sitting amongst the perfect set you got on your wedding day and couldn't dispose of because it was one of the others. I was the damaged housewife.

Straddling him, I clenched my eyes shut as he sighed loudly, gripping my waist and moving me up and down his length. Suddenly, my body tensed up, not from an impeding high or orgasm but from sadness. I felt sad that it wasn't Archer Collins. I was betraying him.

In that moment when I was pumping my body on another man—who wasn't my husband—I realized I was in love with Archer Collins. Picturing Archer's lips against my body, feeling his fingers on my skin, my back arched and my body shuddered as an orgasm rippled through me.

Opening my eyes, I felt disgusted. I just got off picturing my husband's boss while riding my best friend's husband. Pulling myself off, I grabbed my leggings, bunny hopping away, stuffing one leg into each part before slamming the door shut behind me. Tears burned my eyes, shame rode through me harder than surfers on their most desired waves.

Jogging home, I hunched over, letting out a heavy breath. Turning the knob, I heard the TV on and the kids singing along to yet another watered-down version of an adult song. Brody stood over the sink washing dishes, while a plate sat on the table for me, filled with food and a glass of wine next to it.

"Hey, are you okay, Sage? You just darted out with a bleeding hand. I know the sight of blood bothers you, but I could have cleaned it up for you." Brody wiped a plate carefully.

"Um, yeah... Harlow had texted me and needed a hand, even a bloody hand," I added and waved the paper-towel clad hand with a small smile.

Brody let out a laugh and came closer to me. "Babe, I'm sorry. I've been a complete ass lately. I know you're overwhelmed caring for the kids and balancing everything. How's your book coming? I'd love to read some..." Brody pulled me into him, but I stood there like a statue, no longer used to his affections.

"Thank you. It's not ready; I had a bit of writers block lately. Maybe I just need to get away for a weekend and really write." I looked up at him.

He gently kissed the tip of my nose before placing a

soft kiss on my lips. "You know, that's a great idea. I've been stressed with this Smith case and feel like I've been really absent from the kids... Babe, I know I've been a complete jerk to you. You need a break." He tilted my chin up and sympathy seemed to actually be embedded in his eyes for once. "Go to that nice, new B&B on Sullivan's Island and get your writing and relaxing in." He slowly pulled away. "I love you, Sage." He smiled and walked to the living room before rallying the kids up for bath time.

Looking over at him, I realized something.

I didn't love my husband... and I never had.

"Hey, Sage!" Harlow called out from the parking lot, waving excitedly at me.

Sliding my sunglasses over my eyes, and in my sick mind, it was a way I could shield the fact that I had just fucked her husband the night before. "Hey, Harlow, how was bible study?"

She wrapped me in a warm hug—a hug I didn't realize I genuinely needed until this moment. "It was great. You should come... How many years have I begged you to join? A lil' Jesus would be good for you, honey." She tapped her hip into mine, with her arm around my shoulder as we walked toward the school.

"Yeah, maybe," I replied, knowing there was no way I'd ever join a bible study.

Besides, my spot in hell was already reserved. What was the point when the only person I needed to get good with, was the devil himself.

"Isn't this spring so much hotter than usual. Gosh, you'd think living on an island by the water, we'd feel that so-called sea breeze. It's hot as Hades." Harlow wafted her hand over her face.

She was right, the sticky humid air was growing more and more uncomfortable; it was only a matter of time before summer brought a suffocating heat of its own. The summer also meant my kids would be home all day, every day with me. Any hobbies I was interested in would soon be significantly harder to do. Days would be spent at the beach, or playgrounds sweating my ass off while my kids whined about being bored day three of their summer break or begging for a third popsicle. But maybe that's what I needed? Maybe my kids could be my chaperones so I'd stay in line and not stray.

"So, Jake told me you're going to the new B&B on Sullivan's Island for the weekend." Harlow and I walked into the school library and took a seat before we went through the piles of books the librarian left for us to help sort through.

Fucking PTA.

I tilted my head in wonder. "How'd Jake know?"

"Brody told him that he booked it for you, which, um… husband of the year. Lord knows, I'd kill for a weekend away from my family." Harlow giggled and began shuffling through the books.

"Yeah, I just want to work on my book and I guess have a bit of a breather." I rubbed my face. "It's been a rough time."

"Honey, if I didn't have to go to the kids' game this weekend, I'd beg you to pack me in your suitcase and let me come with."

"How about we plan for a girls' weekend sometime soon? Until then, I'll be sure to bring you back a slice of blueberry pie from that bakery nearby."

"Indigo's Cafe? Bring me back an entire blueberry pie… it's seriously to die for." Harlow pretended she was drooling.

I laughed and feigned to care about which books needed to be retired for bent pages and ripped covers. A weekend away by myself is just what I needed.

It wasn't like I was going to bathe in holy water and come back a saint, but maybe, just maybe, I could purge a little of the sinner out of me.

Pulling up to Magnolia's B&B on Sullivan's Island was nothing like what I thought it would be. In my mind, I pictured the beach version of one of those Hallmark Christmas movie rustic homes with an older couple greeting you on the wraparound patio. Nope, this was a mansion on the beach that reminded me of Archer's house. Speaking of... Archer happened to live somewhere right along this very stretch of the ocean. The temptation to invite him over tonight was great, but I needed to get some damn words on my laptop in the event my husband finally insisted on seeing my supposed book. And secondly, a spa treatment and waxing are something no man was worth giving it up for in this moment.

Greeted by a young woman who looked like a Barbie doll, I was given a glass of champagne with a strawberry neatly nestled on the rim. Yes, this is exactly what I needed.

Once in my room, I stripped and was ready for my massage. Tugging on the soft robe, I tied my hair into a messy top bun. I chugged the rest of my champagne —rather ungracefully, I might add—and headed down the winding mahogany stairwell to the spa.

"Hello, ma'am, how may I help you today?" Rob, the concierge in a white two-piece linen suit, asked.

"I have a massage scheduled. I'm Sage, Sage Miller."

"Ah, wonderful. Mrs. Miller, I see you right here. Your husband actually called and asked for us to upgrade it, so you're in for an ultimate treat," Rob replied with a robotic smile. His face showed no wrinkles and was stretched like plastic… kind of like a creepy, Ken doll.

"Wow, great. I'm such a lucky girl." I rolled my lips to suppress my impeding laughter. I was led back into a dimly lit room, the soft sounds of ocean waves crashing against the shore providing the perfect background noise.

"You can get undressed and choose to keep on whatever you'd like or take off as much as you want." Rob nodded at me and quickly left.

I took off my robe, panties, and bra, then planted my face in the massage table hole. If there was one thing about me, I was never worried about the way I looked. I knew I was beautiful, and after having two children, my body still looked incredible.

My only weapon in this world, and I intended on keeping it locked and loaded as long as possible.

I heard the door crack and quickly positioned

myself. I didn't care to look up and make small talk with the masseuse—this was for peace and quiet, two things a mother never got. They didn't say anything, which I appreciated. I had already filled out the form of exactly what I wanted. I let myself drift off as their soft hands—which felt rather masculine, with both size, pressure, and technique, and I immediately pictured a sexy man—planted on my back with warm oil.

This was good. Really good.

I let out a soft moan. Maybe this could be my new hobby. He began rubbing out the knots in my upper shoulders, and less than a minute later, his hands moved from my back to my scalp. Just as I was about to open my mouth to ask him to focus on my back, a violent force shoved my face into the headrest further. I could feel two hands pressing down and the cotton fibers from the towel draped under me muffled my attempts at shrieking. I tried lifting my arms, but they were frozen. Trying to wiggle my legs and feet to plummet off the table, I couldn't. I was paralyzed. Fear iced my body over. Why couldn't I move? Was it the champagne I tossed back without a second thought…? My breaths became shallow as darkness overtook me.

I was done.

CHAPTER SIXTEEN

*W*armth brushed my face, and I opened my eyes to the scent of the ocean and the sound of the waves crashing. I looked over and jerked up. A woman with stunning deep blue eyes and dark hair was sitting near me, watching me. I jolted again, my lips parted to speak, but I couldn't remember what I wanted to say.

The pretty doctor quickly reached and patted my arm. "Mrs. Miller, this is Dr. Serena Indigo, she's a frequent guest here and found you unresponsive by the fireplace in our spa."

I looked between the doctor and staff member, whose badge had the name Tish scribbled on it. "I've had one too many before I came here, it's easy when you're so relaxed," the doctor said, her voice reassuring and calm. No wonder she was a physician.

"I think I was getting a massage..." I rubbed my head, hoping this small gesture may unleash memories I couldn't recall.

"Well, we checked our records, and it seems you missed your massage and never checked in for it," Tish added.

I sunk back into my pillow and stretched my arms over my head. "I'm starving." I yawned, tilting my head side-to-side. My neck and scalp were aching.

"Why don't we have breakfast brought up for you?" Tish stood quickly and nodded at me.

"You know what? Have them send some for me as well. I'd love to stay and have some company, if that's okay with you, Sage?" Dr. Indigo smiled at me again.

"Yeah, that actually sounds nice." I felt grateful; being alone wasn't as fun as I thought it was.

Why can't I remember anything? Did I just get drunk and black out?

Moments later, a trolley full of every breakfast item, coffee, and juices came up into my beautiful, large room. We decided to go out on the balcony and sit at the table that overlooked the ocean. "Dr. Indigo, do you live here?"

"Please, call me Serena, I'm not even practicing

right now… Taking a bit of a break. But yes, I moved here a few years ago for a… change." Her eyes sparkled as the steam from her coffee rose up from her lips.

"Oh, cool. Did you find it?" I asked while stabbing my fork into a piece of freshly cut watermelon.

"Find what…?" Serena trailed, her eyes filled with wonder.

"Change?" I spoke as the watermelon juice trickled from my mouth.

"Perhaps in the scenery. But you can only find something that's lost, and I never felt lost… more so, forced to be. Forced to be what I'm not." She placed her coffee down and lifted a piece of whole grain toast, delicately biting into the corner.

I quickly lifted my napkin and dabbed around my mouth, taking in what Serena just said. Was that true? *Have I always just been forced to be something, someone I'm not?* I checked my phone and realized Brody hadn't called or texted me. I quickly messaged him and asked about the kids.

I glanced up at her as my fingers glided against my phone screen. "Do you have children, Serena?"

"Well, now that's a long story." Her eyes drifted toward the crashing waves.

I followed her gaze. "I have time."

"Oh, sweetie, it's not just a long story, it's… a story

long enough to be a book." She offered a light, but sad laugh, lifting her coffee back to her lips, which were covered in a beautiful, red lipstick.

My phone buzzed. I flipped it over and Brody had texted a picture of him with the kids, smiling big. I turned my phone to Serena, and her frown turned into a grin. "How beautiful…" She looked at me carefully. "You're blessed, Sage."

"Then why do I feel like I'm being forced to be someone I'm not. I… This life just feels like it isn't enough to me." I looked at the complete stranger in front of me, wondering what made me want to pour my soul out to her.

Her hand that donned a large, beautiful ring gently brushed mine. "One day you'll look at your reflection in the mirror and see the girl you have always wanted to be. It's up to you to decide if that girl is worth fighting for or if the girl you already are, is worth salvaging." She stood. "I've actually got to be going now, but this was absolutely lovely, Sage. I own the Indigo Café just down the road; we are known for our blueberry pie. Please grab a few boxes when you leave to take home to your family… my treat." She smiled at me.

"Oh, what a small world! We love that pie. Thank you for this… it's been… everything I didn't know I needed." I stood and wrapped her small frame in my arms in a hug. She was taken aback for a moment, but reciprocated with a small pat on my back.

"Goodbye, darling." She winked at me and left.

I looked out at the rolling waves ahead; this part of Charleston seemed so different from the suburbs we lived in. One night here, and the best part so far had been no text messages from whoever had been harassing me. My head still ached a bit, so I stood to go look for some ibuprofen. *How much and what the hell did I drink last night?* The last time I blacked out from booze was when I was single, but I hardly drank because of my mother. I didn't want to share the same addiction. I didn't want to share anything with her.

I walked back into my room, and decided a long, warm bath was calling my name. Afterward, I definitely needed to get some writing done. The giant standalone tub had tiny bottles of bubbles, soap, and shampoo neatly lined with a bamboo tray set across. A few chocolate pieces and mini bottles of champagne were perched beside it all. I took the alcohol and quickly put it in the vanity drawer. I didn't need another repeat of blacking out and embarrassing myself. Climbing in, I let the hot water fill the tub as I watched the bubbles grow bigger and fill the entire tub. Leaning my head back, I took a few deep breaths in and out. It was nice taking a bath where a plastic toy my child had left behind wasn't stabbing me in my ass.

Looking down at my fingers, they resembled raisins. I must have drifted off. When you weren't with your kids, time flew by, especially when you did anything for yourself. I stood and wrapped myself in the soft, plush towel and headed to get dressed. As I towel dried my hair, a light knock sounded against the door of my room. My lips pursed together as I looked at the unmade bed and trays from breakfast lingering. *Probably housekeeping.* My fingers slid against the cool metal, tugging the chain off. I feigned a friendly smile, but dropped it just as fast when my eyes met no one else's. Instead, my breathing grew heavy as the giant bouquet of bright blue-purple violets sat on the ground in front of me with a card attached, taunting me.

My eyes shifted side to side, but the hall was empty. I could have sworn my breathing was echoing against the stillness. I lifted the bouquet into my cold hands and plucked the card out. I didn't want to give the sender the satisfaction of reading it, but I would be crazy not to know what it said.

Violets are blue.

Three words… Three simple words, yet ever fiber in my being was shaken. A simple rhyme, haunting me and proving to me that someone was still out there lurking. Lurking and waiting for me. Backing into my room, I let the door slam shut, quickly fastening the lock.

My phone lit up, buzzing repeatedly. I quickly pulled on an eyelet dress and let my messy bun down. My hair fell into waves from the steam of the tub. Again, my phone went off. I grabbed it from the table outside, and my eyes widened. I had twelve missed calls from Brody, and a million messages from my mother-in-law.

Oh my god, my kids.

I called Brody, and suddenly, the only thing I could do during the never-ending ringing was to… *pray.* Whether it was to God or the Devil, I didn't care. *Someone please, please, protect my babies.*

It's sad, isn't it? When there are times of distress, your life suddenly flashes in front of you, and you beg for forgiveness, for a second chance. You vow to be a better person, and swear to never take anything and anyone for granted.

"Sage! Babe, are you alright? Sage... you need to come home. I've sent a driver to come get you. There's been..." he spewed out.

"Brody, the kids?" I cried out, my voice cracking between each syllable.

"Oh Sage, the kids... They... they are fine. It's the Davis house. You need to come home. Your driver has arrived, they are driving a silver car. Hurry." Brody hung up the phone before I could even process his words.

Harlow? Her kids? Jake? *What the hell was going on?* I quickly threw my things into a bag. Glancing over my shoulder, I turned back, the bright flowers teasing me as I crammed the card from the bouquet into my purse.

Sick bastard.

Outside, I looked around to match the picture of the car with the one in front of me. Even in a moment of panic, I wasn't about to jump into a random car, especially after everything that had been happening. Climbing in, the car began moving and I started to call and text Brody and Harlow.

Why was no one answering? Clutching my phone against my chest, the minutes went by increasingly slower. We went over bridges and hit every damn red light physically possible. As soon as we turned onto our street, my pulse pounded, radiating into my head. Sirens roared through the air, lights flashed brightly, and police, medics, and firefighters were racing around in front of Harlow's house. It looked like a scene from a movie, not our suburban neighborhood full of families and Goldendoodle puppies. *The only thing out of place in the suburbs was an occasional stray cat... or me.*

I jumped out the car, and raced toward the Davis house. An officer quickly flung his arms out to stop me. "I'm... I'm a good friend of the family. Please, I need to see them," I yelled, pushing his arms off me.

"Sage!" I turned over my shoulder. Pulling out of the officer's grip, I ran to Brody. He held me tightly, and I swore in that moment he was scared to let go.

"Brody..." I didn't even know where to begin.

"It's Jake..." His voice trembled as he clenched his eyes shut. "He's dead."

My heart sunk. Dead? *Jake was dead?* I pressed my face into Brody's chest. Was this the saddest moment of my marriage? The closest I had ever felt to my husband was when our friend—a man I had an affair with—was dead?

"Where's Harlow?" I whispered, tears pouring out my eyes.

"They took her in for questioning. My mom took

Andi and Tate to stay with her, and the Davis kids are with Harlow's mom." Brody rubbed my back and whispered reassurance against my hair. *Questioning? Was Harlow a suspect?*

"Mr. and Mrs. Miller?" I quickly turned around. My eyes met with short man with gray hair and small black glasses. "Detective Burton." He flung his hand out. Brody took it, while I just stared.

Would they find out about our affair? How did Jake die? Natural causes? I mean, people in their thirties were dropping dead all the time now. I even read an article about some super healthy twenty-seven-year-old man having a heart attack mid-run.

"Sage?" Brody gently nudged my shoulder and I looked at him, "Detective Burton would like to come to our house and ask us some questions." Turning my attention to the detective, I nodded slowly. We turned away and began walking. I looked down at my overnight bag clutched in my hand and back to Brody. *This was an actual fucking nightmare.*

"Nice house... pays to be a lawyer, I bet," Detective Burton scoffed as we entered. "Look, I'm going to cut to the chase. I'm sure Mr. Miller is well aware of the rules of this game."

"*Game?* One of our best friends has been murdered… and you're calling it a game?" I shouted.

"How do you know he was murdered, Mrs. Miller?" The detective tapped his chin with a ballpoint pen that had clearly been chewed up on one end.

I looked over at Brody. "Detective Burton, you know, I'm not sure this is a good time. My wife and I are processing this very devastating and disturbing news, and I think we'll be in touch when we are ready. I'm friends with Detective Hartley, so I'll be sure to convey any information I have to him." Brody stood and ushered the suspicious detective out of our home.

"I'm just saying it always looks guiltier when you can't have a basic conversation, Mr. and Mrs. Miller." The detective paused mid-way to the door, eyeing us up and down.

"Detective Burton, I'm positive you wouldn't want me to call in your station in regards to my case against you for harassment," Brody said with sheer confidence. *Perks of being married to a lawyer.*

I had to get in touch with Harlow. I quickly ran down the hall and dialed her contact, hoping she'd answer. "Harlow…" I whispered into the phone. The call was answered and all I could hear was crying.

"Sage, he's gone… Jake's gone." She choked on her words, and my heart shattered for her, for their children, for Jake. "They have me here at the station, questioning me like I'm some evil witch. I found his body, Sage. That monster shaved his head, and... the blood, oh—" Hysterical crying and sobs ensued.

"Hey, babe, is that Harlow?" Brody whispered, his eyes stringed with red, and I realized he must have been crying. My husband lost his best friend. I nodded, covering the speaker with my palm.

Brody mouthed, "Let me talk to her," And I handed over my phone. Harlow was still hysterical on the other end. "Hey, Harlow, I'm coming down to the station now. You know we are here for you." He ventured off with my phone and continued to talk to Harlow, using his best attorney voice to reassure her. A moment later, Brody came back. I felt like glue was coating my chair, I couldn't move. "I'm obviously going to be representing, Harlow, and I'll be home as soon as I can, babe. I think you should go stay with the kids and my mom." He grabbed his coat off a chair and tugged it on.

"I'm going to stay home. I want to be here, with you..." I whispered, my eyes fixed on my hands.

"Okay, babe. Lock up, and I'll see you soon." He planted a swift kiss against my head and left. I heard the door lock from the outside and sunk back. The house was silent, making it easier to hear the commotion outside. I walked to the front window, slightly pushing away the curtain. News vans were lined up like hungry vultures and yellow police tape was wrapped all over the Davis' house.

I walked backward and quickly went upstairs, sliding through my contacts. I anxiously tapped my screen, knowing I shouldn't but what does an addict do in times of distress? They need a fix. "Archer, hey…" I swallowed, not sure exactly what I needed here.

"Sage, I'm so sorry about your friend. Brody called me as soon as he found out Harlow was being taken in. Where are you?" he added softly.

"Home, but I don't want to be." I softly cried into the phone.

"Look, why don't you come over? Brody is going to be there all night, and it's not safe for you to be home alone… Besides, I miss you. I'll text you my house address. I'm in my downtown place, not the beach house."

"Okay." I hung up and ran to the bathroom, quickly brushing my hair and washing my face. I applied a generous layer of mascara and lipstick. But then, I froze. I was getting dolled up moments after finding out my best friend's husband—who I had an affair with—was murdered in a neighboring house, and adrenaline was pumping through me for a booty call. I used to laugh when I attended a few sex addiction anonymous meetings. I mean, come on, a woman wanting to screw all the time? Wasn't that just called "every man's fantasy?" But now, I'm realizing that *I was every man's dream, but my own nightmare.*

I walked down the stairs, passing portraits of my children neatly lining the wall. Pictures of us a family, lovingly looking into one another's eyes, and images that were plastered to prove we were that picture-perfect family everyone hoped to be. Gorgeous wife and mother, educated and providing husband and father, a daughter, and a son. Hell, all we needed was a fluffy dog named Buddy, and we'd be ready to be featured on the cover of the next local home magazine.

Sliding into my car, I wove through the media circus and police cars, driving over bridges and into downtown Charleston. Minutes passed quickly, considering my brain was on fire and my body felt numb. Maybe that's why I needed these fixes—it helped me feel alive when I felt otherwise already dead.

I turned onto Broad Street and pulled into a historic home. White, with a two-story wrap-around porch, this was easily a seven-million-dollar home based on the size and location alone. Well, and the fact that just as soon as Archer sent me his address, I immediately searched it online. Brody dreamed of living in one of these historic houses that were renovated but retained history.

The front door swung open, and Archer appeared. He was wearing a full cream linen suit, with a light gray V-neck under it. His dark brown hair was slightly tousled and his eyes lit up as soon as they met mine.

I quickly glanced into the rearview and using my index finger, I swiped around my lips, dabbing away the hurried job I did on my lipstick.

He came to my door and opened it for me, ushering me out with one hand. "Sage, I'm so sorry, baby…" He wrapped me in his arms, quickly leading me inside his home. I paused to take it all in. It was magnificent, in a time-warp kind of way. Unlike his beach mansion, this place was a tribute to history. The dark mahogany wrap-around stairs, the deep red rugs, heavy gold curtains, and portraits framed hung neatly against stylish, yet dated wallpaper.

I looked up at Archer. "This is a museum."

His face broke into a smile as his eyes filled with amusement. "That's… that's not usually what people say when they walk in."

"I'm sure it's not. I'm sure they kiss your perfect,

firm ass and tell you history facts they Googled in your driveway to impress you. Sorry to disappoint." I winked.

"God, I love—" The stare I shot at him made him stop in his tracks. "I love your wit." He winked back at me as laughter erupted from inside of me—a sound I so rarely heard emitting from my own diaphragm.

Kicking my shoes off in the foyer, I sink into the sofa. It was soft, worn, and cozy, yet the deep blue velvet couch was sleek. "I am really, truly sorry for your friend and her husband. I can't even imagine…" Archer brought over two cocktails and handed me one.

"This better be top-shelf, Suit." I took a sip and hummed my approval before I set it on the table in front of me. "I'm still not sure I believe it. I haven't seen Harlow, and I'm not really good at this stuff. Death…it just, I don't know. It doesn't faze me the way it does others. It doesn't impact me. Does that make me a sociopath or a bitch?" I looked over at Archer, who's dark brown eyes were fixed on me.

"Neither. It just makes you stronger than most." He sat, balancing his leg over his knee as he sipped his drink. He looked like he was about to film an ad for Grey Goose.

"Harlow mentioned the killer shaved Jake's head," I whispered against my glass, averting my eyes from his.

"So, from what my buddy at the station said, it's the same killer as the Smith case. Jake's head was shaved perfectly, and again, something shiny and metal was found lodged into the chest cavity, sticking out, wanting to be found." Archer pulled in closer to me. "Sage…"

I took a long sip of my cocktail before turning back toward him. "I was at the spa; I have an alibi. I'm not a serial killer, Archer. And if you thought for even a moment that I was, then that makes you a psychopath for being in love with me." I placed the glass down and eyed him.

"Well, that was a mouthful of the truth."

"Harlow's got an alibi—bible study. Brody was with your kids. You were at the B&B. That leaves random people as suspects, but you're not here to talk about the case, are you?" He pushed my hair to one side before his lips brushed against the crevice of my neck, sending chills up my spine and warmth between my legs.

"I'm not here to discuss anything… because everything I want to do requires no words." I tugged his jacket off, while he quickly unzipped his pants. Standing, he was in nothing but his briefs, and I tugged my dress off over my head. His eyes dropped and scanned over me, sending electricity through my body.

The way Archer Collins looked at me was a love story in its own. Your husband, no, he'd never look at you this way, especially after he saw your giant melon-headed children push through your vagina. This look Archer was giving me—much to what he didn't know —was not a look of love and admiration; it was a look filled with lust and desire. If lust wasn't anything, then why was it that the forbidden fruit is what is sought after? No one gives a damn about the generic, mass-marketed apples and bananas lining the shelves of the grocery store. Every single person, you and me included, wants what they can't have, especially if it's forbidden, because that makes it all that sweeter. The grass is not only greener on the other side, but it's also trimmed and waxed to perfection.

I let Archer lead me up the magnificent stairs that narrowed and curved as we made our way up. Walking into his bedroom, I let out a small laugh. "Kind sir, how did it feel to sign the Declaration of Independence?" His room was huge, with a fireplace to boot, but the décor matched the rest of the house— a historical tribute to a lifetime ago.

Archer snickered and I looked back at him, and with both palms, pushed him onto his four-poster bed.

"Come on, sugar, let me fuck your brains out before you get called to protect our freedom against those damn Yankees." I let out with my best attempt at the Southern drawl with deep sarcasm.

With a salute, he leaned his head back and helped move me on top of him. A loud, hungry moan left my lips as I tossed my head back. I clenched my muscles around his width as he glided me up and down over him.

"Fuck, Sage... you're perfect."

I loved how I made him lose control; his eyes were clenched, and his breathing grew dense. Moving his hands over my breasts, I pumped my body faster. A moment later, he flipped me onto my back and held both of my wrists over my head. Plunging inside me, the movement of his hips were in harmony with my breathing—long, deep, and intense. Moments later, I couldn't hold out any longer, and I let myself get my release, my high, my fix. Suddenly, everything washed away. All the sadness, the pain, the regret... nothing mattered in this moment.

Collapsing next to me, he let out a satisfied laugh. I turned my face to his as he ran his hand through his hair. "Wow..."

Just as I was about to say something, my phone rang loudly. I jerked up and quickly grabbed it. "Harlow, hi!" I answered excitedly, quickly shaking my head and realizing I needed to tone it down. *What the hell is wrong with me?* This was a question I had asked myself daily.

"Sage, I'm coming over. I… I don't want to go be with the kids right now. I can't stand to tell them about—" She began to cry quietly. "I can't tell them their daddy is gone. I can't do it, Sage. I'm not strong enough. I'm not like you."

"Harlow, honey, I'm here. I'm here for you, for the kids, everything," I whispered.

"Brody's going to bring me over to stay with y'all tonight," she sniffled, "if that's not a burden."

"Harlow Davis, you are my best friend and could never be a burden. I'll see you soon." I jumped out of Archer's bed and hung up. "I'm sorry, Archer. That was Harlow. She's going to stay with us tonight. I gotta go."

Archer got up swiftly and grabbed his robe, wrapping himself in it. "It pains me that when you say us, it really isn't *us*." He pulled me into him and kissed my forehead.

I looked up at him. "Don't do that."

His lips brushed against my skin. "Don't do what?"

"Make me fall in love with you…" Tears stung my eyes and I quickly turned away, jogging down the stairs completely naked. I grabbed my dress off the floor and pulled it over my head.

"Sage, I have to ask you something."

"Yeah?" I tugged my sandals on quickly.

"Did you ever sleep with Jake Davis?"

My sandal fell from my hand, and I looked up at him.

"Oh, Sage…"

"Archer, I swear, this is some sick coincidence between Payton and Jake…" I rambled out, panic officially setting inside me.

"Sage, does anyone have any idea?" He cupped my elbows as I covered my face.

"No, I don't think so… I mean, I haven't gotten any texts from whoever was sending them to me ever since I went to the B&B. Just a floral delivery." I paused and realized, what if it had truly been Jake all along? Now, he was dead. Was that it? Were the flowers one last straw? The end of the torment and harassment?

"Look at me. You need to stay under the radar. This kind of shit will be found out. Brody representing Harlow means this is going to my firm, and I can do whatever it takes to protect you with the Payton case, too. But you have to be honest as hell with me, Sage. I'm going to ask you one time and one time only…" His usual soft expression turned intense and serious. "Did you kill Payton Smith or Jake Davis?"

"Archer, I swear to you, I didn't kill either of them. I've never killed anyone in my life," I said with complete confidence because unbeknown to Archer, I was the queen of lying to everyone, including myself. A woman who can stand on stage in front of thousands of gawking eyes in nothing but a bikini and a sash while lying about what she wants for the world or why she wants to win the pageant... that's a talent of its own.

"I believe you, baby. I believe you. I promise, no one will find out your connection to either person." He tilted my chin up and parted my lips with his. That kiss was filled with possession and protection, and the reason I believed him the most was because that kiss was one of love. And when you love someone, you have rose-colored glasses on; that person is flawless and you are at your weakest and most vulnerable—a deadly combination.

Poor Archer.

CHAPTER SEVENTEEN

$\mathcal{I}$ made it home just before Brody and Harlow pulled in our driveway. I quickly changed out of my dress and into worn-out sweats, while tying my hair on top of my head in a quick messy bun. I sucked at the emotional element of grief, so I most definitely needed to look the part to be more convincing. The creaking of the door made my heart race. I walked slowly as Brody came in first, and then Harlow. Her eyes were red and swollen; she wore no makeup, besides the tear streaks from her black mascara, and her hair looked like a bird's nest.

"Harlow…" I opened my arms wide and took her in them, which caused her to immediately cry into my shoulder. I rubbed her back in rhythmic motions, guiding her to my bedroom. Brody nodded with understanding as he stayed back. We walked up each step until I led her into the bedroom, and she collapsed into my bed.

"Sage… he's really gone."

I handed her a box of tissues, climbing under the covers beside her and whispered, "I know sweetie, I know… I'm so sorry." I clenched my eyes shut and blinked, hoping something, anything would come out to show my sympathy. But my body deceived me—it knew me better than anyone.

Temptation? It's revved up and ready to go. *Sympathy and grief?* You better believe it's not going to crack on me. *Call it survival mechanism or a defense mechanism… either way, I was constantly defending myself to survive.*

I rested my chin on the top of her head and rubbed her arm. Reaching for the remote, I flipped on the TV and played Clueless, one of our favorite movies. Harlow pulled away from me and a small smile appeared on her face.

"Do you want me to order some pizza?" I asked while she clutched my hand tightly. She looked at me and shook her head. "Okay."

"Sage, who is going to take care of me? I mean, the kids have me and their grandparents and teachers… but me…? Jake was my whole world." She shielded her eyes with her hands, tears seeping through her fingers.

"I am. You have nothing to worry about, Harlow. I love you." I pulled her back into me and squeezed her tightly. I meant it; Harlow was someone I actually, really loved. I mean, my kids, obviously, I loved them. Brody... I cared about him, and maybe that was its own form of love, but our entire relationship was based on a surprise pregnancy and me looking for an easy out of New York. Harlow was the one person who was really there for me and loved me, even though I was the black sheep.

"I love you, too, Sage." She kissed my arm and sniffled. We watched Clueless and eventually fell asleep where no one could hurt us.

The morning came quicker than I wished and shined light on the cruel reality that was in front of us. My mother-in-law was taking the kids to school and really stepped up to care for them so we could be there for Harlow. Her kids were with their grandparents. I guess that was a perk of people like Brody, Harlow, and Jake. The kind of people who all grew up in this area and flocked right back home after school to settle their new families, knowing they'd have a support system within easy reach. For me, nothing ever felt like home.

When you're damaged like me, you seemingly only find darkness, even in the sunniest of places.

"Hey." Brody offered a small smile over the steam from his coffee.

"Hey..." I grabbed a coffee mug, and suddenly, the memory of Brody shoving me with his hand around my throat into these very cabinets flashed in front of me. I quickly stepped away from him and placed my mug down.

"You don't want coffee?" Brody looked over at me, completely oblivious. I let my hand rub against my neck and looked at him with pain embedded in me. "Oh, shit... Sage. Babe, I'm so sorry about that."

It was rare for us to be home in the morning and to be making coffee at the same time because I was usually darting out with the kids for school and he was usually long gone for work. He stuck my coffee mug under the Keurig and came around the island to me. "Babe, I love you. I'm so sorry." He grabbed me from behind, letting his hands rub my shoulders while kissing the top of my head.

I pushed his hand off me and looked up. "If I was murdered... would you be sad?"

His face dropped and paled. "Why would you ever say that? Sage, you're the mother of my children."

I spun around on the stool, tears stinging my eyes. "Is that all that I am to you?"

"No, of course not. We are just in the trenches of life. Two kids, a mortgage, car payments, my demanding hours, you... busy with writing, and then all the kid stuff. We don't have time to appreciate or enjoy each other. That's normal, Sage. What did you expect? In marriage, the honeymoon phase ends as soon as you land at the airport." Brody walked back to the Keurig and slid my filled mug over to me. Maybe it was true. The only abnormal part of my normal life was *me*.

"Mommy!" a little voice called out from the foyer and instantly, the pattering of feet came toward us.

"What the hell? I told my mom to keep them with her and take them to school." Brody raced to the front door but he couldn't beat the excited faces of Andi and Tate. They came running and both kids with wide arms swallowed me whole. I grabbed them tightly and sunk to my knees, inhaling them. The tears that teased my eyes stood no chance with these two. Rivers ran down my cheeks as I kissed them both ferociously.

Tate looked up at me with his bright eyes and a frown. "Mommy, Granny said Mr. Jake is dead."

Suddenly, my heart fell out of my chest when I realized something I always knew but had filed it away, because that's what I did best in life. I brushed his blonde hair to the side and gripped his chin between my thumb and index finger. "Oh, Tate." I sighed, closing my eyes.

What did I do? I turned slightly and saw Brody staring at us intently. Andi had run off to get a snack, and I was frozen in this moment as a wave of pity and grief washed over me for my son. He'd never get to know his father—his biological father. Jake would never know that he had another child, a son... one who should have carried his name.

"It's a shame." Brody's jaw clenched and he shook his head with disappointment before grabbing his jacket and leaving. What did he mean by that? Brody had made comments before, but I thought it was more of an assumption not certainty. Suddenly, things started to piece together. Brody was on the case for Payton, and now Jake. Brody had access to me at all times and our home.

The texts, the pictures, the stalking...

Was the man I began my new life with the one who was trying to end it?

My mother-in-law's soft voice broke me out of my trance. "Sage, sweetie, I put a casserole in the fridge, and I'm going to swing by upstairs to give Harlow my sympathies before leaving with the kids. They can stay with me for as long as needed. You have too much going on and besides, I'm worried about the k-i-l-l-e-r on the loose around here." Tate was watching her intently as he tried to figure out the word she spelled out. She came over and gave me a big hug.

I gripped her tightly. She was a good one, especially compared to my friends, who all told me about their shitty mother-in-law. The ones who were always just trying to fill their husband's heads with negativity or call them crying on the phone to stir up drama; the ones who didn't love their child enough to let them be happy with their spouse and family. But mine was kind and helped at any chance she could. If anything happened to me, if her son— My chest tightened. Andi and Tate would be okay, no matter what happened, they'd be okay.

"Bye, baby, I'll come over to Granny's and see you and Andi. You both be good. I love you so much, my sweeties." I crouched down and held my children tightly.

Knowing I could have been a better mother to them, for them, churned guilt inside me. I tried my best… considering that a monster lurked inside me, one that never stopped taunting me and was put there by my own shitty parents. But I took every day with them for granted. I wished away the time, found every way possible to run and indulge in my dirty little secret and addiction. *Men.* Random, strange men were more important than being present for my children. But then again, maybe I was being too hard on myself. I mean, just because I'm a stay-at-home mom doesn't mean every waking moment has to circle around my children.

Yes, I'm an addict, and yes, I have a problem, but at least my addiction allowed me to be conscious and available for my children. I wasn't knocked out from booze or high as a kite from drugs. My addiction... well, it's like going to the gym. Yes, physical health.

Sage, you're a good fucking mom.

I trekked upstairs and opened my bedroom door. Harlow wasn't in bed, so I turned and walked toward the bathroom, holding my breath, "Harlow?" I knocked against the door.

A moment of silence passed, and just as I was about to knock again, the door slowly opened and steam clouded behind her. "Sorry, I just needed a shower." Her voice was hoarse and her face was still swollen from the tears she basically drowned in through the night.

"You don't need to apologize for showering, sis." I

rolled my lips and leaned in to cover her in a hug. "How are you holding up?" I whispered against her ear.

"I keep wishing and waiting that... I don't know, that this will all be some cruel nightmare and I'll magically wake up from it, and I can just go home to my husband." She sniffled and pulled away.

"Harlow, I can't even imagine what you must feel..." I didn't know what more to say. I had lost someone close to me—my own mother. I mean, sure, we weren't close by the emotional connection, but she was my blood, my mother, the one who gave me life, and I... took hers away. Shuddering at the memories, I quickly ushered Harlow downstairs so we could eat.

"I'm going to head home to collect some of my things, especially from my craft room. I want to make some scrapbooks for the kids." Harlow stared off while barely eating.

"Scrapbooks? Harlow, don't you think maybe you should just rest?" I put the fork down in the fattening casserole dish in front of me.

"Rest? Sage, my husband was fucking murdered. I found his body, bleeding out, with his head completely shaved because some psychopath used the love of my life and father of my children as a piece in their sick, killing game. I'll never know how to rest without fear again." She closed her eyes and rested her face in her palms.

"I'm so sorry, Harlow... I didn't mean to upset you." This was so uncomfortable and a disaster. I didn't know how to comfort someone when they lost an elderly relative, let alone lost a spouse to a horrifying murder. Jake's death was shocking and heartbreaking, but also some form of sick relief. There would never be any way someone could prove or care to prove that Tate was his son. No one was going to dishonor a widowed wife and her deceased husband's memory. The temptation of an easy high from my neighbor was now buried in the ground with him. Maybe the killer wasn't the only psychopath on the loose; maybe I was just as crazy. The only difference was the killer probably wasn't an SUV-driving stay-at-home, PTA mom of two who was once Miss USA. Then again, who knew?

I mean, after all, wasn't that what insanity was? Letting go of the control and allowing madness to consume you.

Luckily, a knock on the door saved me from my disastrous attempt to comfort my friend. "I'll be right back." I rubbed Harlow's back and made my way to the front door. I peeked out to see who it was and found two men dressed in all black standing there.

"Who is it?" I called out through the door between us.

"Mrs. Miller? I'm Detective Matthews, and this is my partner, Detective Cary. Will you please open the door?"

Shit. I glanced around. Should I call Brody? Would that make me look suspicious? My heart pounded as the detectives knocked again, confused by my silence. Opening the door slightly, I peeked out, holding one palm against the door, keeping it halfway closed. "I'd like to see badges. There's a serial killer on the loose." I swallowed and waited.

They looked at me, not breaking their serious expressions but nodded, holding up their shiny bronze badges. "Okay." I offered a crooked smile, opening the door and motioning my hand like a game show host for them to enter. "Um, just letting you both know, Harlow Davis is staying with us, so please, be courteous and try not to upset her." I followed behind as the detectives didn't answer and continued to the living room. Their eyes wandered around our home like snakes slithering through the grass, eager to find weakness so they could plunge forward.

"Harlow, uh... this is Detective..." I paused, already forgetting their names.

"Matthews and Cary," the shorter, older detective stated.

"Sorry, mom brain." I awkwardly chuckled and could feel heat grow in my cheeks.

"Mrs. Davis, we are extremely sorry about your husband. We are doing everything in our power to make sure whoever..." Detective Cary's eyes left Harlow and connected with mine. I could feel sweat building in the crook of my neck.

Shit, shit, shit. I'm not guilty, stop making me feel like it, asshole.

"Whoever has done this will be found, and we will make sure justice is served."

My hands were trembling and suddenly, I felt an icy wave wash over me. "Can I get you all something to drink? Coffee, tea...?" I quickly stood and laced my fingers together.

"Sure. Coffee would be great." Detective Matthews, the taller and more attractive detective smiled at me.

"Great. Harlow? Detective Cary?" I smiled through clenched teeth.

"Sure," Detective Cary replied callously while Harlow offered a simple nod.

"I'll be right back." I quickly shuffled to the kitchen

and glanced over my shoulder. Detective Cary was watching me. Rolling my lips, I smiled again. *Should I be smiling?* What looked more suspicious, a bitchy frown or a welcoming smile?

I lifted my phone once I got to the kitchen. "Hey, some detectives are here, and I'm nervous. Am I supposed to have an attorney present, like you or Brody?" I whispered, cupping the speaker to further muffle my voice.

"Sage, hey… I mean, are they questioning you or Harlow? Archer cleared his throat, and I heard a door shut behind him through the phone.

"Yeah, I'm…like, why are they here? They don't need to ask me anything, right?" I felt my heart race against my chest.

"If you have nothing to bury, then they have nothing to dig up. But you don't have to answer anything you don't want to. You need to call Brody and tell him they are at your house, that way I have a reason to come over and represent you."

I busied myself making each single-serve cup of coffee and buying time to cool my nerves. *If you have nothing to bury, then they have nothing to dig up.* The only issue was that I had a lot to bury. The darkest secrets were buried deep in the ground, and I prayed no one would ever have the strength to dig far enough to find them.

"Mrs. Miller? Need a hand?" Detective Matthews approached me with a bright smile.

I handed him a steaming hot cup. "Oh, please, call me Sage."

"You can call me Jameson." His eyebrow lifted as he took a sip of his coffee, a small, teasing smirk halfway hidden.

Was he flirting with me?

"Detect—" I paused and realized that having a detective on my side may be a lifeline in case anything from my past came to torment me. Licking my bottom lip, I leaned in, squeezing my chest together in just the right way. His eyes dropped down and I knew this would be too easy. "Jameson, I'm just absolutely *terrified*. I mean, can you imagine a serial killer on the loose, and I just... Can you tell me anything to perhaps alleviate my fears?"

"Oh, um... well... I'm not supposed to, but..." He glanced over his shoulder and back.

"Don't worry, I'm sure Detective Cary is occupied with interviewing my poor best friend who," I sniffled, swiping my nose dramatically, "is a widow now." I grabbed a tissue and dabbed my eyes.

"Sage, please don't cry." Jameson reached for my

hand and gently rubbed it. "We have a few leads, but it's just such a peculiar case. We are trying to find out more about Payton and Jake, and what may tie them together. The killings were identical—shaved heads, metal shrapnel left in the body, daytime murders. One was here, obviously, well… at your friend's home, and the other was at Hotel Besos by the airport." Jameson looked at me as I came around the kitchen island, moving closer to him.

"I see… What is this metal shrapnel business? It seems so… creepy." I leaned in closer, and his Adam's apple rose and fell as I ran my fingers up his arm. "Detective…" I let my eyes stay on his.

"They have no clue. There is really no way to trace it back. I mean, it's just a sharp, shiny piece of metal that both bodies had in their chests. The murder weapon seems to be a knife, but the killer is planting this strange metal inside like a… signature."

I cleared my throat. "What kind of knife?" I titled my head. *There was no way…*

"Just a normal butcher knife. Why do you want to know this, Sage?" Jameson's forehead creased as if he was thinking clearly for the first time during our entire conversation.

My hand fell to his crotch, that, as I assumed, was hard as a rock. *Men, so damn weak and easy.* Rubbing him, his lips parted as he watched my hand stroke him over his pants. I leaned in close to his ear and whispered, "Like I said, detective, a serial killer is on the loose in our sweet little suburb. I'm just worried for my safety and my family's." I pulled away and grabbed Harlow and Detective Cary's coffee. His mouth opened wider, his thighs twitching together. *Leave them wanting more, and they'll always protect you.*

CHAPTER EIGHTEEN

"*H*ow well did you know Mr. Davis?" Detective Cary looked at me with the eyes of a shark.

I was sitting next to Harlow, my hands gripping hers. "Oh, well, Jake and Harlow are… were, I mean, *are* our best friends." I cleared my throat and grabbed my coffee to prolong the next answer.

"Did you ever meet with Mr. Davis privately?" My eyes darted from over my cup to Detective Cary's, who I wished would shut the fuck up.

"Privately?" I repeated and glanced over to Detective Matthews, whose face was still flushed from a simple rub down. I had to hide my grin behind the steaming mug.

"I think Mrs. Davis could be relieved from this

interview, don't you agree, Cary?" Jameson cut through and offered a small smile my way.

My hero. I rolled my eyes inside.

Harlow looked at me concerned, straightening her back and letting go of my hands. "No, it's okay. I have nothing to hide, especially from Harlow." I nodded at her. "I don't think we ever purposely met privately. I mean, that sounds presumptuous, but you know, I'd stop by to see if Harlow was home or if the kids were playing. Jake was my friend, too." I averted my eyes and glanced at bright sunshine through the back doors.

"Did you know Mr. Payton Smith, by any chance, Mrs. Miller?" Detective Cary looked at his notepad and back up at me. "Mrs. Davis said you frequently visited Hotel Besos. May I ask why?"

My palms grew sweaty and a wave of heat splashed over me. I turned and looked at Harlow. *Thanks, bestie.* "I'm an aspiring author, and I am in the process of writing my first novel. I spend some time over there... well, I used to, in order to get some peace and quiet and a change. Are you a parent, Detective Cary?"

"Yes. I am," he replied curiously.

"Well, then you know that our lives revolve around our children, especially as a stay-at-home mom. I need a change of pace sometimes, and Hotel Besos was far enough that I wouldn't run into nosy PTA moms who would end up wasting my time with endless conversation. I didn't know Mr. Smith, and after he was killed, I never went back to that hotel. I'm not trying to be the next victim, detective." I let my hands fold in my lap.

He nodded and quickly wrote something down. "Mrs. Miller, you were once Miss USA, correct?"

Oh, fuck. I wouldn't do good in prison. I'd be someone's bitch on day one. My kids would visit me behind bars. I don't look good in orange... it washed me out, especially without my spray tan. I didn't kill anyone. No, I didn't.

"Mrs. Miller?" Detective Cary's voice rose.

"Yes, I was. I was also Miss New York and a million other titles." I looked away.

"Do you have your crowns?" Detective Cary tapped his pen against his skinny, dried lips.

"No. They were left with my dad, and he left me. I have no clue where they are or where my dad is for that matter." I quickly swiped at my eye and added a small sniffle. Suddenly, a knock at the front made us all jolt, and I grabbed my heart.

"I can get that, Mrs. Miller." Detective Matthews smiled at me and quickly went to answer it. Moments later, he and Archer walked in. My eyes widened when Archer sat next to me, wearing a three-piece navy-blue suit and looked like he was about to film an episode of Law and Order.

"Detectives." Archer nodded at them, unbuttoning his suit jacket with the flick of two fingers. His fingers were truly crafted of magic, and my body shuddered at just the thought of the magic they could wield.

"As you both are aware, Mrs. Harlow Davis is being represented by my partner, Brody Miller, and I'll be representing Mrs. Sage Miller since it seems rather than respecting my client's grief and time to process such a traumatic event that just happened, you both have chosen to come down on these innocent ladies like heartless savages. Any further questions can be directed to me at another time." Archer immediately stood and nodded in the direction of the front door. His presence made me feel so at ease. That was the biggest difference between Archer and any other person in this world. For the first time in my life, someone made me feel like I could breathe without a guard up. For the first time in my life, I felt like I didn't have to protect myself, alone.

"Sage, I'm going to head over to my mom's and see the kids. I'm a terrible mother for not being with them right now. Thank you so much for everything. You're the best friend a girl could have, and I'm just so sorry you guys are being dragged into this mess because of us…" Harlow pulled me in close and hugged me.

"Anytime, I love you," I whispered against her cheek.

"I love you…" She frowned and got up.

"You okay to drive?" I called after her.

"Yeah," she sighed, "I'll be okay." The front door closed, and footsteps grew near.

"So, this is a fucking mess." Archer came back to me and sank into the vacant spot.

"What? Why?"

"Detective Cary is really interested in you. He wants to know more about where you were when Jake was killed, about your pageant days, any kind of relationship you and Jake may have had…" Archer's eyes darkened as he studied my reaction.

"Look, I slept with him out of desperation and… I don't know, okay? But I didn't kill him, and I sure as hell don't need to hash out details of my beauty pageant days during a fucking murder investigation. Clearly, these fools are incompetent, and that's why the killer is on the loose making his way through Charleston." I folded my arms across my chest defensively and waited for Archer to agree with me.

His eyes wandered to the giant frame of Andi and

Tate, which was proudly displayed in the living room. "Sage, who is Tate's father?"

Shit.

"My husband and your colleague. What is this, some episode of Maury? Are you guys going to gang up on me and force a paternity test? I'm done... You can see yourself out, Mr. Collins." My feet hit the floor and I was halfway up when I felt his hand pull me back down onto the couch.

"Sage, this isn't a game anymore. Don't be cute. You could be charged with murder, or at least, listed as a fucking suspect if you aren't already. If you have something you're hiding, you better tell me now. I can't help you when I don't know what's reality and what's fiction. This isn't a chapter in your romance book."

My hands were ice-cold, yet I was sweating. "I think Tate is Jake's son..." My voice trembled. "I mean, no one knows, and I never told Jake. But the resemblance is uncanny, and the timeline matches up." I let my face fall into my palms, trying to conceal the humiliation that plagued me.

"Fuck." Archer ran his hand through his hair. "That gives you motive," he mumbled, lost in thought.

"You think I killed Jake so no one would know he fathered Tate?"

"Sage, it doesn't matter what I think. It matters what the detectives think, and what they choose to dig around for. Then, it matters what the jury thinks. Fuck!"

Suddenly, and for the first time, I realized I wasn't invincible. What happened with my mother was an easy cover-up. An alcoholic, older woman with no friends and a broken marriage, living paycheck to paycheck, wouldn't be missed. Police in New York had gangs, serial killers, terrorists, and way bigger crimes to worry about than that shit.

But now, especially in Charleston, South Carolina, whose nickname was literally The Holy City, they'd do anything and everything to make sure they found their resident Satan.

"Sage, you slept with Payton Smith and Jake Davis. You… Oh my God." Archer jumped up and stared at me with his mouth partly opened, as if a film played in front of his eyes and he realized he'd missed an entire portion of a movie.

"Archer, I swear to you, please… I didn't kill anyone… I would never. You have to help me. I have children." I began crying, and this time it wasn't a farce; this time I was fucking scared. "You saw the texts. You know someone is setting me up!" I quickly ran to the front office, grabbing the box of sashes and all the crowns I had long ago hidden away, just in case. Pulling the lid off, I tugged out the two notes. One read, **Roses are red** and the other, *Violets are blue*. I handed them over to Archer. "Can you see if these have fingerprints or anything? I mean, they have to be from whoever texted me. They both were attached to flowers."

Archer glanced at them and me, letting out a long sigh. "Where's the third one?"

I raised my eyebrows and studied him carefully. "Third one?"

"Roses are red, violets are blue... I love you? Shouldn't there be a third one?"

"I don't know... I didn't get a third one. These came at two separate times."

Archer lifted my chin in with his index finger, his eyes piercing into mine. "Swear to me you didn't kill them."

"Archer, I swear to you, I didn't kill them. The only lie I've been telling you is... to not fall in love with me because I'm a fucking hypocrite. I fell in love with you." I closed my eyes as tears rolled down my cheek, quickly landing on my lips.

"Damnit, I love you, Sage... and I am going to protect you." His lips parted mine, intertwining with mine.

Just as soon as my eyes opened from the most intimate, raw kiss of my life, he was gone. Even though I was scared for myself, for my children, and panic was still coursing through me, I didn't feel the need or urge to just run and find a fix. I didn't need to seek male attention to make my worries dissipate. Maybe Archer Collins was the antidote to my poisonous self-destruction after all.

Hours went by, and I busied myself with doing the dishes, making dinner, and cleaning the baseboards. I mean, who the hell actually cleaned their baseboards? I did everything I physically could to keep my mind off the fact that the detectives were interested in me. Interested in me as a potential suspect in the murders of two men—two men I slept with. The jingle of keys hitting the small glass bowl on our foyer console table broke me out of my self-pity.

"Brody?" I called out,

"Yeah, it's me." He appeared in the kitchen and he looked exhausted. Tugging his suit jacket off, he threw it over the stool. "I know Jake is Tate's dad, and I know years ago, just before we met, you killed your mother. Now, what I don't know is how my wife and the mother of my… child, is connected to these murders." He sunk into the seat and pulled the plate of chicken risotto I had moments ago in front of him. Picking up the fork, he began to eat as if he didn't say the craziest thing a husband could say to his wife.

"Brody..." I clenched my fists so tightly that my knuckles had gone white. "Brody, I... I'm so sorry about Tate. It was a one-time thing." *Lie number one.* "He loves you, and you *are* his dad, Brody. It doesn't matter about blood, I know you love him." I choked on my words. "I have no idea why on earth you'd think I had something to do with my mother's death, but that's just spiteful to say. I didn't kill my mother." *Lie number two.* "What kind of monster would do that?" I scoffed, wiping away the tears that had already budded at my waterline.

"Sage, cut the fucking shit. I read your journal entry right after we had started dating. I mean, that's when I really knew you were just an empty shell. A beautiful, empty, little shell I could mold into what I needed." He set his fork down and tilted his head. "Who the hell journals about killing someone?"

My heart felt like it would explode at any given second. I glanced down at the knife that was clutched in my hand as I chopped the lettuce in front of me for my salad. The sharp, shiny steel cut the crisp greens so easily... just the way they cut through the woman who tormented me, used me, and hurt me. I picked the knife up higher, my reflection staring back at me.

Something Dr. Serena Indigo said over at the B&B rang inside of me. *You'll look at your reflection in the mirror and see the girl you have always wanted to be. It's up to you to decide if that girl is worth fighting for or if the girl you already are, is worth salvaging.*

Tears streamed down my cheeks. "Did you know I started competing in pageants when I was five? By the time I was fourteen, my mother loved getting the winning checks, the lavish gifts, and tormenting me by ripping the scholarship checks in half. She always said I was too dumb for college. She paraded me in those pageants for her own gain. *I was the main attraction in her own circus, and she thrived off being the ringmaster of my life.* When I was sixteen, this older judge came around back and pushed me into a corner. He told me if I didn't fuck him, I'd lose. It was a huge pageant, and I knew if I didn't win, my mother would destroy me. So, I turned around and let him." I paused and looked up from the knife.

Brody's eyes met mine. "Sage… I didn't know that. I'm so sorry, babe. Why don't you put the knife down, and…" He stood quickly and backed away.

A smile broke out on my face. "You think I'd actually kill you, don't you?" I giggled at how his face looked like he had seen a ghost.

"No, because you are just hurting, and you and I

have two beautiful children." His voice shook between words,

"Oh, so now you'll claim Tate as your son? Because I have a fucking knife in my hand, and you know I dug one into my mothers' body several times with zero remorse or regret?" I tapped the shiny metal against the smooth marble, crafting a scratching sound that irked my ears.

"Sage…" Brody stepped back so many times that he ran backward into the back of our couch.

Turning the water on at the sink, I grabbed the sponge and slowly washed the knife, scrubbing the vegetable remnants away. Once done, I grabbed a dish towel and wiped it clean. With a smile, I lifted it up high and turned back to the butcher's block, placing it in its spot. "You know the best part is when that judge fucked me… *I liked it.* That's when I knew physical gains could be so much better than emotional pains."

"Sage…" His voice trembled, and I loved that I induced that level of fear in him.

"Brody, I'm not going to kill you. Why would you ever think that? Why would you ever assume I killed them?"

"Where there's smoke, there's fire." He gripped the back of the sofa tightly.

I let out a small laugh. "Oh, sweetheart, I'm a damn diamond. Fires can't even scathe me."

A light knock on the door made me break my stare from my husband's terrified gaze. "I'll go get that, honey." I winked at him and made my way to the door. "Harlow…"

"Can I just stay here with you guys for a few more days? The kids… they—" She whimpered. "They said they wished it was me and not their dad." She cried into her hands, and I tugged her into my chest. "No one loves me, Sage. The one man who did is gone…" Her entire body convulsed with the force of her sobs.

"That's not true, sweetie; they are just upset and in pain. Besides, you know I love you." I kissed the top of her head and guided her inside. Coming into the living room, I looked around and could hear footsteps moving up the stairs. Brody took this as an opportunity to make sure he was safe and away from me.

"Come on. I'll make some popcorn and we'll watch a movie." I sat her down on the couch and went back to quickly grab some snacks. Jake's funeral would be a cruel reminder of death and its permanence. Until then, I could offer Harlow a small safe haven, considering reality was nothing more than her worst nightmare.

"Okay, *NSYNC or Backstreet Boys?" I tossed some buttery popcorn into my mouth.

A small smile grew on Harlow's face. "Is that even a question? *NSYNC, all the way." Harlow reached into the bowl and grabbed some popcorn.

"See, if you answered Backstreet Boys, I would never have trusted you." I laughed and sipped on the ice-cold diet Coke.

"Do you remember those Juicy Couture track suits with bedazzled words across your ass?" Harlow smiled to herself as she reminisced on a happier time.

"Ugh, yes. Can we please bring them back? I'm pretty sure I have some in storage. I used to rock those while getting my hair and makeup done before pageants."

"Let's totally bring them back, and then you can throw on your fur coat over it when it's cold." Harlow nudged her shoulder into mine.

I sighed. "I'll never find a fur coat like the one my mom sold from Miss USA. It was beautiful." I closed my eyes and rested my head back into the couch. I remembered the way it felt over my bare shoulders as I left wearing the Miss USA crown on top of my head and going to an after-party to celebrate with the most incredible people. Celebrities, gorgeous title holders, sexy and wealthy men... they all had their eyes on me.

Dom Perigone ran wildly, the claps that radiated around me still jolted through my body. I felt so wanted in that moment, so desired. It was the only time I felt that way without a man doting on me or pushing himself inside me.

But just like a balloon at a party that sways and floats high in the air, it will eventually come crashing down and deflate to nothing more than a sad piece of plastic.

"You deserve the most beautiful fur coat in the world, Sage. You are the most beautiful person, inside and out." Harlow let her head rest on my shoulder, and I dropped my head on top of hers.

If there was one thing Charleston, South Carolina gifted me with, it was a friend. For the first time in my life, I had a real friend and I intended to be there for her. Sleeping with her now-dead husband was low, even for me, but I'd like to think as my best friend, she'd understand that my addiction is an illness. She'd probably recognize that I couldn't help something that was overpowering me. I just no longer had to worry about her finding anything out and risking my only friend. Reprieve from one sin made me feel almost…angelic.

"Everything is going to be okay…" I whispered as I stroked Harlow's hair.

CHAPTER NINETEEN

"We are gathered here today to honor the life of Jake Davis, beloved son, husband, father, and friend," the preacher's deep Southern accent drew out.

I looked down at the grass below my feet. Wearing black at the end of spring in Charleston was a punishment of its own. Summer heat and humidity teased us daily, but wearing all black while the sun roasted you felt suffocating. Andi and Tate were sitting between Brody and me. Harlow sat in the front row, her head bowed with her children, parents, and in-laws surrounding her. The light sob that emitted from her was somewhat muffled by a monogrammed handkerchief she clutched in her hands. The preacher went on and on about how God sacrificed his son, or something along the lines of a bible story I must have missed sometime in my life. Jake was being compared to Jesus, and I had to bite my bottom lip to suppress the smirk on my face. Religion was a funny concept. You could be the most immoral person, but if you showed up to church, bright-eyed and bushy-tailed, then you were washed away of your transgressions.

"Thank you all for coming…" I looked up. Harlow had taken the small stage in front of a microphone. I glanced around, seeing tons of people. Jake was well-loved.

I gripped Tate's hand tightly. Would I ever tell him about Jake? Did I owe him the truth? Or was telling someone the truth selfish? It really only hurt the party who didn't know and only benefitted the person who got to take the burden off their shoulders. Maybe carrying this secret, this burden, was the best gift I could ever give my son.

"Jake was always the guy at the party who made everyone laugh and smile. He didn't think twice before helping a stranger or a best friend. He was the most loyal man in this world, and I don't know how I'll do this life without him… but my sweet Jakey, I'll try my best for you. I want to make you proud, my sweet-heart." Harlow's sobs choked her words as she moved down to the casket, carefully placing her hand over it while the other hand clutched her heart. Her children moved toward her, and one by one, they all dropped a rose and then… a violet.

I froze as I looked around—luckily, my eyes were shielded by sunglasses.

This was just a coincidence. I mean, the stupid poem was so popular, it was romantic. I hadn't received any strange texts, pictures, and no sketchy black cars were following me. This was paranoia. I was being paranoid. What if between Payton and Jake, I had been freed? What if they were working together in some sick game to mess with me? I let the air from my lungs release and sank back into the hard-plastic chair. One by one people started to leave. Brody finally stood and walked to Harlow, wrapping her in a hug, respectfully keeping his hands up toward the top of her back. He then dropped down and hugged her children. I watched him carefully as he moved away and nodded at me. Grabbing Tate and Andi's hands, I walked to the casket, each of us dropping a rose and violet on top. "Harlow, I love you."

She gripped her hands around me tightly. "Thank you so much for everything, Sage. You have been my rock. Please thank Brody for donating the flowers." She pulled away and moved to the next person who was waiting to give their condolences.

My chest tightened as I glanced over at Brody. I quickly walked with Andi and Tate to the car. "You guys hungry?" Brody looked over his shoulder and lifted Tate into his booster seat.

"Yes! Pizza!" Andi shouted excitedly.

Oh, childhood, wasn't it so beautiful? You could literally attend your best friends' dad's funeral, or in Tate's case, your biological dad's funeral, and skip away to get some pizza and Coke. Death wasn't permanent to children; the concept was too complex for their innocent minds to understand.

I pulled the seatbelt across my chest and buckled. "Let's go to Santino's."

"S-sure, that's a... that's a great idea, babe," Brody stammered. He was so on edge around me since our not-so-happy conversation. But these flowers? This had to be a coincidence. The detectives had shame-lessly called me countless times today, and they even showed up at Jake's funeral. Archer told me to decline to comment on anything further, but I thought that made me look guiltier than they already pinned me to be.

Pizza grease stained our lips and ice cream cones with rainbow sprinkles lifted the morose cloud of death. Once we ate and talked as if nothing had happened, we went home. Tomorrow was the first day the kids would be home with us and me going back to my days of carpool, changing from pjs to athleisure, meal planning, and PTA meetings. With the ongoing investigation, I knew the only way I'd stay sane and not lose my mind would be resuming my normal life. Part of that being to keep my hands to myself and my damn legs closed. I didn't need any more enemies or anyone following me and finding out things that shouldn't be found.

After Brody gave the kids their baths, Andi asked for me instead of her dad. She sat on my lap as I carefully brushed her hair. She was beautiful; she looked just like me, which I hoped for her sake would be a blessing and not a curse. I wanted her to be everything and more. She was already so smart, and I hoped she'd make something of herself and never have to use men as a stepping-stone to get what she dreamed of. She laid next to me in her bed, the fluffy blush-pink comforter tucked around both of us. She turned her small face toward mine. "Mommy, why do you love Tate more than me?"

My heart sunk that she even thought that. "Baby, I don't love him more than you. I love you both equally," I whispered, tapping the tip of her nose.

She looked away. "I think you do."

"Andi, you can't love one eye more than the other. I

love them both, they both help me see clearly." I smiled and nuzzled my face into her neck.

"You can love one eye more than the other, because what if one of them is weaker or has an *amistagism*." She looked back at me with a frown.

I couldn't help but giggle. "You are so smart, Andi, and absolutely right about the eye thing, but the love thing… you couldn't be more wrong. Tate and you make up my whole heart. I love you both more than anything in this world." Leaning in, I kissed her, which made her laugh. I didn't have the heart to correct her and tell her it was *astigmatism*. She was brilliant and maybe she was on to something—maybe deep down I did keep a small distance from her. I was the result of a horrific mother, and what if that passed down and in some crazy way, it was genetic to just be a fuck-up. I wanted my daughter to have a fighting chance at a better, smoother life than my own.

Once Andi fell asleep, I tip-toed downstairs, and surprisingly, Brody was sitting on the couch with the TV on. He had been avoiding me at all costs, spending time in his office or heading up to bed immediately after the kids. I couldn't blame him; I'd be scared of me, too. "Hey." I sat next to him.

"Hi." He looked away from the screen, seemingly waiting for me to say something else.

"Brody, look, I don't even know how you're still sharing the same space as me after what you know about me. Hell, I don't know why you even married me when you read my journal, but look, I am the product of a messy marriage and even messier parents. I just want Andi and Tate to have better than that." I rested my head in my hand and looked at him.

"I know, and I do, too." His voice was low and hushed. "Look, Sage, I married you even though I knew about your mom because you got pregnant with Andi. I was scared that you couldn't be trusted alone with my child. But then, I also knew I didn't want you in prison... I didn't want the mother of my child in a jail cell. That would have destroyed you, me, and Andi. I also knew you were protecting yourself because no one else ever did. I married you because you're a fighter, you always have been. When I found out about your affair with Jake, I wanted to make you suffer. I wanted to inflict the pain and humiliation on you that you did on me. But then, I thought about Andi... if she had the childhood and life you did, then I'd want her to have someone who loved her, even amongst her faults. And while you may think I don't, I really do love you, Sage Miller. I fell in love with you the moment you put that beer in front of me with nothing but that old, wooden bar dividing us."

Well, damn. He said everything I never knew I needed to hear. I leaned in and let my head rest in his lap as tears teased my eyes. His hands brushed my hair from my face and stroked through gently. "Thank you for saving me, Brody," I whispered, wiping the tears that smuggled out. We watched an hour of some rom-com before heading up to bed, hand in hand. The room was pitch-black and we slowly began to undress, and while no words were exchanged, the weightiness of our breathing did. After a very long time, I laid in bed and didn't think of it as a fix or a high. Instead, I let my husband make love to me, thinking maybe there was hope for this damaged broken girl from New York City who had spent her life suffocating on her secrets.

I looked over as the warmth of the sun grazed my cheeks, letting my hand brush the pillow next me. Realizing Brody wasn't there, I opened my eyes and rolled away, glancing at the time. "Shit." I jumped up and rushed to the kids' rooms, but they weren't there. "Brody? Andi? Tate?" I yelled out as panic suddenly set in. My phone rang, and I answered before a second ring could even come through.

"Hey, babe. You looked so peaceful sleeping, so I dropped the kids off at school. I have a busy day with this Smith, and now Davis case, so I'll see you tonight, but I love you. Last night was... amazing." I could hear him smiling through the phone with the joy that lined his tone.

"I love you, too, Brody." I hung up and decided that maybe today, I would start really writing after all.

One long hot shower and a steaming cup of coffee later, I opened my laptop and began to type. It would be a story about a boy and a girl who met at a bar in New York. I smiled as my fingers hit the keyboard. Writing could be my new hobby; it could fill the void that I always had in life, rather than filling that void with my addiction. *I could do something normal... I could be someone normal.* Author Sage Miller, I liked the sound of that. Inspiration coursed through me as I took a sip of coffee, and as the porcelain hit the kitchen island, my doorbell rang. I considered ignoring it, but then again, it could be Harlow or it could be a package. We'd had an increase in porch pirates lately, so I hopped off my stool and walked to the front door.

Opening the door, I realized just as much as I found a sliver of light and possibly a new, improved part of myself. Unfortunately, darkness always, always found its wrath and overshadowed any chance for happiness in me. I bent down and lifted the vase of violets and roses in a large vase. Peering out to both sides, my legs felt like Jell-O as my shaking fingers unfolded the small card.

Someone is dead, let's hope it's not you.

My heart stopped, the vase fell from my grip and crashed to the ground below. The bright red and purple flowers broke into pieces, just like my life.

Andi and Tate...

I ran back inside and grabbed my phone, quickly dialing the school. The ringing seemed to last longer than necessary while fear and panic meshed together, torturing me. My fingers tapping against the kitchen counter. Once the receptionist finally answered, I shouted like a maniac, asking her to check on my children. I grasped my hands together and prayed. I prayed so hard, I figured some god, any god, would help my babies.

"Mrs. Miller, Andi and Tate are both in class. Is everything okay?" the school receptionist asked calmly.

My lips quivered. "Yes, yes everything's okay. I'll pick them up this afternoon. Thank you." I exhaled and placed my phone down, then I massaged my pulsing temples as I tried to steady my heart.

My phone buzzed and I looked down at the anonymous text, my stomach acid rising into my throat.

You are so beautiful, baby. We are so close to finally being together.

The message came in right before an image. Tears rushed out of my eyes, and I turned in a complete circle. It was a picture of me in the moment I had just called the school.

"Leave me alone! Fuck you!" I screeched so loudly that my voice went hoarse, and my sobbing grew more intense. The ringing of my phone competed with the animal-like sounds that tore from my own body.

"Archer? Archer, did you just send me a picture? Is it you? Are you..." I shouted, crying in between each word. I was having a full-blown panic attack, and my mind spun faster than my body could keep up.

"Sage? Sage, where are you? You need to come to the office. It's... it's Brody," Archer stammered while sirens bellowed in the background.

"Archer? *What?* What is happening?" I yelled into the phone, which suddenly went silent. I looked up at the ceiling and let my hands grip both sides of my face as I continued to shriek. This was it.

There was no light at the end of the tunnel when your tunnel was sealed. Trapped inside, you just suffocated and died.

I sped over to the office, running through red lights, stop signs, swerving around other cars, not caring if I smashed into one. Tears blurred my vision as I drove in a worse mental state than if I had been inebriated on any substance imaginable. Pulling into Brody's law firm, my heart fell. Cops, EMTs, and fire-fighters all raced around, just as they did at the Davis house.

No, no, no. Was this penance for my sins?

I ran inside, ducking through the raised arms of the police and pulled out of their attempted grasps. "Brody! Brody!" I called out, my chest constricting as I forced the words out. Archer appeared, his eyes red and his face fell as soon as he saw me.

"Archer?" I held no more strength, just like my soul.

"Sage…" He shook his head and didn't move. My eyes lifted from his, and I walked toward my husband's office. "No, Sage, don't…" Archer protested, but it didn't mean anything, and he knew it. My feet dragged forward, but it felt as if I were running through thick, wet sand.

"Ma'am, you can't be in here." Words blurred around me as I stared forward. My hand jerked over my mouth. My throat was throbbing from my screams, and I didn't have anything left. *Brody Miller, my husband…* The man I had a family with was sitting in his chair, hunched over. Blood was splattered everywhere—all over the walls, all over his desk. His head was completely shaved. I couldn't move, I couldn't think. This was when life ended. You couldn't recover from this. I was messed up enough, and this… there was no way. I was more gone than Brody. Tears streamed down my face. I didn't have strength to fight or question. I just sank to my knees, rocking back and forth as tears dripped off my chin, hoping to just disappear. It looked like a paintball tournament gone wrong. Blood stained the curtains behind him, plastered over a family photo of the four of us. The scent of tangy blood permeated all around me in a cloud of death.

Life was cruel and unfair. Life was pointless.

"Sage Miller, you are under arrest for the murders of Payton Smith, Jake Davis, and Brody Miller. Anything you say or do can and will be used against you in the court of law…" the officer continued, and I didn't hear anything else. Calloused hands lifted me, the gasps of Brody's coworkers barely scathing me as the officers shoved me into the back of the police car.

A loud knock against the glass echoed, repeatedly. Looking up, I met Archer's gaze. "Sage, Sage… don't say anything. I'll meet you at the station. Don't say anything!" he yelled out desperately.

You only had something to say when it was worth

sharing. I didn't care to ever speak about anything ever again. This pain was embedded in me for a long time, but now it had finally hit the surface... the surface I had thought I could protect.

Silly, foolish woman.

I pressed my forehead against the glass and stared out. I wonder what Andi and Tate were doing in school right now... Who would pick them up? Would my mother-in-law know how to participate in the end of the year events? Would she know how to buy them new swimsuits, or that Tate liked his sandwich cut diagonally and Andi had to have it cut horizontally? Would they hate me when they found out I was in prison and their dad was dead? Would people bully them? My head spun, just like the blue light that sat atop this car. We got to the station and I walked in, guided by an officer of course. Hungry eyes peered at me, the stale scent of burnt coffee and disinfectant lingered in the air. The tiles beneath my shoes were faded and yellowed.

"Mrs. Miller..." The arresting officer and Detective Cary sat across from me.

Where was Detective Matthews? Had he told them I got handsy and excused himself from the case. What a waste...

I stared down at my fingers, chipping away at the pale, pink polish that adorned my nails. I exhaled and didn't move my eyes upward. I didn't care anymore. Two hours passed, and I didn't even know what they were asking or taking from me at the station.

"Excuse me. You all were aware that I happen to be representing Mrs. Miller and there was to be no questioning without me." Archer's breathless voice rumbled in the room and he sunk into the chair next to me. His eyes met mine for a moment and suddenly, I wondered if maybe it wasn't Brody who saved me after all. Maybe my knight in shining armor was sitting right next to me. "You should all be ashamed of yourselves. What evidence do you have to even make such an outlandish accusation on my client? She had only just seen her deceased husband, and may I add, my colleague's body, bleeding out in his office."

"Mr. Collins, we do have evidence. This."

Detective Cary slid over a black and white image, with two other images below it, and my heart fell out of my body. It was my crown from Miss USA, cut into three pieces. The photos laid stitched together to complete it. "You see, your client may not just be the sweet, stay-at-home mom and wife of your beloved colleague. The metal shrapnel found in each body of the deceased has been a piece of this crown. What a way to leave a mark, Mrs. Miller. Probably the most iconic and creative we've seen in years. Of course, we are still very much wondering about the shaved head fetish and where the knife you used to slaughter these innocent men is, but I'm sure you'll enlighten us on your own time."

I leaned back into my chair. This had to be some sick joke. My lips parted and I pleaded with myself to say something, anything, but the words didn't form. I looked up at Archer, who immediately looked back at me. His face had defeat plastered over it and the game had only begun. I shook my head. "This is a set-up. I've been getting these texts and deliveries, and… someone had been in my house while I was showering." Tears and snot collided together as my words rambled out pitifully.

"Sage, Sage… stop." Archer's voice lost its dominance, but he put his hand up for extra support. "There has been plenty of Miss USA winners." He shoved the images away angrily. "Anyone could have broken into my client's home and stolen the item, and truthfully, why on earth would my client leave such a clear-cut mark? This is ridiculous." Archer didn't sound as confident as he usually did, and that was because I knew he didn't believe the words that were coming out from his mouth.

Hours had come and gone. Archer and I sat alone before I got booked. Apparently, my bail hearing was scheduled for tomorrow, but I'd have to spend the night in a cell. Archer had filed a motion and luckily, he was well-connected and had me in the first slot.

"Sage, look at me…" Archer tilted my head up and looked down at my lips. "Don't say anything and don't do anything. Keep your mouth shut, keep your head down, and just sleep. I'll have you out of here by the afternoon."

I glanced at the darkened glass wall beside us, knowing it was a one-way mirror. He released his hold and sighed. "I'm innocent, Archer. I was at home; you know I wasn't at the office. Just check the cameras," I whispered.

"Sage, I know. But the cameras… they were tampered with. Just, don't worry. I'll figure it out." Then he glanced over his shoulder and mouthed, "I love you."

I looked back at him with tears and mouthed, "Me too." My husband was dead… No, my husband had been brutally murdered, and my attorney was his boss and the man I'd been having an affair with. I exhausted myself.

I laid on the shitty, worn-down mattress in a cell by myself. There wasn't anyone else in it, maybe because our beautiful city wasn't full of female criminals. The small window had bars running down it and a glimpse of the moon shimmered through. Andi and Tate must be wondering where I was. Where their dad was? I should be there with them, and instead, I'm here, locked up like a monkey at the zoo. This didn't scare me, though—being in a physical jail was nothing compared to the mental jail I had been imprisoned in for my entire life. I closed my eyes and hoped sleep would just overtake me so I could wake up and hopefully, reunite with my babies. It's ironic, really. Every day I thought I lived the same repetitive day of giving, giving, and more giving, and how that was a prison of its own. But now I realized, perhaps I was being punished for being such an ungrateful bitch.

CHAPTER TWENTY

$\mathcal{I}$ walked outside and took a deep breath; the fresh air was a welcome scent compared to the stench of the county jail. I was wearing a baggy T-shirt and leggings. One night in jail and my hair looked like spaghetti, draped and stringy. Archer looked over at me and continued to drive. "Let's go grab a bite before we see the kids." Thankfully, due to Archer's relationships with the judges, he had my bail posted earlier, and because there was no true evidence that was one-hundred percent traced to me, I wasn't a flight risk. Archer bought me time.

"Okay." I nodded, licking my lips that were dry and cracked. I guess the ten-step nightly regime I used—along with the lip balms and masks—wouldn't be the usual routine in prison.

We pulled into a small diner parking lot and walked in together. Archer's aftershave was a comforting smell, and I let my hand brush the back of his but he didn't even look at me. Quietly, we sat across from one another until our food arrived. Archer basically ordered the entire menu. Gooey stacks of pancakes dripping with syrup, covered in thick slivers of butter, with fluffy eggs, grits, toast, and hot coffee sat between us. I hungrily dove in while Archer silently observed me, barely taking sips of his coffee. I swallowed an overly large bite of the sweet pancakes. "You're not hungry?"

He shook his head. "Sage, I looked through your phone, and every single text from the anonymous number was gone."

My mouth dropped. "What?" Placing my fork down, I waited for him to speak.

"Yeah… I just… fuck."

"The notes, the floral delivery notes… The roses are red, violets are blue, someone is dead, let's hope it's not you…? They are all in a pale pink box of sashes in our office," I said full of hope.

He shook his head again. "It's not enough." He took a sip of his coffee. "Sage, you have to think long and hard about this. Do you have any enemies, any ex-boyfriends or anyone with a vendetta? I mean, you have to give me something." He was pleading with me, and it broke my heart knowing that I couldn't think of a single useful thing.

"I thought it was Jake sending me the flowers and pictures. Then briefly, I thought it was Brody..." I closed my eyes. Between all the madness of my arrest, I didn't even have a moment in time to process the fact that my husband was dead. Images of him hunched over with blood everywhere, with his head shaved, made me shudder.

What did he think before he died?

We had such a beautiful night together, and part of me thought it was a turning point for our family and our marriage. Maybe I could have sought out help and treatment for my addiction; I could have broken things off with Archer. Maybe we could have moved away and started fresh. He didn't deserve to die, and he definitely didn't deserve to be murdered. I softly cried into my palms. "Brody's dead..."

"Sage, I know... I'm so sorry." Archer's voice grew low and sympathetic as his hand reached for mine, gripping it tightly.

"I didn't kill him, Archer. I didn't kill my husband. I didn't..." I began coughing violently, nearly hyperventilating. Quickly grabbing my water, I took a sip as the saliva in my mouth thickened and choked me further.

People were staring with their eyes wide with judgment. *Oh, clutch your fucking pearls somewhere else, Karen.*

I didn't care, I had to fight. My children and my life depended on it. I gave up everything my entire life for someone else. I had to do this for them, because there was no more *him*.

"I believe you… I know you didn't." Archer came around and sat next to me. I planted my face into his shoulder and let myself grieve.

Another funeral, and similar people who attended Jake's were at Brody's. Glancing at me, they kept their distance as if death was contagious. Some of them were on fantasy football leagues together, they coached soccer together, and they shared poker nights with the same friends. Jake and Brody were truly best friends.

I had my arms around Tate and Andi, with my mother-in-law sitting right next to us. She didn't say much, except when she told me that she knew I didn't hurt her son. I think she didn't get to process the pain yet—after all, she'd been busy caring for our children and staying strong for them. I felt guilty that I took away her chance to cope, to really give herself a minute to grieve.

I watched the priest speak and couldn't take my eyes off the enormous, framed photo of Brody. He looked so handsome, his big eyes sparkling and his white teeth on display in a big smile.

He was a good man for the most part, considering who he was married to. They say when you point one finger, always remember that at least four more fingers are pointing right back to you. Maybe Brody and I were just on two different frequencies and would have done better as friends and co-parents. Maybe that was the next chapter in our story.

I would do anything to have him here and be alive. To have him be able to walk his daughter down the aisle and to be able to teach his son how to drive. Tears continued to drain down my face. There were a few, long stares because people had heard about my arrest. Some assumed I was the guilty housewife while others glanced at my long legs, small waist, and painted face, knowing a beauty queen turned stay-at-home mom wasn't capable of butchering her own meat, let alone her husband.

"Sage, honey, baby, goodness… I just hope you know we are with you and yours during this time," Caroline purred out. I think this was the part she wanted me to bow down and thank the mighty Lord that the PTA president from our kids' school missed Pilates in order to attend my husband's funeral.

"Thank you, Caroline." I gripped Andi and Tate's hands tighter and nodded at Archer, who stood behind her.

"Hey, guys, I'm so sorry about your dad. I loved working with him. He was such a great man." Archer crouched down and gently tapped Andi's shoulder and offered a small smile to Tate.

"Thank you for coming… and for everything, Archer." I spoke quietly and didn't dare move closer to him while everyone was around. He looked at me longingly before taking a deep breath and walking away.

Death was ironic. People you haven't heard from or talked to in months or even years all came together and showered you in support, food, over-the-top flower arrangements, not to mention the long, senti-mental messages…

But once the hype around the shock of death wears off, just like rain against pavement, it eventually all stops and disappears as soon as the sun comes out. As soon as everyone goes back to their happy lives and the sun rises again, the grieving family is forgotten. Everyone moves on. One by one, each guest leaves.

My mother-in-law stood next to Brody's casket as she cried. Burying your child had to be the worst thing in the entire universe. Nothing could ever be worse than that.

She took her time and whispered something against the wood just before letting her hand rub against the smooth casket. "Sage, I'm going to head to the car and take some time to just…" She dabbed her eyes while her other hand sat on her heart.

I nodded at her. There weren't words to be spoken; I didn't know what I was supposed to do. How the hell was I supposed to be strong for Andi, Tate, and my mother-in-law while I was still very much the primary suspect as a serial killer?

"Mommy, can we just sit with Daddy for a few more minutes." Andi loosened her grip on my hand.

I looked down at her, slowly brushing her hair through my fingers. "Okay, baby," I whispered before kissing the top of her head.

We sat back down, and Tate was fidgeting and wiggling non-stop. Andi had her hands neatly folded in her lap, just staring at her father's casket. Birth order at its finest. Their lives were forever changed, and so was mine.

In my peripheral, I saw a figure in all black grow closer and I turned my head slightly. "Guys, I'll be right back." I quickly stood and pushed my sunglasses on top of my head, moving closer to her.

"I'm so sorry…" Her words were hushed and tears began trickling down her bare face.

"Why are you sorry? I'm sorry," I whimpered as she pulled me into her arms.

"No, I should have been here… I should have been there for you when you got arrested. I'm the worst friend in the world, Sage. I just… I didn't know how I could handle all of this when they said you were being arrested for Jake's—" She cried harder and tried to wipe the tears away.

"Harlow, I didn't—" I clutched my chest tightly, and finally mustered the courage to pull away and look at her.

"I know, I know." She sighed and looked over at Brody's casket. "This is crazy, Sage."

"I have no clue how I'm going to take care of us…"

"I guess you're stuck with me." Harlow laughed lightly through her tears and glanced up at the sky. "You think Brody and Jake are playing fantasy football up there?"

"Definitely. Not to mention they're probably chugging beers, thrilled they don't have to go to work the next day," I added, nudging my shoulder into hers.

"He was such a good man. Such a good man." She

shook her head with her forehead creased. "How are the kids?" She looped her arm in mine as we began walking closer to the casket.

"I don't think Tate understands at all, and Andi... you know she's so mature for her age and conceals her emotions. Unfortunately, she's too much like me." I stared at my daughter who hadn't moved from her seat and hadn't taken her gaze off her father's photo.

Tate had found some sticks and rocks that he was playing with on his hands and knees. Mud stained on his pants and his blonde hair was all over the place. "Sage, I love you, and you know I'll be here for you and the kids. You're going to be okay. They can't charge someone just because they have tiara pieces... it's ridiculous."

I paused and looked over at her. *How did she know about the pieces of metal being my Miss USA crown?*

This case was sealed tight; they didn't have anything out yet. "How did you know about that?" I let go of her arm and moved away.

"Your mother-in-law told me..." She tilted her head and looked at me completely confused.

Of course. In the south, any tidbit of your life, even murder case details, were grape-vined faster than lightning. We sat together in silence, letting the grief stick to our skin, just like the Charleston humidity did. Except this wouldn't just wash away in the shower. This was forever. I couldn't get the image of Brody's lifeless body out of my mind.

Permanence.

It's such a strange concept, one I had struggled with the most. I always thought of marriage as a constricting bond I had no way out of. Brody had made it clear from the beginning that divorce was never an option, and he eventually made it clear that he knew more of my secrets than I realized, especially my role in my mother's death. That meant if I left him, he'd make sure I never saw my children. I married Brody because I was pregnant, and it was the easiest way out of New York. It was the easiest way to forget who I was and become who I needed to be. It was stability—financial and so much more. We chose our house based on the top schools in our area, we bought our SUV based on the highest crash-safety standards… everything we did was for them. Now I was alone, with two kids and a mortgage I'd never be able to carry on my own.

The kids were fast asleep, sharing a bed because they missed him too much. I sat downstairs in front of the TV, with a glass of wine that was filled to the brim. Suddenly, I heard something, almost like a buzzing, but maybe more of the sound of something electronic turning? I muted the TV and looked around. The curtains were wide open and the dark night sky painted across them.

There it was again. What the hell was that? I placed my glass down and stood with my neck craned as I stared at the ceiling. Again, a creaking sound. Glancing around, I looked at our built-in that surrounded the TV and froze. On the very top shelf, nestled in a decorative conch shell, was something small, something black that moved.

The air escaped my mouth as I crept toward it. Planting my palms on the cabinet, I pushed up and stood on the narrow bit before gripping the shell and tugging it out. My feet landed wrong and my ankle twisted. I yelped as I landed on my ass. "Fucking hell," I hissed while pulling the shell closer to me.

Blinking, I shook my head. "Oh my god..." My fingers shook against the groove as I tugged a tiny camera from the shell.

Someone was watching me when I didn't want to be seen. Someone knew what I was doing every single day. Someone had been in my house. Someone was still out there, lurking, stalking... *hunting me.*

I jumped to my feet, even though the weight of my body made me cringe as pain shot down to my ankle. I took the meat masher out of the kitchen drawer, and in one swift motion, with tears of fury burning my eyes, I let out a scream and smashed the camera on the counter harder and harder until the metal was only damaging the marble underneath. Sobbing and defeated, I sank to the floor, cradling myself with my knees pulled into my chest.

I asked for this. I complained about stupid shit. Kiddie songs on repeat, dance class being too close to dinner, PTA meetings wasting my life, not enough time to do what I wanted or needed. I complained about how I had to suppress my urges and needs that went with my addiction. I complained about every fucking thing, and now… nothing was left.

I was nothing.

CHAPTER TWENTY-ONE

"*I* mean, it would have been helpful if you didn't reduce the camera of taco meat." Archer looked at the Ziploc bag that had bits and pieces of the camera inside.

"Archer, I bet you anything there are more cameras inside my house. I mean, whoever was, or is trying to kill me has had full access to everything I've been doing. The pictures of me… it all makes sense. I showered today with my towel wrapped around me for god's sake. I took the kids over to Harlow's to bathe them. I can't live like this." I dropped my face into my hands.

"Baby, look at me. Why don't you guys come stay with me?" Archer reached over his desk and grabbed my arm, pulling my hand.

"Um, because I'm being accused with the murder of three men, and you're my attorney? Not to mention that my husband has only recently been buried." I yanked my hand out of his.

Details about the case had been leaked, and I had officially been labeled the *Stay-at-home mom slayer.* The school even left a message, telling me they thought it would be beneficial for the kids to homeschool. Obviously, I told them that I'd be suing if they discriminated against my children. Archer even reached out to them as well. The only blessing was that my kids were still young and their classmates didn't have a clue as to what was going on. Their parents wouldn't talk about it around them because who would want to fuck up their own child on purpose? *See that mommy over there, she's a serial killer.* No one would want little Timmy pissing his pants or crying in the middle of the night because of me.

"Sage, everything's going to be okay." Archer broke me out of my thoughts.

"Really? Are you being accused of murder? Did you see your dead husband lying on his desk? Do you have two children who have no idea why their dad is never going to come home again? I mean, you have zero leads. A monkey in a suit could have collected more information than you have." I crossed my arms and turned my head. That was low, even for me. Archer had been nothing but kind to me. If it was any other man, they'd have hit the ground running and screaming by now.

"I know, and I'm sorry. You're right. I don't have much to go on, but I do think I may have some leads. I just don't want to get your hopes up until I can confirm things. Sage, you know I love you. This is my top priority. You are my top priority." He came around and crouched next to me, getting eye level and lifted my chin. "I'm not going to let you go to prison. No matter what I have to do." His lips met mine, the scent of his aftershave brushed against my nose, and all I wanted to do was get lost in him.

"I told you I have more baggage than an airport." I let out a small laugh and looked into his dark brown eyes.

"And I have two hands that will carry as much as I fucking can for you, baby." He helped me to my feet before he lifted me onto his desk. Mischief danced in his eyes and a devious smile grew on his face. "You are so beautiful, just Sage." His lips parted mine and his tongue crept inside, meeting mine.

"You're not so bad yourself, Suit." He smiled against my lips and pushed my skirt up. "Mr. Collins, I think this is quite the conflict of interest..." I pulled him by his tie, needing him closer as he unzipped his pants.

"Well, it's a good thing I enjoy combining business with pleasure," he whispered against my lips.

Pushing inside me, I let out a cry, gripping his shoulders and allowing him to take over my entire body. This is what I needed. I needed to forget—forget the pain, forget the cruel game life continued to play with me, forget that everyone always needed me to keep my shit together.

"Harder," I said through clenched teeth. My head tossed back and suddenly, everything washed away. It was just me and him. Mourning looked different for everyone, and so what if this was my way to grieve?

Once in a while there are moments in life that make you feel real, raw pain. You feel like your heart won't be able to handle it, and no matter what you do, you can't fix it. That was today.

I got a call from school because Andi was shoved on the playground because some low-life kid was bullying her... about me. I stormed through the school doors and into the office. There she was, sitting with her head hung down, tears marking her pale, pink skirt below. The rage I felt to go slash that bully's mom's tires melted when I saw my child. She didn't need me to raise hell; she needed me to hold her. I sank to my knees in front of her and lifted her chin up. "I'm so sorry, baby girl," I whispered, blinking hard against my own tears.

"It's okay, Mommy. I know you're not a bad person." She sniffled and wiped her nose on the sleeve of her gray cardigan. Her big bow had loosened against her soft curls, and her knees were scuffed up from the fall on the playground.

"You have to promise me one thing. No matter who tries to tear you down, you'll keep your head up. You can't let your crown fall, because if you let it fall, it'll break and that's when they know they've broken you." She slowly lifted her head and straightened her shoulders. "Atta girl." I gripped her head and pulled it close, kissing her forehead.

I did chew out the principal and Ginny Slater's douche parents. Just as everyone started to leave the office, I stopped in my tracks next to Ginny. "Look, Ginny... if you ever lay a finger on my kid again, or even speak to her, I'll make sure her mommy comes out to play with you... and I don't play nice. Got it?" I hissed at her. Her freckled face turned bright red as she nodded. With a smile, I patted her head and left.

I took Andi and Tate home early, after we grabbed a dozen cookies from their favorite bakery. We sank into the couch with a movie on, with nothing but love and cookie crumbs between us. The thing about motherhood is that you want to be with them all the time, but at the same time, you want space. But once you get that space, you miss them. It's a constant battle.

Looking side to side, I didn't know how much time I'd get to do this. All signs and evidence of the case pointed to me, and the jury would definitely think of me as this evil, psychotic, serial killer. What if these moments were going to truly be fleeting, evaporating between my fingers just the way sand does on the beach. I closed my eyes and held them tightly. The only reason I was even out on bail was because of Archer's connections in the judicial system. He gave them his word that he'd essentially babysit me or his job as an attorney was over.

The next few days passed in a blur. Andi and Tate were no longer being bullied. It seemed that Ginny Slater was the ringleader, and my little conversation with her had kept her lips sealed. I might not have been the murderer for this case, but blood was already on my hands, and when it came to my babies, no one would hurt them.

"What do you think about this one?" Harlow lifted a neon-yellow blouse against her chest and stood in front of me.

"Oh, it's... bright." I fingered through the rows and rows of clothes at the quaint, Charleston boutique. The store clerk had her eyes on me like I was going to actually steal some damn shirts.

I think I'm past petty larceny at this point in my life of crime.

"Sage! Look!" Harlow grabbed my hand and tugged me to a corner. "Oh my gosh, you need this fur coat!" She lifted a stunning cream-colored fur coat in front of me.

That was the strangest thing... What kind of Charleston boutique had fur coats at the beginning of summer?

I let my finger brush against the soft fur and looked up at her. "It won't go well over the orange jumpsuit." Turning away, I fought back the tears of distress.

"Sage, honey..." she hugged me from behind, "let me buy it for you."

I reached and held her hand and shook my head.

"Harlow, it's eight hundred dollars. Let's just go. Neither of us need to be spending money right now, or for the foreseeable future." I shuddered at the thought of sitting down and looking at my finances.

"Have you not looked into Brody's life insurance policy?" Harlow put the fur coat down and crossed her arms over her chest.

I shook my head slowly. "No, between getting arrested and everything else going on, I just... I'll be honest, I never touched our finances, bills, or anything. I was in charge of the kids, and Brody did the rest." I sighed, rubbing my face and dropping my sunglasses over my eyes.

"Well, it's time for you to start, honey. That's the first thing I did after Jake's funeral. There's a serial killer on the loose, too close to home, connecting all of us together, so you better believe I'm setting everything for my kids, and you should, too."

I nodded and sighed. This was too much, too fast.

I got home and ran upstairs to change out of the summer dress I had forced myself into. Everything seemed to have a time stamp, including wearing nice clothes. The doorbell rang, so just before I was about to collapse onto my bed for a mid-day nap before picking the kids up from school, I headed down. My sleep had suffered because every squeak, every motion in the house terrified me. Peeking through the window, I had to double-check it wasn't another vulture news reporter. How many times could one woman say "no comment" was beyond me. The door creaked open, and I saw a yellow envelope sitting on the worn doormat. I glanced around before I lifted the envelope. Walking backward, I locked the door behind me and quickly opened the seal. A small sticky note was on a stack of large, black-and-white images.

Your dirty little secrets are safe with me, baby...

No, no, no... I collapsed to the ground and pinned each image in a circle around me, spinning around like a dog chasing his tail. An image of me burying the knife I had killed my mother with, an image of me having sex with Archer on his desk the other day, an image of me with Jake the last time I saw him, an image of me clearly fighting with Brody, and finally, an image of me laughing at the Hotel Besos bar with Payton Smith.

This was every single image of every single secret I had.

This was a stack of my own death sentence. My world closed in around me. The show would not go on. I couldn't go on. Begrudgingly, I stood in a haze. My mind was blank. I didn't have anything left. I was a shit wife, an even shittier mother, and there was no need to even call me a friend.

I stood on my tiptoes and reached for the prescription bottle of sleeping pills my doctor had called in for me after Brody died. Popping the thick white lid off with my thumb, it hit the floor and I poured them out in my open palm. I then grabbed the opened bottle of wine from the fridge.

"Cheers, you bastard. You win." I lifted the bottle and fistful of pills to the ceiling, knowing someone was still watching me, even though Archer had someone come and scale the entire house, to which they found nothing. I knew some sick son of a bitch was stalking me, and I was tired. I couldn't run any more.

I was nothing more than his weak prey, who had finally been hunted.

Dumping them into my mouth, I tilted my head back and took the longest sip of wine. "I'm so sorry, Andi and Tate... but you'll be so much better off without me. I love you both. I love you both. I love you..." I repeated those three little, yet meaningful words over and over again before the world decided it had enough of me.

CHAPTER TWENTY-TWO

a soft humming rung in my ears as I slowly opened my eyes. The florescent lights above me made me close them tightly. "Sage?" I felt my arm that was covered in wires. "Sage..." I didn't want to look. "Sage, look at me. We don't have much time."

Oh shit, I was dying. I opened my eyes and saw Archer. He wasn't wearing a suit; he was in joggers and a T-shirt. He had dark circles around his eyes, and his hair was a mess. "Oh my god, Sage. You're okay. You're okay, baby." He sat next to me on the small bed, which, after looking around, I realized wasn't a pit-stop to hell, it was a hospital room. He pressed his face against mine. "What were you thinking, my love?"

"I can't do this, Archer." I softly cried against him. "Archer, who found me? There were pictures...

pictures sent to me. I'm screwed. It's over, Archer."
Panic radiated through me, making my body ripple
with fear. I looked around the room and toward the
glass windows, waiting for officers to swarm in and
take me.

"Shh, Sage. I was the one who found you, and I saw
the images. I have them. Don't worry, no one saw
them. I think… I think I found something I can really
work with." He rubbed his head. "Sage, whoever is
doing this has known you for a really long time. The
image of you with…"

"Archer, it wasn't here. That image was years ago in
New York… I can explain…" I looked away.

"I already know. Brody told me. He didn't know
about our relationship, but he was worried if you ever
snapped, and for the kid's safety… even though there
wasn't a shred of doubt in his mind that what you did
was self-defense. I mean, he married you. Sage, what
you were forced to do to your mother was self-
defense, but with the mess you're in now, that can
never ever see the light of day. You need to think long
and hard now, for yourself and for me and for your
kids. Someone you've known since New York is here."

Chills shot up my spine. Someone has been
watching me, following me, stalking me for years?
Someone had made it their life mission to wreck

mine? Who did I ever hurt that badly? "I don't know..." I shook my head and sank back into the pillow.

"I have to get to the office and start working with my private investigators, but Sage, baby, you have to help me here. You have to try..." He kissed my cheek and quickly stood. "Don't you dare ever think about hurting yourself again. Andi, Tate, and I need you, Sage. We can't live without you." He turned and shut the door behind him.

I spent the next two days in the hospital. The psychiatrist had me on an involuntary psych hold for further evaluation. I didn't care, because suddenly, this stark room seemed like the only place I could feel safe. My mother-in-law took the kids to her house for an undetermined amount of time. Archer even helped to arrange a small moving truck so they could have plenty of their belongings. My home wasn't safe, and truthfully, it was no longer my home. It was a house that had become a catacomb. Maybe prison wouldn't be so bad; maybe it would be the only place I could live out the rest of my life without being tormented. Besides, didn't I deserve it? This was karma. I took a life, and now it demanded mine in return. I spent the rest of my psych hold eating Chipotle that Archer had dropped off and catching up on The Real Housewives of every city imaginable. If I was heading for prison, I might as well enjoy the simple luxuries of life first.

"You know, if you had told me you were going to try to overdose of pills, I'd have killed you myself for hurting my best friend." Harlow looked over at me while her hands stayed on the steering wheel. I rested my head against the seatbelt and watched as Charleston passed us by before we crossed the bridges to get back to our little island. I wasn't ready to go to my mother-in-law's house and face my children or her. I was an embarrassment. "Sage, I love you. Why didn't you talk to me? I thought we made a pact that we'd be there for each other. We are all that is left now... for each other and our babies." I could see her eyes filling with tears as she stared straight ahead. Her kids were with their grandparents, and it would just be us two at her house so I could get through this fog before I had my court hearing.

"You know I was talking to Archer, and I told him he should pull the insanity card for you..." Harlow kept talking even though I hadn't replied.

I let out a small laugh but kept my eyes on the window. "You talked to Archer?" *He hadn't told me that.*

"I'm serious, Sage... I mean, you tried to kill yourself; it might be the best way out of this. You can go to some mental health facility, which for us stay-at-home moms, would be like a vacation, and then get released for good behavior or whatever."

She had a point. Maybe spending the rest of my life in some psychiatric hospital would be better than jail. "I don't want to leave Andi and Tate..." I whispered.

"I know, honey. I'm just trying to tell you that there might be options, but look, I already told Archer he better work that pretty little ass of his off and save my girl." She glanced over and offered a small smile. "Everything's going to be okay, Sage. We have each other." She held my hand as we pulled into her driveway.

"You sure you don't mind me crashing here for a bit? I feel bad your kids left." Pangs of guilt and embarrassment coursed through me. Even Harlow didn't trust me to share a roof with her children. I didn't blame her, though, who would want a murder suspect sleeping next door to their kids.

I walked inside, it was so clean and smelled like freshly baked cookies. Harlow Davis was the best mom I knew and the kindest friend. Maybe if I had found Jesus the way she did or found joy in the life I was living, I could have been better, too. Women suffered through infertility, miscarriage, and stillbirth, yet here I was, complaining because I got accidentally knocked up twice and had to live behind a white picket fence. I needed more help than anyone could ever find me. I was my own worst enemy.

My kids made me look for monsters under their bed every night, but what they didn't realize was that the true monster was right there, tucking them in.

"Listen, honey, I have to go get the kids from school, yours included, and take them to my mom's. I'll be back as soon as I get them all set up for dinner and everything. Are you going to be alright alone here?" She grabbed five apples out of the glass bowl and tucked them into her purse. Even amongst the mess of our lives, she still remembered to bring a healthy after-school snack for the kids.

"I could come with... It'd be nice to see the kids and thank your mom for having them over tonight." I stood from the stool. My mother-in-law had two doctor appointments today, so it made sense for the kids to stay somewhere else so she didn't have to rush around. It really does take a village.

Harlow clicked her tongue. "Sweetie, and I mean this in the nicest way possible, but I think it'd be best to give the kids some time. They are a bit shaken up." She came around and gave me a tight hug before glancing at her phone, "I'm going to be late for pickup. There are plenty of leftovers in the fridge, and every takeout menu and number you can imagine are in the first drawer. I'll be back in a few hours." She waved at me and paused. "I already locked up all the pills, so don't think about doing anything crazy. I just mopped the floors; I don't need to find my friend foaming at the mouth and messing them up." She winked and left, and I couldn't help but laugh.

Harlow's car pulled out of the driveway and I started to look around her house. I found myself in front of an oversized picture from Harlow and Jake's wedding. They were looking into one another's eyes, smiling. Jake was such an asshole for cheating on her, but I was an even bigger one for being his easy lay. They really did make a good team and couple, and I was just something fun for a bored married man. He loved Harlow, and I knew that—I could see it in the way he looked at her, and how she looked at him, and how their kids idolized them both.

Harlow was going to therapy three times a week and working with a grief counselor. She had mastered the ability of putting on a strong front for the rest of us, when inside, I knew she was fighting her own battles. Her ability to push aside her own pain and struggles to make sure those she loved could burden her with their own struggles and pain is what made her the most amazing mother.

Going up the stairs, I let my hand graze along the shiny wooden banister. The silence and loneliness were making the devil work wonders in my head, so I decided to just snoop around my best friend's house to fill the time instead. The kids' rooms were nice and tidy, beds made and everything in its place. Opening the master bedroom, I looked inside. Harlow's bed was also neatly made, a pair of bedroom slippers tucked on her side. She had neatly folded Jake's pajamas next to hers on the end of the bed and his slippers on the other side. My heart sank seeing the pain my best friend was in, and I never even took a minute to truly ask her how she was. I let my hand brush their soft bedding and smiled at the pictures of Jake and Harlow from their honeymoon, where they both had their tongues out and were swimming with dolphins. Turning out of the room, I shut the door quietly behind me. There was something so thrilling about looking through other people's homes; you could see a real glimpse of who they really were.

I walked out and passed the playroom, which was sort of messy and made me realize Harlow and her kids were really humans like the rest of us. Approaching the end of the hallway, I stood in front of

Harlow's craft room. I always teased her that she was probably the only person in their early thirties who spent hours on end scrapbooking and doing crafts to the point where she needed a craft room. I turned the knob, but it didn't budge.

Why would she lock her craft room?

I pursed my lips and stared at the shiny bronze knob. Then again, it made sense considering she did have three young kids and there were probably scissors and sharp objects behind the door. I nodded at my own rationale, but I had to go in. What's locked is meant to be opened. I wanted to see what she was working on. She spent hours in there when the kids were at school, to the point she often turned down lunch or workouts with me to do whatever she was working on. I tapped the top of the doorframe, hoping to find a key, since this wasn't a lock I could finagle with a bobby pin—this one was deadbolted.

I quickly made my way back to Harlow's room and tugged each dresser drawer open. Everything was in its place—jewelry lined and then… photos. I tilted my head and reached for a small, faded stack of photos that were pushed back into the drawer.

I recognized that stage and those images all too well… because I had the same ones. The images were from the Miss USA pageant. My heart began to beat harder as my fingers slid against the smooth images. One by one, I began flipping through, freezing on an image of Miss South Carolina on stage alone. Squinting and holding the image closer to my face, I blinked for what felt like a hundred of times. A woman with long, red curly hair was waving in the image. Harlow didn't have long red hair… she had short, light brown hair—the mom-cut. I flipped through the rest and stopped at a close-up image.

"Oh my god…" My voice trembled along with my fingers. There was no mistaking her. This image had a close up. It was Harlow. Harlow Davis was in the Miss USA pageant the same year I was. She had never mentioned that she was even in a pageant, let alone the biggest one in the country. With me…?

Placing the photos down, I looked through the rest, sliding my fingers against them. My breathing stopped when I lifted the last one up. It was me. I was on one side, another girl stood in the middle, and Harlow was on the other end. Harlow's eyes were fixed on me, even though the other girl and I were smiling, facing the camera. I shook my head so hard, my neck hurt.

What's happening?

I needed to find that damn key and go inside that room. I tucked the photos in the waist of my pants and forced my legs to move. Each creak in the wooden floors underneath my feet sent chills across my body. I opened every drawer, and even laid flat on the floor to peer under the bed.

Nothing. Absolutely nothing.

Just as I sat up from looking through each and every nightstand drawer, I stared at the thick gold photo frame in front of me and lifted it into my hands. "What are you hiding from me, Harlow?" I whispered at the smiling image of the woman I thought was the most transparent woman on the planet. The woman who was my best friend, my only friend. Just as I placed it down on the table, I heard a slight jingle. Lifting it back up, I shook it.

Shit.

I quickly flipped the frame over and let my finger jam against the dense black cardboard backing until I felt a divot. My finger pushed straight through and out came a golden key. My chest tightened as I lifted it into my hands. Pushing myself up from the floor, I stood and looked up. My eyes caught the reflection in the mirror of a woman with red hair behind me. My hand flung to my mouth as a gasp seeped through my fingers. I blinked again, and when I forced myself to focus, no one was there. My chest heaved as the key dug into my strong grasp, as if I were scared of opening it and seeing nothing in my palm.

I quickly shuffled back down the long, darkened hallway to the craft room. Just as I passed the stairwell, I could hear my phone ring loudly downstairs. It would have to wait. I continued to pace forward, but my phone rang again. *Damnit, what if it's an emergency with Andi or Tate?* I gripped the key tightly and raced down the stairs. Turning into the kitchen, I saw my phone sitting on the countertop. *It was Harlow.* I looked around and I squeaked, "Hello?"

"Sage, are you okay? You weren't picking up, and I got worried. I was about to get in the car and speed home to check on you." Her voice was laced with concern.

"No, no… don't worry, I'm fine. I dozed off on the couch. The hospital administered so many meds, and it must have all just hit me. I'm sorry. You should spend time with the kids. I already feel like shit. Andi and Tate should have someone motherly around…" I forced the words to sound desperate and pleading.

"Aww, honey, you are an amazing mom. They were just saying how they can't wait to see you soon. Did you heat up the lasagna up yet?"

I rolled my neck and head around. "Yeah, I'm just about to. Thank you." I paused. "Harlow, are you with your mom?" I realized my kids were with her, and that made me feel uneasy.

I don't know this woman at all.

"Oh, actually I'm not with the kids now. I'm heading to get some groceries for Mom, but they are with her and fine. Don't worry about a thing, Sage. You have her number, right? Just call her if you want to talk to Andi and Tate. Okay, I really gotta go. Love you and see you soon!"

The kids had to be okay. I mean, she wouldn't tell me to call her mom and talk to them if they weren't. Maybe I should just double-check. My fingers slid through my contacts. The phone rang over and over, making my heart beat faster.

"Hello?" a deep Southern voice answered.

Relief washed over me. "Janie? This is Sage... Sage Miller. I just wanted to check in on the kids," I stammered, and before she could answer, I heard the kids yelling and fighting in the background over some video game. My puffed cheeks blew out the air I had held.

"They are just fine, dear. But they are all rippin' my house apart, so I have to go. Harlow is out runnin' some errands and will be back soon. Take care, sweetie." She ended the call before I could speak. I wanted to ask Janie about Harlow being in the Miss USA pageant, but I also didn't want her telling Harlow I was digging up dirt when they had my children.

Before going back upstairs, I needed to do one more thing to make sure my babies were safe. The phone rang and rang until his voice to leave a message came through. He was probably in a meeting or working his ass off to help me with this mess.

"Archer, listen it's me. I need a favor... Can you please go get Andi and Tate from 415 Forest Drive? They are with Harlow's mom, and something's not right. I'll explain everything soon, but please, just go get them." I hung up knowing he'd do it; he always came through for me. Once this nightmare was over, I'd make everything up to him.

I swiftly made my way back upstairs. Sliding the key into the doorknob, I exhaled when it fit. Turning the handle with the other hand, I walked into the darkness.

They say a surprise is an emotion. It's an actual brief physiological and mental state. What they don't tell you is that surprises aren't always a good thing... and this moment was just that. As soon as my cold fingers flipped the light switch on, I also flipped the switch on an entire new side of my so-called best friend—the one person in the world who I had truly trusted and even loved. My hand flung to my open mouth and bone-chilling fear overtook ever single fiber of my body. I slowly walked closer to her desk in a room that was so unlike the rest of the house—a complete mess and disaster. Maybe I had died after the overdose after all. Maybe this was hell, it had to be, because suddenly, I was sweating and I knew this had to be from the inferno I was in. Images of me before I was married, images of me in pageants and bartending were plastered all over the wall. Images of me in my house just two steps away, where I was completely naked while showering, bathing, changing my clothes were all pinned in neat, organized rows. My skin was crawling with what felt like small spiders racing up and down it.

I felt dizzy, stomach acid teasing my esophagus. Bending over, I looked at her desk. Three pairs of scissors and a trimmer were lined in a neat row, each one covered in something. I squinted and leaned closer. "Oh my god…"

Brushing against one pair, I lifted my fingertips in front of my eyes. *It was human hair.* Payton, Jake, Brody… all were left with their head shaved. That was the killer's sick mark. His signature. *Her signature.*

Harlow Davis had known me for years before I even knew her. She knew everything about me, every little secret and worst of all, she was trying to frame me and ruin me. But before she did that, she was taking away everyone I had ever been intimate with or cared for. I could feel my pulse pounding in my temples. Harlow Davis was playing a game of chess. She wanted to make sure the queen went down last. The broken tiara, the pageant images... this was all some meticulous game of revenge. But why?

What was her next move? *My kids? Archer?* I pulled open one of her desk drawers and my eyes stung with tears. Nestled neatly in the drawer were pairs of my panties, as well as a tube of lip gloss I had thought I had lost somewhere in my purse. This room was a shrine...

A shrine for me.

My fingers trembled so hard, I didn't think I could even call for help, but I had to. My kids and Archer's lives depended on it. Just as I dialed the number nine, a voice sliced through me.

"I wouldn't do that if I were you..."

My body froze, and in that moment as panic choked me, I really wished I was dead. Slowly turning around, I saw her standing in the doorway, the lights in the hall off.

"Harlow..." I hated how weak my voice sounded. "Harlow, what is all this?" I looked behind her, hoping there would be an escape, but there wasn't. This was a windowless room, which was probably once intended to be a storage closet. There was only one way in and one way out.

"Sage, oh honey... Why did you have to be so rude and snoop around my home? I don't think that's very good manners. But then again... I know New Yorkers aren't really known for that. I just figured you'd have acclimated to our Southern hospitality and charm by now." She let out a menacing laugh.

Suddenly, I realized something. I wasn't the only one with an addiction and needing a high... *Harlow Davis had her own dark secrets, her own addiction... and that addiction was me.*

"Harlow, why didn't you tell me you were in the same pageant as I was?" I had to buy time, I had to find a way to make her not find her next fix by killing me.

"Isn't it so heart breaking? I had taken to you so much in that pageant. You were so different from all the other girls. So lost in a world that wasn't here. So lonely, so sad. I was fascinated by you. You even spoke to me; actually, you were one of the only girls who was even nice to me. I heard many of them snicker about me, but you... you were kind and gentle. I gave you my phone number, and you promised to keep in touch. Did you know that? But you never called." She looked down at the large bag that was in her hand.

"Harlow, that was a really hard time in my life… I mean, you must know how fucking damaged I am. I had basically no friends. I still don't have any friends, except for you. I'm so sorry. I just… Please, just tell me what this is, Harlow?" I forced the words to piece together because I knew the silence would set the stage for her next act. I looked toward the shrine of pictures of me, the light reflected against the cool metal of the desk taunting me. My eyes stayed on the scissors as I whispered, "Harlow, did you kill them?"

"Oh, Sage, can you just focus on *me* for once. You are always so caught up with men that you could never see the one and only person who loves you the most…" Her smile grew larger, her eyes desolate like a lost, hungry animal in the woods. "Me."

"Harlow… I just need to leave. I need to see my kids. I swear, we can forget all of this, and I can get you some help." I moved toward her and the door.

"So, you just want to, what…? *Forget* me? You want me to go to prison?" Her voice grew louder as she emphasized every word.

"No, no, I just… Harlow, if you love me, you'll let me go." My eyes filled with tears. "Holding me here and scaring me… that's not love."

She let out a rumbustious laugh, one that was tormenting. "Love? Sage, you wouldn't know the first thing about love. I'm the only one who really does love you. You just kept fucking every man you could, giving them your love... and me...? You didn't even care to love me. You even fucked my husband, you had a child with him... You never loved me, even though I gave you my entire heart." Her face was flushed and her words poured out as if she'd rehearsed this moment countless times, anticipating it.

Like she knew it would come.

"Please, please, let me go," I pleaded with her. "I do love you, Harlow. I just... I'm not..." Words jumbled out of my mouth, but I knew there was no point. Not only was she in some trance, but she was looking at me in a way that I knew all too well. She wasn't here; she was lost in another world—a world full of darkness and motive. She even knew about Tate, which terrified me all that more. "You are a good person, Harlow. You are *good*."

"I know I am, Sage. But even good people get tired of being good to bad people, and you, Sage... you are bad. You are selfish and self-absorbed." She clicked her tongue while shaking her head.

With a swift kick, she slammed the door closed. "I have been working on a very special gift for you, my love." She let the bag fall open and she tugged out a thick fur coat—the same fur coat we saw in the boutique. "Will you humor me and just put it on? Then... *then* I'll let you go to the kids, I promise. Really, our kids. I mean, in one sense we share Tate now. We're a real family." She smiled big and let the bag drop by her feet. "I have to say it's not finished. You caught me off-guard. I actually decided to customize it for you. You know, you're one of a kind to me, and I wanted you to have the coat that you looked gorgeous in the day I fell in love with you." She paused and stared into my eyes. My body trembled as each word came out of her mouth. "When you were crowned Miss USA, and they wrapped you in that fur coat... You looked like an angel. My angel."

My eyes moved to the door, but I didn't know how I could get out of here. All I wanted was to run to my children. Leave this hell behind us, and live.

In this moment, I realized I had spent so many of my days living to die and now, I was dying to live.

"Harlow, please. I'll do whatever you want me to. Just let me see my kids one more time, please."

"Put. The. Coat. On. Sage," she screeched.

I nodded quickly and turned around, letting my arms stick out so she could slide it on me. A moment later, I was wearing the heavy coat. Spinning back around, I forced a small smile out with my lips rolled tightly. "I love it, Harlow. Thank you." I brushed the fur on the front, the entire coat was cream and instantly, my hand froze over the uneven patches that were embedded all over. "Harlow... what kind of animal is this?" The erratic dark brown and sandy blonde patches had my stomach churning.

She laughed, quietly at first, then louder and louder. "Your favorite animal." I lifted my head, my eyes frozen, unable to blink.

The scissors behind me covered in hair... the needles and thread... She had shaved each man's head that I had slept with and embedded it in this coat. I had once told her that my favorite animals were men; she took that literally and made a sick joke into a reality. Vomit pooled in my mouth and I gagged. Bending over, the thick acid spewed onto the floor.

"Sage! Honey!" She ran to me, cradling me in her arms. I shrugged my shoulders hard and shoved her off, running to the door. I grasped the handle and as soon I tried to turn it, a hand gripped my ponytail and a rip radiated through the air between us. I crashed to the floor as screams rose between us. My hands flailed as images of my mother and I flashed between this very scene.

"You didn't let me finish the coat... I had one more

for you…one more animal, baby. I think it was your most favorite one." She grabbed a fistful of hair from the bag, and it didn't take me a second longer to recognize it.

Archer. It was Archer's thick, dark beautiful hair. Tears plummeted out as a scream so loud boomed through my body. I started kicking hard, releasing myself from her grip before crawling to the door. But I didn't stand a chance, because as much as my head throbbed, in that moment, Harlow wasn't going to give up. I reached up for the doorknob, but Harlow grabbed my legs and pulled me back, and that's when something seared through me.

I fell onto my chest and turned my head slightly. "Harlow…"

She held a pair of sharp, shiny scissors in my back while she sat on top of me to keep me pinned down.

With a swift motion, she tugged it out. I screamed, the burn coursing throughout my body as I cried, but my voice was gone. But unlike my voice, I still had some fight left. I kicked back as hard as I could and heard Harlow let out a cry. Swinging the door open and slamming it shut, I ran as fast as I could down the stairs, tripping along each step as my body begged to keep up with the adrenaline pumping through me. My phone was clutched in my hand, and I looked over my shoulder. Harlow wasn't there, and I had barely kicked her. My hands trembled against my phone. I had dozens of missed calls from Archer. Without thinking, I hit his name on my screen, terrified I would fuck up dialing for 9-1-1.

"Sage…" His voice was weak and cracked.

"Archer! Archer!" I cried into the phone, running for the front door. My body was slow from the sheer shock and pain radiating from my wound and blood dripped behind me like footsteps in the sand. My fingers slid against the locks, shaking as I pulled at the knob.

"It's Harlow, Sage… it's Harlow," he let out with his raspy voice just before the phone suddenly went dead.

"Archer!" I called out, knowing he was probably somewhere bleeding out and I couldn't help him. I couldn't even help myself.

As soon as my feet hit the doormat, I took a leap to run. I felt cold hands tug me with intense force. I started to scream as loud as I physically could. "Harlow, get off me!" I thrashed my arms around again and again, but my body was pressed against the concrete. Our street was silent, with not a person in sight. My back arched and muscles tightened as she flung a blade into my back. This felt different; it didn't feel like the scissors, this object cut through me with ease. I sank into the ground, crying against the earth below me. I let my cheek fall to the side and pulled my face up slightly, gripping the rough concrete below. Harlow's hair was scattered around her face wildly, her eyes glossed over, and when my eyes met, I knew that I was dead from the moment she met me on that stage all those years ago.

In her hand was the knife I had used to kill my mother. She followed me, she stalked me, and she unearthed it. She had used that knife to kill Payton, Jake, my husband, and Archer… And now, she was going to slaughter me with it.

She plunged it inside me again and again, and I realized it was true… She and I were more alike than I ever knew. She had demons lurking inside her that couldn't be tamed. She needed a high and a fix to live. I just so badly wished it wasn't this way.

Everything grew black around me, and just before my eyes closed, I saw Andi and Tate. Their smiling beautiful faces, the sounds of their laughter, the feel of them hugging me tightly. I reached out in front of me. "I love you…"

"I love you, too, sweetheart…" Harlow giggled from behind me.

I closed my eyes, and let go…

CHAPTER TWENTY-THREE

"We are gathered here today to pay our tribute and respect to a mother and wife. A child of God. We are here to pray for her soul, because my brothers and sisters, even tormented souls deserve redemption. Leaving behind her children, but joining her husband, she will be missed by many. May we pray she finds a safe haven and rest," the preacher's Southern drawl rang out over the pounding rain that beat against the flimsy green tent above our heads. My two-seasons' old Jimmy Choo's dug into the moist ground below. Charleston humidity had finally found solace by showering its wrath down on us through its somber skies. The sticky smell of heat mixed with the mounds of fresh dirt radiated around us.

"You ready to go, baby?" I looked up and met his

dark brown eyes—the ones that made me think of hot chocolate on a cold, winter day back in New York. The ones that gave me hope. When I married Brody, I thought that was my second chance at life, but this… this was my real second chance. The one where I finally laid my demons to rest, the one where I could live, knowing no one was left to blackmail me, to hurt me.

I was free.

Harlow Davis, a wife, mother, active church member, and PTA-loving, bake-sale winning woman had darker secrets than I'd ever imagined. After she violently attacked me, a neighbor found me unconscious and bleeding out. Authorities found Archer, who was tethering the weak rope between life and death with a picture of me clutched in his hands, against his heart. We fought for our lives side by side at the Medical University of South Carolina hospital. Harlow left a suicide note. She jumped from the famed Ravenel bridge, and according to witnesses, they saw a woman who matched the description. Weeks later, her clothes were found in the water below, but no body was ever discovered. Detectives reassured me there was no way someone could survive that fall, and there was no way she could have hidden and escaped a place like Charleston when they had closed every bridge leading in and out of the city immediately after Archer and I were found. I was cleared of all charges, considering the police compiled all the evidence they could ever need from Harlow's house.

I looked around, not even her children had attended their mother's funeral. They were living with Harlow's mom, and I had visited them a handful of times. Children having to pay for the sins of their parents was something I could sympathize with.

"I just need a little more time. I'll meet you in the car." I smiled at Archer, letting my hand squeeze his. He nodded back and turned away. His once thick, dark brown hair was mostly gone. Harlow had come into his office, shared a coffee with him, which she had drugged. She then stabbed him countless times before shaving his head to add to the gift she'd been creating for me. The fur coat, which in her sick and twisted mind, she thought I'd appreciate the so-called grand gesture and run away into the sunset with her.

It had hair embedded into the fur from each man I had been with in Charleston, as if it were a souvenir. It was what my nightmares were crafted of. The fact that I wore something over my body, that came off the scalps of men, of human beings... *my own husband*. I shuddered at the thought of it on my skin. How many times I sat on the shower floor, screaming and scrubbing my arms until my skin peeled and blood trickled out.

Harlow's mother didn't say much, but she handed over some scrapbooks Harlow had collected through the years to the authorities. Pages after pages were filled with photos of me. Each pageant I won, every news articles I was featured in as Miss USA. Photos of me bartending, and so much more.

What no one knew, not even Archer, was that I had gone back into the Davis house before the funeral, pretending to help the kids pack their belongings. Instead, I went back into Harlow's craft room, which, for the most part, had been swiped clean for evidence. I dropped to the floor, letting my palm rest against the ground. It was a hollow floorboard, something I had felt when I was in here with Harlow fighting for my life. I pressed on it multiple times before half of it sunk in, and I let my hand fall deep inside. I found a small box tucked away. In that moment, sadness filled me for the friendship I had lost.

Ultrasound images of her children, snapshots of Jake and her in their dating days, movie ticket stubs, and concert mementos. *Even monsters had hearts.* Harlow Davis was a monster driving a minivan, and somewhere along the hopscotch-covered sidewalks she fell off. Just before I was about to place the small box back under the floor, my eyes caught something. A small black diary. I pulled it out and flipped through it.

"Ms. Sage, we are ready to go," Harlow's oldest called out from the hall.

I tucked the diary under my shirt and put the box back. It could wait.

I pulled a folding chair closer to the light wood coffin in front of me. This funeral was different, it was closure. Closure for a slew of murders, a serial killer haunting an otherwise secure community, and most of all, closure for my fears and secrets. I traced the creases and grooves of the pine. I pulled the small diary out and began to read the perfect cursive writing and the eloquently flowing words. Flipping through the first few pages, I got to the dates that matched with the Miss USA pageant. I read on and on until finally, I stopped when I saw Brody's name. My heart sped and my fingers paged through as I begged my eyes and brain to process the words in front of me.

Harlow Davis had known Brody since they were teenagers, something I was already aware of because they grew up in the same area of Charleston. But what I had to read over and over again and what made me terrified to even be by the empty coffin in front of me was the fact that Harlow had insisted Brody visit the bar I worked at in New York City. Brody was a pawn in Harlow's game from the very beginning. She knew I'd fall for him, and he'd fall for me. *I was his type, and he was my way out.* She knew it was an easy way to potentially have me move here to be closer *to her.*

Our friendship, our houses, my fucking marriage… everything and everyone was a mere puppet and Harlow was a puppeteer in her show that was my life. She had meticulously crafted every shred of my life.

"You bitch…" Tears streamed down my face. A gust of wind picked up and brushed my neck, and in that moment, I could have sworn I heard her. I stood up quickly and spun around. *Nothing.*

Archer was sitting in the distance, patiently waiting in the car. Behind a larger tombstone, I saw a glimpse of a woman in the distance wearing a flowing white gown, red hair swaying behind her. Harlow had light brown hair, but she was originally a redhead.

"Harlow is dead. She jumped off the bridge," I murmured to myself.

The figure in the distance peeked out from behind the tombstone. Charleston cemeteries were the worst —old and more pain-filled from its long, dark history.

You could feel the negative energy and haunted souls that lurked around.

Shaking my head, I turned toward the car. I needed to lay Harlow to rest. "Sage…" a voice mixed with the rain that had grown lighter and an abnormally cool breeze had rippled through. I looked over my shoulder and saw the woman in the white dress looking at me before she walked farther. Picking up my pace, my heels continued to dig deep into the wet ground and my hair matted around my face uncomfortably.

"Harlow!" I screamed out, but the woman began to jog away. "Harlow!"

"Sage? Baby!" Archer yelled out behind me, I hunched over, releasing a deep, shallow breath as I gagged on my own saliva pooling in my mouth. Archer gripped me from behind, and I let myself fall into his arms.

"I swear I saw her, Archer… They have to find her body. I can't…" I wrapped my arms around myself tightly as if I actually believed I could protect myself.

"Sage, shh. Sage, baby, Charleston isn't big… The bridges were completely closed. No one got in or out for days when they were searching for her." Archer brushed my straggling hair out from my face and kissed my forehead multiple times for me to calm down and be centered to reality.

"I saw her…" I whispered against his chest.

For years, I had felt so alone, but I never was actually alone, was I? There was a person lurking in my shadows every single day. Harlow was watching me and crafting my life, piece by piece. The police found twenty cameras all over my house. *Twenty.* Embedded in different places to have clear access to me showering, eating, living my life every single day. The only joy I had ever found through pageants was that I loved the feeling of being watched, admired, and appreciated. But this was me being watched in my most vulnerable of times when I hadn't rehearsed a smile or a strut. This was me being exposed and stealing away any ounce of security I had ever felt. That's the most terrifying thing in life. Knowing your private moments aren't really yours, they never were.

So now, every single day, I'd live my life sitting on the couch and looking over my shoulder, everyday I'd live my life thinking the footsteps behind me on a busy sidewalk belonged to someone who wanted to hurt me. I'd live my life in a prison that she created.

I gripped Archer's hand as we left the cemetery. Glancing back, I looked at the coffin. Just like the inside of a coffin, *I had to let the darkness of my life stay closed and allow for light to seep in, even if it were through the cracks.*

"Andi! Tate!" My voice echoed against the high ceilings. Light filtered in through the oversized window skylight above. I placed a large cardboard box down and squatted next to it. Undoing the flaps, I lifted out a picture of Brody and the kids. I had kept the wedding pictures packed away, assuming that maybe the kids would like them one day. But this one was for them to see daily, to help them remember him and to know I would never try to bury him away. I owed them, and him, that. Letting my fingers brush over Brody's smiling face in the image, I couldn't help but wonder if he would have even shown interest in me if Harlow hadn't pushed him my way.

After reading more of her journal, I found out that she had told Brody her old friend who was Miss USA worked at the bar, and she was exactly his type. She made him promise to not mention her because she lied and said she had stolen a past boyfriend from me. How stupid Brody was to believe her, I wasn't sure. But what I knew for a fact was that she wasn't lying... well slightly. I wasn't exactly his type; I was exactly *her* type. Chills grow along my arms every time I think about timing. That night was supposed to be one of my last shifts, becoming Miss USA was about to change my life, but then, that morning, I killed my own mother. I knew better than to jump into the spotlight, being with Brody was an easy escape. An excuse to even myself, I didn't need this dream come true, I could settle safely in the suburbs. What a joke that was.

"Mommy, Andi picked the bigger room!" Tate came down whining with crocodile tears.

"Honey, you get the better view from your window, though." I wrapped him in my arms. "Go grab a slice of pizza, and then we will all go out for some ice cream." I kissed the top of his lush blonde hair. The sun felt so nice coming in from the skylight above, it warmed me in a way I didn't realize I needed. Our new Goldendoodle puppy, Row pranced around my feet. I had made sure we got a male dog, because after Harlow I realized there was a surplus of conniving bitches in the world, and I didn't want to live with one, too.

Standing back up, I walked into our bedroom, Archer was pulling a T-shirt on over his head. His hair had started to grow back, and his face lit up in a big smile while his eyes twinkled as soon I came inside. "Hi, baby."

"Hey, Suit." I winked at him, letting my fingers lock behind his waist. I took a deep breath in. Damn, he smelled delicious. I was going to therapy four times a week, not just for the Harlow and dead husband trauma, but also to work on learning impulse control. Even though I loved Archer and felt wholeness with him, temptation teased me on every corner. I loved when I'd be walking down the sidewalk with our puppy, and the hungry eyes of men would graze over me. I loved knowing I still had it. I was still in control, because control became my newest addiction. Finding out Harlow had been controlling my life in so many ways made me lash out even more when it came to sex. I craved danger and irresponsible sex because it made me feel alive and in control of that man—his thoughts and his body.

So, rather than spiral out of control, I tried therapy. It wasn't perfect, but I sure as hell wasn't, either. Did I fuck a random stranger in the backseat of my car after I met him at a local dog park? Yes. Did I tell Archer? No. Because, *secrets will always hurt everyone, except you.*

"You are so beautiful..." Archer gripped my waist and pulled me in closer.

"The kids are going to barge in any second...I promised them ice cream." I grinned up at him.

"Cock-blockers," he whispered against my lips.

I sighed. "I know I'm not good for you, I have never been good for you... But thank you for sticking with me and being crazy enough to marry me." I smiled, lifting our intertwined hands that were both adorned with gold bands.

His was thick and curved, while mine was embedded with diamonds neatly nestled with an enormous engagement ring. He tilted my head up and whispered before kissing my lips, "Even when you burn, you get rid of all the bad around me, just Sage."

I paused and looked at him. "Very cute alluding to my name." I winked at him and kissed him back.

"I just have to check the roof really quickly. There's been some scratching sound and I just want to make sure it's not some animal up there damaging it." Archer opened the door and led me out of our bedroom. I walked to the kitchen and sat on the stool next to Andi and Tate, grabbing a slice of pizza.

Life was good. We moved to Calabasas, California where Archer had lived before Charleston. He still had his gated house there, so it was perfcct. We switched coasts, swapped hurricanes for earthquakes, and even changed the Atlantic for the Pacific. We couldn't have altered much more if we tried. This change of scenery was exactly what I needed, what we needed. I had started sleeping slightly better, though I was still medicated—considering when I closed my eyes it was her face I saw. When I was home alone, when the kids were at school and Archer was at work, it was her voice I heard. I supposed knowing she had been around me for years had engrained into me and I never truly felt alone. When I showered, my eyes would wander to the ceiling, scoping out a hidden camera that didn't exist.

But I learned to live in the moment, because that was the only guarantee I had. *When you get a taste of how bitter death can be, you realize how sweet life truly is.*

"All done, Mommy!" Andi's pink lips were shining in pizza grease, and Tate's chin had streaks of sauce running down his chin.

I couldn't help but smile. I wished away so many days with them, the sleepless nights, holding my breath, and crying, counting seconds until they'd sleep through the night. The days they would cling to me, and my back ached from lifting them in my arms because separation anxiety coursed through their little bodies. I wished away the days where my ears stung from the word mommy, and I just wanted to be Sage again. Now, I knew time was a thief, and moments were fleeting.

My life wasn't what I planned it to be... it was filled with trauma and pain. I was a sinner in every way possible, and maybe Harlow was sent by Lucifer himself to ensure I paid for those very sins. I clung onto the hope that repentance was erasable and redemption was possible.

"Andi, Tate, go wash your hands in the sink, and I'll grab my purse. We can meet Archer outside. Ice cream time!" I sang out as their faces lit up with excitement. I quickly walked back to the living room with a goofy smiled plastered over my face. It felt nice to just… *live.* Andi and Tate were giggling away over the sink, splashing one another as they washed their hands— something I would have once yelled at them for, but now, life was good. It was so good because it was truly and finally ours.

The doorbell rang. "Archer, did you lock yourself out again?" I laughed and walked to the front door, turning the heavy doorknob. My feet froze in an awkward position just before the next foot went in front of the other. "No… no…" I said under a hushed gasp. "Archer?" I squatted down, lifting the vase in my quivering hands, prying the cream-colored note from the vivid red rose and deep blue-purple violet bouquet.

Roses are red, violets are blue, someone is dead, let's hope it's not you, too. Because baby, I will be the only one who loves every single, shade of you…

A loud crash sounded, and I glanced up at the bright blue sky, but before I could think twice, Andi and Tate yelled inside so deafeningly, it forced my trembling legs to sprint back to them.

I looked at their faces, which were both tilted up toward the living room skylight, horror painted across their eyes. Tate began crying hysterically, and I slowed my pace as my feet slid across the shiny wood floors. My eyes followed theirs upward, but the rest of my body sunk into the ground below. I didn't even realize that the echoes of shrill screams were coming from my own mouth.

The clear glass skylight above slowly clouded with a pool of deep, red blood. Archer's palms faced us, his face pressed down. "No, no, no…." I sobbed and yelled simultaneously, gasping for air in between.

Andi and Tate stood there next to me, weeping. I didn't even have the strength to shield them, I couldn't. I didn't know how to protect myself, let alone my own children. Archer's body was limp, and blood continued to pour out of him the way waves crash into the ocean. Just as I was about to close my eyes, his darted open while his mouth parted and formed the word, *run.*

Chills shot up my spine, and as if his words fueled inside of me, I jumped to my feet and grabbed Andi by the hand, flinging Tate over my hip. Reaching inside my purse, I tugged the keys and sprinted as fast as I could to the side door with them. Adrenaline surged through me as I hurled Andi and Tate into the front passenger seat and slid into the driver side. Locking the doors, I opened the garage and stabbed the key into the ignition. With one swift movement, the car roared. The garage door stopped mid-way, letting just enough light into the darkness. I glanced at the rearview and frantically hitting the garage opener with trembling fingers. "Open, you fucker," I shouted, staring in my rearview at the jammed garage door.

"Mommy—" Andi's voice broke under a whispered tone.

My wild eyes looked over at hers, but she was staring out of my window. Exhaling slowly, I turned.

Harlow stood there, her face pressed against my window, her hair wasn't light brown but back to its original shade of red. My eyes widened and her lips that were painted in red began to part, while her hands clenched together and shot open. "Boo!" She tapped the glass with the blood-covered knife. The knife that had haunted me for years; the one she had used to carve every single person I loved out of my life.

A sinister smile grew on her face. "Andi, Tate, I want you to close your eyes... none of this is real. None of this is real. Think of us at the beach." My body shook, but something rose inside of me and with my foot on the pedal, through clenched teeth, I screamed, "You crazy bitch…"

I slammed my foot down and reversed, ramming backward. The car jammed against the thick garage door; Harlow threw her head back and began laughing hysterically. I looked at Andi and Tate, their faces drained from fear. "Close your eyes! Close your eyes! It's not real!" I chanted over and over to them. Their eyes stayed closed, yet tears trickled down while their sobs radiated around the small space. She began walking slowly towards us, swinging the knife around with a smile on her face that made my stomach curl. I shifted from reverse to drive, pressing the gas harder than possible.

Harlow's eyes broadened as I smashed into her body, driving over and letting the rubber of my wheels crush over half her body before braking. The sound of her bones crunching underneath was one I knew would never leave me.

Sorry, bestie, there's only room for one fucked up stay-at-home mommy in this town.

I pressed my forehead against the steering wheel, clutching it tightly, and let myself cry as I reversed the car. My tires vibrated as they reversed over Harlow's body. Her hand twitched slightly, and I gripped the gear again, I'd run this bitch over again if I needed to. But then her hand fell flat, and her chest seemed to stop rising and falling. It just…fell.

I exhaled what felt like trapped air in my lungs as my body trembled and tears burned my raw cheeks, and the garage door began to creak before it opened fully.

Slowly, I looked over at Andi and Tate, who still had their eyes clenched shut and arms wrapped around one another. Suddenly, a shadow passed my window, my eyes burned through the tears and my vision stayed hazy. Leaning in, I blinked over and over.

Archer. He was in front of my car and crouched over Harlow's lifeless body. His hand brushed against her straggling hair. *What was he doing? How was he alive?* Just as my hand gripped the handle of the door to get out and see him, my fingers froze. He grew closer to her face and kissed her lips. My tires had smashed only half of her body into the ground because the sound alone scared me too much to continue, and her face seemed unscathed. He kissed her again, and my heart that had slowed began to pound against my chest. He stood and turned, looking at me with his eyes desolate and tears streaking his cheeks.

No… this can't be happening. Archer and Harlow?

Before I could think twice, unfreeze myself from the moment, he lifted the sharp knife that laid next to Harlow's body and plunged it into my front tire. My eyes widened, but my mind was two steps behind my body as I quickly turned my key in the ignition. The car was jammed, it was making a noise that I knew was the sound of my own death. Glancing at my children, I screamed, turning the key in and out, slamming the gas. Archer walked unhurriedly and slashed the second front tire before walking over to the kids' window, my eyes trailing him in sheer shock.

"Mommy, it's Archer! He's okay!" Andi reached for the door and unlocked it.

"No, Andi!" I yelled.

Archer's face lit up in an ominous smile as he opened their door. "Archer! Don't you dare touch them." I screeched. I grabbed Andi and Tate as Archer sunk lower, grinning at them. They cried out as I pulled them over the gear shift, trying to wiggle out of my grasp. Clutching them into my body, Archer threw his head back, laughing hysterically.

"Archer—" My voice cracked as I began hyperventilating and tears soaked the top of my children's hair. "Please, Archer… why are you doing this?"

"Get out of the car, Sage." His voice was hoarse and filled with rage.

"I'll do anything, but don't hurt them, please... please... don't hurt my babies." His lips curved into a conniving grin, then he stood straight and began walking back around to my side. I nodded, knowing this was truly it.

The curtains were closing in on me, my chest tightened as I quickly kissed the tops of Andi and Tate's heads, brushing their hair back, hoping I could bottle the scent of their innocence into my soul because that would be all I was about to have left.

"As soon as I get out of the car," I whispered into Andi's ear, "you and Tate need to run. Don't stop running until you find help. And no matter what, don't come back for me. I love you both so much." I whimpered, barely making it through each word that felt more painful than a bullet into my flesh.

"Mommy..." Andi's eyes darted to mine, terror filling them but also a glimmer of acceptance. The tapping against my window made me flinch. Archer had the blood-covered knife in one hand, picking the pace up of its sound against the glass.

"Run..." I yelled, fear paralyzing every limb in my body. Andi and Tate jumped off me and scrambled to the open passenger door as I rammed my door into Archer, who let out a cry.

"You bitch!" he screamed, holding his abdomen which was already covered in blood.

Andi and Tate sprinted hand in hand, turning away onto the street. I slowed my run; I had to give them a fighting chance. Archer's fingers aggressively dug into my skin and pulled me into him from behind. *If he has me, he can't get them.* I let my body go limp as he jerked me back through the opened front doors.

"You just won't die, will you, you little slut? I mean, I was so close at that B&B spa... suffocating you during your peaceful massage, but you just won't die," he said through clenched teeth as he shoved me inside by the collar of my shirt.

Pushing me harder, I fell to the ground, catching myself by my palms and knees. "Ah!" I shouted as Archer dug his foot into my ribs, kicking me again and again while laughing.

I sobbed into the floor, my cheek grazing the hardwood. "Please...stop." Each word crackled against my tongue. Terror pulsated through me as I recalled waking up and not remembering anything about my massage, thinking I was dreaming when small slivers of someone shoving me into the pillow arose. Jake died the same day, and there I was, sleeping with the Grim Reaper.

My own Grim Reaper.

"You killed her. You killed the love of my life!" he yelled.

My mind was blank. I didn't even know how to begin to piece together what he was saying. It was as if he was speaking a different language.

Grabbing my collar, he pulled me upright, dragging me while my knees slid across the floor until we reached the sofa, my skin raw and red. Tossing me onto the sofa like a rag doll, he sunk beside me. I used to watch horror movies and roll my eyes, thinking why those idiots didn't jolt up and run, but now I knew... My body was aching, bleeding and paralyzed by fear. Fear of what was going to come, knowing there was no longer a reason to run. *I had nowhere to hide.*

"I loved you..." My voice was hushed, there was no strength in it, only weakness and vulnerability.

Archer snickered. "You aren't worthy of love. You're a selfish bitch."

"Harlow... she, she wanted to be with me." My hand was firmly against my ribs, and it felt as if fire had blazed through them.

"No. That's where you're wrong, just like everything. She did love you; she did want to be with you... but then she realized how selfish and disgusting you are and found solace in me. *With me.* But you just had to take that away. We were in the home stretch." He waved the knife close to my face. I flinched as the tip pressed into my neck. His laughter roared, but his breath was shallow.

"I guess I cut myself a little too deep for the act." His eyes shifted to his abdomen, where his blood dripped onto the couch. "I'll be okay after I finish this." He swayed the knife between us.

"Everything between us was a lie?" Tears ran from my eyes as I tried to buy time, time where I could think of Andi and Tate and hope they had found someone, anyone to help them, protect them—two things I failed them in.

He chuckled. "I actually did enjoy you at one point, you are a good fuck," he scoffed. "But I met Harlow at Hotel Besos the day before I met you, actually. She was there to check out the spot you seemingly frequented often... and then I eventually realized she was so much more than you. She was just caught in your shadows, so I thought if I helped her with her little project, which was you, then I could show her just how much she could have with me." He brushed his finger across his bottom lip and smirked. Pushing onto his feet, he gasped, clutching his core.

I felt emotionless, and knew that I couldn't handle

anything else. This was not just a shock, this was my life turning into a joke, a spectacle.

"Wow, talk about love triangle from hell. I guess I just prefer my twisted love triangles in movies about vampires and werewolves." I let out a soft laugh, which made me cringe at the pain it caused in my body. "She would have never been with you; she was just using you. She was obsessed with me, you moron." I coughed as I spewed the words out at the man I thought I loved, the man I assumed I was building a new life with… my second chance.

"Shut your fucking mouth!" He grabbed me aggressively, letting my body fall to the ground like it was nothing. He pinned me down as he collapsed onto my legs, his weight making my thighs ache. "For Harlow, my love, I'm finishing what you started, baby." Archer kissed the dirty blade and waved it once in the air just before lifting it higher in between his clutched hands.

Five seconds, that's all I had. Five seconds between life and death, and I sure as hell wasn't going to give it up. In his dramatics, he pinned my legs assuming I wouldn't fight back with my arms. He thought I was weak, and maybe in another life, I would have been, but this was it. *All or nothing.*

With all my might, I clenched my fist and punched straight into his abdomen where the blood had stained the most, where I knew the Grim Reaper had already left his mark.

He was taken by surprise as he cried out, releasing the grip on the knife as his hands jerked to his own weak spot. I shoved him hard, crawling away on all fours, sliding the knife away with my hand. "Fuck!" I yelled out as he turned and grabbed me from behind. Kicking backward into the air, I picked the knife off the ground with our arms flailing until I felt it dig into flesh. Screams so loud from both of our bodies collided into one. I heard a crash, and slowly turned, terrified I had wrecked my one shot at life.

Archer was on knees, the knife plunged into the side of his neck. Blood splattering from his jugular. Choking on air and suffocating on his own blood, he fell face-first. The weight of his body plummeted into the floor, shaking me to my core. My whole body trembled as I watched the red pool around him. Holding my knees into my chest, I sobbed harder than my body thought possible. Seeing the life leave a human being was something I had seen, I had caused. But this... It was over.

It was finally over.

Peeling myself off the floor, my ribs shifting with every step I took, I clutched them and whimpered in agony. Limping outside, the fresh air brushed against my face as I tilted my head to the sun. It felt different today; it felt like a sensation I had never experience before. *Hope.*

I cried out in pain as I walked down the sidewalk. My arms and hands were covered in blood, not just visibly, but deep-rooted. *These hands had killed and taken life.* My breath was raspy as I pushed myself forward. The closest neighbor was still a distance away. No cars were driving by, and even if they were, who would stop for me? My entire shirt was soaked in sweat and blood.

Suddenly, I heard light sniffles in the bushes and froze. Turning, I squatted and saw them. Andi and Tate sat huddled together, hidden away, waiting for me. *Their mom.*

Collapsing into the soft green grass, I pulled them into my chest. The two people in the world—no matter what secrets I held, no matter what sins I had committed—who loved me without limits. They believed I'd live. I'd survive.

There's a monster inside of each of us, some just suppress it better than others. Others unleash it and cause nothing but pain and destruction. The main difference is how long until each of us can contain that monster and darkness before letting it come to the surface. I knew the monster in me only came out when it had to... at least, that's what I told myself.

They say when you're about to die, you get some kind of highlight reel, and I've decided I'm just not ready to watch mine yet. *All good things must come to an end, but in my life, I've learned that all good things never truly start.* But I know I'll die trying to make them happen. *For them.*

ABOUT THE AUTHOR

Monica Arya is a Charlotte, North Carolina native currently residing in South Carolina with her husband, two beautiful children, and Goldendoodle. Besides writing and her family, she is passionate about the beach, spicy food, chocolate and spontaneous dance parties. She adores writing twisted thrillers, and angst-filled romance novels that provide an escape.

Monica absolutely enjoys connecting with readers, you can learn more about her, current and upcoming releases by finding her:

Official Website: *www.monicaarya.com*
Instagram: *@monicaaryaauthor*

Facebook Reader Group: *Monica Arya's Misfits*

Facebook: */monicaaryaauthor*
TikTok: *@monicaaryaauthor*

If you enjoyed the story I loved telling, please consider leaving a review on Amazon, and Goodreads.

And, if you're looking for your next read, *Girl in the Reflection*, my chilling and twisted psychological thriller is a wild ride of its own.

ACKNOWLEDGMENTS

To my children, Mila and Ari, the two parts that craft my soul. You both made me a mother, tested my sanity, patience and heart in ways I didn't know was possible. We threw a pandemic into the mix and had to learn to navigate so much together. You both made me want time to speed up, but also for it to stand still. Mostly, stand still. Motherhood, isn't a destination, it's a wild, roller coaster journey. My loves, you taught me to throw my hands up, let go and enjoy the ride because it is truly the thrill of a lifetime. I love you both more than anything in the world, and although there are days I miss being Monica, being called Mom by you both, is the highest honor of my life. Thank you for making me a better human with your love.

Mom and Pop, every book I write, I can't help but think of you two. Thank you for teaching me hard work no matter how many obstacles there may have been, thank you for your sacrifices that I didn't even know of, until I became a parent myself and most of all thank you for loving me and letting me thrive as the person I was destined to be. I love you both so much. *Mom*, you get a special shout out because I never realized all that you went through for us, until I became a mother myself. Thank you for being strong, even when you could have been weak. Thank you for loving us, even when we were brats. You're the best.

My older brother, Neal, thank you for your support, and the laughs. I appreciate you being honest when I'm stressing about covers, and all the small details. You're an awesome big brother.

To my dear friend, Shanora Williams I am so thankful for our friendship and unfiltered conversations. When you read my first thriller, Girl in the Reflection, it gave me even more courage to push forward when I was starting out in a new genre which made such a difference in my heart and believing in myself. You have a heart of gold and I appreciate you so much.

My incredible author friends from both thriller and romance worlds, along with my editor, Silvia, thank you for being such an integral part of the creation of my books. You all understand how much goes into each page, each chapter and each story. Thank you for being there to vent, to laugh and to always just be there. Love you all!

A special, heartfelt thank you to Jessica, Gabby, Cristina, Allyson, Marisha, Kori and Jessica. Thank you so much for your support, laughter, and friendships. I'm so thankful my books connected us and turned into wonderful friendships. I love you ladies, thank you for having the most beautiful hearts that make the world a better place. I appreciate you all so much.

My amazing readers, thank you so much for reading my book, and allowing me to tell the stories that run rampant in my heart, mind and soul. Your support means so much to me and I truly appreciate the time you take to read my books. *Thank you to the amazing bookstagrammers, and book bloggers,* I appreciate you celebrating my books and the friendships that form through this journey.

And finally, to every mother, and motherly figure, you have changed lives even when you may have felt invisible. The sacrifices, the madness and the exhaustion are appreciated by someone and if you don't feel that appreciation, just know I see you. I hear you. I appreciate you. You all have crowns on top of those messy buns so keep your heads up, don't you dare let it fall.

Printed in Great Britain
by Amazon